Table of Contents

Chapter 1

My brother killed my father. The papers described it as a tragic accident, but our mother blamed Tom. I saw how she looked at him, with his knobbly knees and baggy shorts, tears welling up in her eyes. I felt so sorry for him, for us. We were cast adrift by our mother's grief and we clung to each other. For years afterwards, when he cried in his sleep, I climbed into bed to console him. Our mother's bedroom door remained an oblong of shadow, resolutely shut. I stopped when his legs got too hairy and scratchy for comfort.

Of course now, older than she was at the time, I understand. She never really recovered from the shock of our father's sudden death but children don't see that, do they? They just perceive a lack of love. I looked after my little brother and my brother loved me. I loved my brother.

Tom was six and I was eight. The loss of our father reverberated throughout our lives, like the hollow sound of an empty drum. It made us who we were — what we were. Tom tried to please and to succeed, and he was successful; by the age of twenty-five he was a millionaire, able to offer his mother a flat in Chelsea. I, on the other hand, had no real ambition although I did become an acknowledged expert in my field. Tom's success mattered more. It was a vindication of sorts, for our father. He'd been a successful novelist, but we'd never had any money. It was a worry, a recurring theme of our childhood. I was so proud of Tom's achievements.

As the years went by, we saw less of each other but on the rare occasions when we did meet, Tom still confided in me. Earlier this year, it must have been February, so eight months ago now, we met at one of the grand be-flagged hotels off Park Lane. I could hear the excitement in his voice and, despite his protestations, I thought he had found another woman so I was surprised when he moved the cutlery to one side and spread photographs of the château across the damask tablecloth. He looked to me for approval, twinkling with the joy of it all. "Isn't it fantastic?" He wanted me to supervise the renovations for him, and to keep the château secret from his wife. "Please, Sis. I want to surprise Sam and the kids."

"How can I?" I said. "I can't just up and leave. I'm in the middle of a job. And what about Philip?"

"Oh him," Tom teased, "he's just a husband. You'll only ever have one brother, and that's me." He spent months trying to persuade me to go to France and then, one night in June, I changed my mind. Tom didn't ask me why. Besides, my distress must have been evident in my voice. He said simply that I would find the key inside the fifth urn on the terrace.

I caught the first ferry out of Dover and when it docked at Calais, I pressed my foot down on the accelerator. I didn't give any thought to the refugees loitering by the roadside. I drove at a pace, only stopping when I ran out of petrol which happened twice en route down the map of France, once landing me on the edge of a motorway with a long trudge to the petrol station, a few miles back.

By the time I reached Provence, my little car was protesting, having been driven too fast for too long. The

8

final climb up the steep hill from the village proved too much. The car spluttered to a halt at the gates, except there were no gates, just two crumbling pillars with a couple of stone lions on top, guarding a remnant of an avenue.

I couldn't see a house behind the wall of vegetation. I couldn't hear anything except the screech of insects. I turned the key in the ignition. The engine clicked. I sat for a second or two, slumped with disappointment, listening to the sudden stillness. Then the strum of cicadas started, pounding and invisible. I opened the door. Even though it was evening, the air still pulsed with heat.

My legs were wobbly after being so long in the car. After a few long deep breaths, I became aware of the sour, dank smell of too many plants in too little light. There was rubbish tangled in the creepers and bushes — a mattress, the frame of a pushchair, a discarded shoe and high up on a branch, a plastic supermarket bag hanging like a deflated flag. I noticed then, the sign for the Château Bellevue, half-hidden by weeds at the base of one of the pillars.

Someone, recently, had beaten a track through the undergrowth. My heart started to pound. I looked back at the way I had come. I was an adult. I had travelled too far. I couldn't retreat.

I took my suitcase out of the car, the thud of the boot causing birds to crash into the sky, momentarily silencing the cicadas. I followed whoever it had been, deeper and deeper into the twilight cast by the trees. I forced myself to put one foot high in front of the other and not to give in to terror. I have a pathological fear of snakes and it doesn't help that I know that it is associated with that last summer, thirty-six years ago, when our father died.

*

We'd been staying in North Devon, in a cottage I called the Gingerbread House. My father was finishing his fifth novel which would be published posthumously to great acclaim, while our mother looked after us, read newspapers and smoked cigarettes in the sun. It was August 1973 and she was riveted by the Watergate scandal in America.

Tom and I were out from the moment we got up to the moment we went to bed. Our parents were lax about bedtime, sitting in the garden over a bottle of beer until they became shapes in the twilight, still talking. Sometimes they argued but not often, not like at home in London.

The Gingerbread garden was a gloriously overgrown wilderness. There were bushes with overhanging branches which became dens, trees that were castles and a well which served as the dragon's lair. I was the bossy princess and Tom my obedient prince, charging to my rescue, a broom between his legs as his steadfast mount.

If I hadn't been searching for our stripy ball in the long grass — everything would have been different.

*

When I stumbled out of the thicket and into the light, I could have been an eight-year-old princess all over again. Half castle, half manor house, the château reared up before me, a breath-taking concoction of pink stone. Great arched doors sliced through its middle. Three rows of long opaque windows reflected the setting sun. A carved stone staircase wound up to the double front door, blue paint almost peeled away. In the right-hand corner, a tower with a green roof and a crooked cockerel for a weathervane pressed into the pale evening sky. Above it all, a solitary bird was wheeling.

The fifth urn on the balustrade was easy to spot. It was the only one with creeper wrenched away. I mounted the steps to the front door, full of trepidation and self-doubt. The key was so long and heavy I needed both hands to turn the lock.

As soon as I pushed the door shut, a sense of peace overwhelmed me. Maybe it was the solidity of the two foot wide stone walls, or the coolness of the shaded air; more probably it was the fact that, after eighteen hours of driving, I'd reached my destination. The broken loveliness of the stained glass window, lit up by a dying sun, rose up from the central landing of the enormous oak staircase, which divided into two to sweep up to a gallery on the floor above. The great window reached almost to the height of the vaulted ceiling. I let my back slide down the door's smooth worn wood and stretched out my legs. It was enough for me, for a while. I was simply glad to have arrived.

There were five doors, three on one side of the stairs, two on the other, either side of an arch which led to a dark corridor. Four doors were shut. I thought I saw a snake which made me nearly pass out — but when I managed to look again, it was a length of thick rope, slung over the only door ajar. The night was closing in, very quickly. I hauled myself up. I snapped on the cheap plastic light switch. A faint pink glow fizzed into the silence from under the chintz shades of twelve pairs of wall lights.

The château wasn't the empty space I'd expected. The hall was full of shadow as happens in old houses and there was furniture: two high-backed winged armchairs set in front of the enormous fireplace, a long low wooden chest against one wall and a pile of old mattresses precariously arranged one on top of the other. A crumpled plastic bottle was chucked into the ashes of the huge grate. A broken chair lay overturned in front of the stairs and a rag had been dropped onto the bottommost tread.

I nearly turned heel and fled when I noticed the set of footprints winding in and out of out of each room and disappearing down the dark corridor. I forced myself to examine the tracks and could tell by the thickness of the dust that they weren't recent. Still though, I called "hello?" and froze, thinking that someone unseen was in the hall with me, as my echo returned my greeting. Eventually it subsided under the weight of the silence.

My footfall sounded strange. Muffled. I opened the first door to the left. I tugged on the light pull. A cavernous brown toilet, thick with dead flies in a stained pan. I let the water from the washbasin trickle over my fingers.

I was too tired to explore the château that evening. I didn't stray from the hall. I just switched on the lights of the adjoining rooms because unfamiliar surroundings and a darkness without ambient light are uncomfortable bedfellows. I liked the fact that all the rooms were furnished. The huge prints of Andy Warhol and Marilyn Monroe in the salon were so incongruous that they made me laugh out loud.

Then an old-fashioned sound almost jolted me out of my skin. It came from the dining hall. I couldn't see a telephone. I couldn't locate the answering machine which clicked and whirred into action.

A man spoke into the room. I didn't understand the French, but his voice was so beguilingly reassuring, he could have been speaking to me. When I heard Philip's light hesitant voice following the beep, the anger deep inside me scorched my throat like bile. "I'm not sure I've got the right place, but I've got this number from Tom

12

Braid, my wife's brother... could you ask my wife to ring me please?"

If I had phoned anyone that evening, it would have been Tom. "Thank you," I would have said. "Thank you for letting me come at such short notice. You're the best brother in the world." I'd have meant it. He'd saved me from myself.

I kept the recorded message for a long time — that is, until it became imperative to erase that voice from the face of the earth. I listened to it in the evening sometimes, when I couldn't think of anything else to do. After Eveline arrived, there was no need. I was no longer rattling about the château on my own in the evening with only shadows for company.

Chapter 2

By the time Eveline arrived in August, I had been at the château for two months. All the major work on the house had been done. I had stripped it back to its beautiful bones. Nothing new had been introduced — no kitchens or bathrooms, no fancy heating or plumbing. The house was functioning but rudimentary, just as Tom wanted, not that he had visited to tell me. Dear Tom. He telephoned regularly — ostensibly to discuss the work on the château, but really to make sure that I was okay.

"Remember, nothing major," he'd bellow reassuringly. "Just habitable. How are you?"

"I'm fine," I'd say, "but..."

"Yes?" And I would tell him about the latest oddity, like the passport I'd found stuffed at the back of a drawer or the three boxes of tongue scrapers, high up on a shelf in the downstairs cloakroom.

He'd be cheerfully insouciant. "Get rid of it/them," he'd say. "Now, tell me how you are," with a heavy emphasis on the word 'you'.

The grounds too had been transformed in that relatively short time, once the fly-tipping had been taken away. The château's façade shimmered, between clumps of water lilies, across the surface of the ornamental pond. There was a semblance of lawns with their little bits of topiary which I'd refashioned into basic toadstool shapes. The flower borders at the front of the house were rampant with verbena, lavender and poppy. At the back of the house, there was a swimming pool with blue and white marble tiles which sparkled beneath a sheet of tantalisingly clear, clean water.

Even the avenue had been reinstated to the gates with three hundred and ten loads of gravel all levelled and raked — except that there were still no gates. Tom said the budget wouldn't stretch to gates. I argued that if he could afford a château, surely he could afford gates. I couldn't understand what he had against gates.

I couldn't have done any of it without Greg, the local English builder. He pitched up at some unearthly hour on my first morning. "Your brother said that you'd be coming. Saw the car at the entrance," he said by way of explanation when I'd finally managed to haul the front door open. I'd bunked down for the night near the door, on a mattress which I'd pulled off the pile in the hall. Greg could see exactly where I'd slept but he didn't make a comment and I liked him instantly for it. Besides, he was a friendly figure: a tall, gangly man with a crooked nose, a shock of yellow hair, and a smile which was so huge that it lifted his large ears. I smiled back, my first genuine smile for months.

"I can't offer you a cup of tea or coffee."

"No worries," he said, pulling a carton of milk out of one of the capacious pockets in his overalls. "I'll make one for you."

He led me through the dark corridor and down a flight of stairs. I found myself in the kitchen which was enormous and basic with a range and sink at one end, and a long well-worn table and dresser at the other. One wall was lined with cupboards. Greg flung open door after door, revealing shelf after shelf of non-perishable foodstuffs, until he found the stash of twenty or more bags of coffee.

He rummaged around the dresser and flourished a percolator at me, like a rabbit out of a hat. He was enjoying my surprise.

"Everything's been left?"

"And then some," he said. "You should see upstairs."

"How many rooms are there?"

"Twenty-one, plus two in the turret."

They were his footsteps I'd seen in the dust in the hall. He'd spent several hours at the château the previous week because Tom had asked him to supervise the reconnection of the services before I arrived. "I see," I said, thinking how prescient Tom had been, as I had no idea that I'd be leaving for France until an hour or so before my departure.

We inspected the château together that first day. In the clear morning light, there was a sense of abandonment about the place — an air of desolation, of lives curtailed. In the salon, for example, there were magazines five years out of date on the coffee table, a man's sweater slung over one of the three white leather sofas, and a pair of leather slippers by the hearth. Everything was covered in a thick layer of dust.

It was not a large château, as châteaux go. The ground floor comprised of the entrance hall, a salon, a dining hall, a small library and down the corridor which led to the backstairs for the kitchen, a bedroom and a bathroom. The bedroom, with a double aspect, was the most beautiful in the house. To the front, a view of the Provençal hills and to the back, a view across the swimming pool terrace to the woods.

On the first floor, the sense of dereliction grew stronger, along with another feeling I couldn't quite place. By then, we'd been silenced by the hush of the house, beckoning each other to come and see bare wires protruding from walls and ceilings, holes in the lath and plaster, water stains where the plumbing had leaked.

Unlike the bedroom off the hall, none of the rooms had a bed. They were furnished very erratically in varying combinations of wardrobes, chests of drawers, tables and chairs. The rooms on the second floor were completely empty apart from one which was full of gym equipment, its expensive machinery reeking machismo from beneath grey cloaks of dust.

It dawned on me then.

Only men had lived there. It explained the atmosphere which lingered in the salon; the cupboards and drawers overflowing with men's clothing and the bathroom cabinets packed with their toiletries. It was the explanation for the rusty razors in the toothbrush mugs, the pin-up tacked to the back of a door, the odd pornographic magazine we'd seen. It explained the almost barrack-like feel of the place. A sense of the absent male permeated the château, as pungent as the odour of a tomcat.

"Who lived here before?" I asked Greg. He had his back to me, checking a window frame for rot.

"On second thoughts, don't tell me," I said, changing my mind. "I'd rather have a blank canvas."

He turned then, to face me. "It's been empty all the time I've been in these parts."

We left the tower to last and I couldn't believe at first what I saw in the lower of the two rooms. For one heady moment, nothing that had preceded my arrival at the château mattered. Nothing mattered except the framed panels depicting episodes from the Cupid and Psyche story. They were sun-lightened but otherwise perfect.

Quickly I closed the curtains that Greg had just drawn back. "These are grisaille panels," I told him breathlessly, my heart thudding with excitement, "circa 1816."

"Grisaille what?"

"Wallpaper. Very rare examples. Dufour."

I announced then that I would sleep in the upper room. I gave Greg the impression that I'd chosen the tower because of the grisaille panels. It wasn't the entire truth. I'd always wanted to sleep in an eyrie but more than that, the tower had an old-fashioned grace that had been erased from the rest of the house. I liked that. I liked that it felt untouched by whoever had lived at the château previously because I knew, even then, that I wouldn't have liked them.

We went back down to the kitchen for another coffee. It was almost lunchtime and Greg cut his baguette in half to share with me.

"What is it with you and wallpaper?"

"It's my job. I'm a conservator of wallpaper."

"A conservator?"

"A bit like a painting restorer."

"I see, the blank canvas etc."

"Greg, please, I don't want to talk about me."

He didn't respond. He put both his elbows on the table and munched through his baguette. I ate mine. When he'd finished he crossed over to the sink. He ran water over the mug and plate. He placed both on the draining board.

"Okay then," he said. "Where do you think we should start?"

I smiled. "What do you think?"

"I'd better have a look at the roof — see what needs to be done."

While Greg investigated the roof, I went back up to the dining hall. I was looking for a vase but when I opened the doors to the enormous walnut sideboard, the two shelves were jam-packed with what I could only describe as jumble — old board games, frayed lampshades, boxes of surgical gloves, dirty tablecloths, fishing gear — all shoved on top of what turned out to be a Sèvres dinner service for a twenty-four place setting. Eventually, right at the back, I found what I was looking for. It was heavy fluted crystal, about two feet tall and just right for my purpose. I'd noticed a mass of canna lilies by the terrace and I filled the vase with them, placing the vase on the wooden chest in the hall. The flowers were tantamount to a flag for me. A woman had taken possession of the house.

I spent the rest of that first day clearing out the personal effects of the previous inhabitants. If I was going to live at the château, I didn't want to feel that I was trespassing on someone else's territory. Besides it was territory which wasn't to my taste, particularly on the first floor. I found eleven balaclava masks, six dildos, and nine pairs of furry, pink handcuffs. I didn't tell Greg about them. I was too embarrassed. I just shoved the sex toys into the sacks I was filling with clothing, hoping that whichever charity received them would welcome the surprise. The clothes were of the finest quality but they smelt — not unpleasant, but with an oily scent which had lingered over the years. I kept aside a couple of linen jackets and shirts handmade in Savile Row, thinking that Greg might like them. He didn't.

I junked everything in the bathroom cabinets. I chucked every magazine I could find. I found rows and rows of pornographic videos in a cupboard in the salon with hideously graphic images of women on their covers. "It's just odd. There isn't a TV anywhere," I said, showing Greg the black bag when he came down from the roof.

He shrugged. "There's nowt so queer as folk," he said helpfully, before launching into a yodel which turned the word folk into another ruder word as the echo bounced around the hall. His humour was so childish sometimes.

Until Eveline arrived, I had nothing and no one to think about except the house. Deliberately so. I locked up my mind, focussing on the house. I locked myself up. I rarely went out. I was consumed by the château.

Hard physical work was enough for the day, but not enough for the nights. There was nothing then to distract me from endlessly replaying in my head that last evening in London: what Philip had said to me, and what I'd said to Philip before I lost all self-control. In the small hours of the morning, I needed a switch to switch myself off. My eyes would strain against the darkness which would throw up shadows — one becoming me and another, Philip. We would be sitting in the garden talking, like the last evening, before I left. Then the shadows would become my parents, pressed up against a wall, dissolving into each other in a passionate clinch.

Chapter 3

The process of writing — the act of inputting word after word on the screen in front of me — I find excoriating. I spend a lot of time gazing at the terrace of narrow houses opposite, typical of so many streets on the outskirts of London. Already it is October. Leaves are falling off spindly trees. Honesty requires self-knowledge and I have always been too frightened by what I might find, if I delved deep. Writing this is like leaves falling inexorably off a tree: leaf by leaf, denuding the branches and leaving me so exposed and so blinded by tears that I can hardly see what I have to write next — but write I will. I owe it to Tom.

*

"Did you see the snake darling?" I remember my mother insisting on an answer, as I howled and my father comforted me.

"A silver one," I cried. Even after all these years, the memory of it slithering into the long grass makes me shudder. My mother glanced over to my father with eyes full of meaning.

"Anything else?" she asked.

"Marks, like zigzags."

My mother ran back to the house. I lay slumped against my father, holding my leg. She returned with a knife. It glinted between her fingers. Tom, having been momentarily silenced by the gravity of our parents' reaction, jiggled about pulling funny faces. Not even he could make me laugh.

Whilst my father cradled me, my mother's hand dipped with a glancing flash. I'll never forget the sharp stab of pain. The next thing I knew, my mother had her head down, her hair fanned out right across my ankle and foot. When she raised her head, her mouth and chin dripped blood. She had to spit out a lot more blood before she could speak. "What a brave girl." She smiled, revealing bloodied teeth like she'd been eating me. I went into hysterics. So did Tom. They had to pull him off me.

When I returned from hospital, my father abandoned his writing to sit at the end of my bed and Tom offered me all his toys which I graciously accepted as my due.

"I tell you what," my father said, "when your leg's better, we'll go for a picnic — all four of us, and afterwards we'll go to the cinema. What do you say?" I said it sounded wonderful. He never did take us to the film. By then, he was dead.

*

The day Eveline arrived, I had spent hours stripping tangerine paint from the wainscoting in the salon. The windows were wide open and my only distraction was listening to the sounds floating up from the village. The sense of anticipation was almost palpable. A circus had pitched camp the day before.

After that hot, arm-achingly, tedious chore, I was glad, come the evening, to be sitting out on the terrace with nothing more taxing to do than to choose the paint colours — gradations of white from chalk to buttermilk — for the interior walls. It must have been a little after six o'clock. Six o'clock and Greg was off, wheeling his bike down the avenue.

I had all the thin strips of card with the paint colours on the rickety little table in front of me. I was watching Greg gradually disappear under the avenue's canopy of lime trees. I couldn't concentrate. I was concerned that all the work Tom wanted done on the château would be soon finished and I had no plans for my future. All I knew was that I had no intention of returning to London.

Everyone in the village must have been at the circus, waiting for the performance to begin. The air was so still it was like varnish. There was no sound — just a dog barking monotonously like it had been shut up or forgotten, and the sudden screech of a car's brakes as it took the steep incline of the hill.

Then there was a shout. Sharp and near. Then another, and another. Greg burst out from under the trees, running, waving his arms. I stood up, so quickly that the table rocked and the strips of card went everywhere.

"I thought it was another bag of rubbish dumped," his voice came out staccato on his breath. "But it's not. It's dead."

Whether he was propelling me, or me him, I don't know. We ran until we reached the gates. I could see Greg's bike crashed to the ground beside a body which was in the foetal position, with one arm flung out and so inert, with its eyes closed, that I thought the worst. I put two fingers on the back of one still wrist just to check.

"Is she dead?"

"She's warm."

The girl couldn't have been more than eighteen, twenty. Not older. Her face was upturned towards the sky, long lashes making deep shadows underneath her eyes. Her skin was the colour of desert sand and her clothes were black, but she looked grey from the chalky dust of the gravel. Luckily, she was wearing a long jacket and jeans.

"Her pulse."

"Quiet, Greg."

"Is she in a coma?"

"How would I know? I'm not a doctor."

"The doctor," he said. "The police." He slapped his back pockets looking for his mobile. I don't know how many times he thumped himself until he found it.

"She's not dying." The outstretched hand was clenched into a tight fist. I started to prise open the fingers ever so gently. Greg managed to dial one wrong number and then the phone slipped out of his hands. It missed the girl's head by a whisker. He ran his palms down his grubby paint-splattered overalls. "What's the emergency number for France?"

"Honestly, Greg. How long have you lived here?"

"Three years, but I've not had call to... Hallo!" he beamed, showing his white even teeth. The girl's eyes were open. She didn't look terrified or distressed by Greg's funny face looming over her. In fact, she had no expression at all.

"Are you okay?" I asked. "Does your back hurt? Your neck?"

Her eyes turned towards me and she started to sit herself up — awkwardly, as if her bones hurt.

She was bruised I thought, hopefully no more than that.

"Hell's bells," Greg said, bending for a closer look at what had fallen out of her hand.

A bullet, a tarnished silver bullet, was lying on the gravel. I looked at the girl and she looked back, with nothing in her eyes except my reflection. I stretched to pick the bullet up but her hand snapped over it, hiding it again.

"Do you need a doctor?" I asked.

She said nothing in response to my barrage of questions. Nothing to who she was or where she had come from.

We stayed outside on the avenue for quite a while, wondering what to do. I squatted beside her, frozen by indecision, unable to decide what to do for best. Greg paced back and forth, hands in pockets. He'd tossed his mobile into the long grass near the swing by the gates.

"Useless. I don't get the lingo half the time."

"Shhh, Greg. I'm thinking." I was deliberating on the wisdom of taking a stranger in, even for an evening. Deep down in my sub-conscious, I must have known that the decision would have consequences — but just how devastating, I could never have guessed.

I remember the moment like it was yesterday. Never again would the sun lie so thick and yellow across our backs, would the blue seep out of a crystal clear sky and the trees lining the avenue fling out their branches with such abandon. The sound of the circus welled up out of the village; a cacophony of yowls and shrieks and snatches of that jolly accordion music which the French seem to like so much.

The girl was beautiful. She had the face of a Modigliani muse, as remote and as impossibly beautiful as a two-dimensional painting but when I turned to look at her again, her eyes connected with mine, wordlessly beseeching me not to abandon her.

"It's okay," I said softly, "you're safe here. I promise."

"Look what I've found," Greg had walked out onto the road, and returned carrying a smart canvas suitcase emblazoned with a designer logo. "Found this on the other side of the pillar. Yours is it?" Greg asked the girl jokingly.

She scrambled to her feet and stretched out her hand.

The girl didn't speak, I realised with a shock. She wasn't going to speak.

"What have you got in here? Rocks?" Greg laughed, moving the case from her reach.

"Stop it, Greg!" He stopped, looked at me, looked at the girl, saw what I meant and, shamefacedly, handed her the suitcase. She insisted on lugging it up the avenue, not allowing either of us to help.

I don't know where Greg located the gendarme but the policeman wasn't any use. By the time he arrived, Greg and I had eaten. Duck pâté out of a tin on stale baguette. The girl wouldn't eat.

It was lucky that the French words '*immigrée clandestine*' sounded so like the English equivalents. How could I have known if the young woman was an illegal immigrant? She had just arrived, hadn't she? Besides, she didn't look like an illegal immigrant. I was more worried that she was a victim of trafficking.

The gendarme shrugged his shoulders. "Then she must be your visitor." He was obdurate. I wasn't to know then that there had been a series of burglaries in a neighbouring village and, as the lone policeman, he was under a lot of pressure.

There was no real need for the French/English dictionary that I'd gone up to my turret to find. The girl sat through the exchange between the three of us with total indifference. Greg was trying to help with his few words of French. I was getting frustrated by our inadequacy. I wanted to shake her and shout "What are you doing here?" To elicit some response.

I asked the girl if she had anything with which to identify herself, but she just looked at me. I drew a rectangle with another small rectangle inside it. I drew a large question mark.

"It's supposed to be a passport," I pre-empted Greg's question.

"You'll have to go through her suitcase."

"I don't like to."

"People don't just land themselves on you."

"Don't they?" I said, looking at the girl sitting still and mute on the other side of the table.

Greg lifted the suitcase onto the table. "Maybe there's an address inside — a contact number."

"Do you mind?" I asked as I tried to press open the locks but they were the combination type. Eyes downcast, the girl reached across the table and swivelled the suitcase to face her. Deftly, she notched the locks so that the lid sprung open. She didn't look at me once. '000,' I thought, 'why didn't I think of that?'

Greg peered over my shoulder. The case was crammed with clothes, thrown in, pell-mell. They were nice clothes, a young person's clothes, all of good quality, most of them designer labels. There was a pair of stiletto shoes and a sponge bag. Nothing else. No address. I folded the clothes and returned them to the case and shut the lid. The suitcase's owner couldn't have looked less interested if she had tried.

"Her jacket?" Greg suggested.

"I can't strip search her." I hadn't meant to snap. He was only trying to help. "I'll look later, when she takes it off." It wasn't easy talking about a person as if she were an unwanted delivery, however beautiful — particularly if that person was sitting opposite you — and she was. Like an unwanted delivery, I mean.

Eventually the gendarme took his leave.

Greg beckoned for me to follow him out into the archway, out of sight of the girl. He bent towards me with his flyaway hair catching in the shaft of light from the kitchen. It was quite dark and, from the snatches of noise, the circus was in full swing.

"There isn't a B&B in the village."

"Then I'll give her a bed for the night."

"She can stay with me, in the caravan."

"There's plenty of room here."

"You don't know where she has come from."

"She's just a young girl," I said. "What possibly could happen?"

"You don't know who is looking for her."

I couldn't allow Greg to have a young girl to stay overnight, more for his protection than hers.

Eventually Greg did leave, reluctantly, despite my reassurances. It didn't occur to either of us that she might have planned to be taken in at the château.

I gave the girl the only room with a bed, off the corridor in the hall.

My unexpected guest stayed sunk in the armchair in front of one of the windows, as I busied myself making the bed. I let her be, wordlessly gesturing to her when the bed was ready. Listlessly she crossed over to her suitcase, her shadow trailing across the ceiling behind her like she'd lost it. She picked out what looked like a silk nightie, clutching it to her chest until I closed the door behind me. No sign of any gratitude. No sign of anything at all, except, perhaps, exhaustion.

I tried to call my brother to ask if he knew anything about a girl turning up unannounced at the château gates. It was highly unlikely but I didn't know what else to do. Samantha, his wife, answered the Oxfordshire landline. She sounded harassed, reluctant to talk.

"I thought you were a journalist, phoning this late."

The press were always plaguing Tom. "Why? What do they want him to comment on now?"

"Try Tom on his mobile."

"I have, but you know what he's like."

"Do I?" Her laugh was bitter. She cut the connection.

I thought, for a second, that the girl was in the room with me — but when I swung round, it was just the draught from a leaky window, playing with the fringe of the lampshade, causing its shadow to quiver on the wall.

On my way up to my room, I peeked in on my uninvited guest. The crack of light slid, almost to the bed. All I could see was a shape hunched under the covers and a mass of shadow beyond.

"Are you alright?" I whispered. "Do you need anything?"

I could tell that she was awake — there was a tautness in the darkened room, like someone was holding her breath.

Chapter 4

"Sis." Tom always called early in the morning. "How are things? Have you run out of readies?"

"Not this time." I asked him about the girl. Did he know her?

He laughed. "Is this a trick question?"

"No," I laughed with him. "But perfectly reasonable given your track record."

"I'm a reformed character these days."

"I know, I know. But listen." I explained the circumstances, about how we'd found her.

"I don't know, Sis." He sounded dubious. "Where's she from?"

"Haven't a clue."

Then he asked the next obvious question.

"How did she get up to the château in the first place?"

"No idea."

"No one with her?"

"No."

He thought for a while. "I don't like the sound of this."

"I've given a young girl a bed for the night. That's all."

"Get rid of her." His urgency took me aback. "You don't know who the hell she is."

"She's young enough to be your daughter."

"For God's sakes, Sis."

"No, not that..." It hadn't actually occurred to me. The girl was far too beautiful — and foreign — to be Tom's progeny.

"Why do you think she's got something to do with me?"

"I can't think of any other explanation."

"No one knows about the château. Why don't you just ask her what she's doing there?"

"I would if I could."

"Stop playing silly buggers."

"She doesn't speak."

"Look Sis," my brother's annoyance gave way to exasperation. "I just want you to be careful. Please. No one just turns up."

There was nothing for breakfast for my uninvited guest, so I went down to the boulangerie. I'd forgotten how delicious a fresh, French croissant can be, so much better than the soft little bits of dough in a plastic bag which I'd been buying from the mini-supermarket on the edge of the village. My croissant was eaten by the time I'd walked back up to the château gates.

I waited for the girl to emerge from the bedroom and while I waited, I resumed the tedious business of stripping away the orange paint from the wainscoting in the salon. The salon's furnishings were completely uncoordinated — it could only have been by chance that the bulbous lampshades which hung over the sofas matched the wainscoting.

Perhaps the sound of my scraping carrying on the heat-laden air woke her. It was almost ten o'clock anyway, with the sun white in the sky, and the dazzle blinding on the windowpanes.

I could feel her presence before I turned to greet her. Her beauty was even more disconcerting in the full light of the day. I felt self-conscious, just to be looking.

"Slept well?"

31

She smiled. She held herself very erect, like a ballerina. She was wearing different clothes: a plain white shirt and khaki pedal pushers. I could see bruises on her arms and legs. She had nothing on her feet.

"I forgot to ask you your name last night."

She said nothing. She didn't look at me. She was looking around the room, her gaze finally resting on the Warhol prints on the back wall.

There was a quality of stillness about her that I was hesitant to break.

"I've got to call you something," I said gently.

"Okay then. It doesn't matter." I was still under the assumption that she would be with me for a couple of hours at most before going on her way.

I took the girl down to the kitchen and warmed up a croissant. She watched me as I lit the ramshackle range — first turning on the gas, then lunging forward with ancient flamethrower before lurching back in case of explosion. She leant against the dresser, its surface covered with the paraphernalia of doing up a château.

"There's plenty of filter coffee, should you like a cup — fifteen bags of it — and if you would like it brewed — " I open another cupboard door with a flourish, "there are five cafetières, four percolators and two filter machines. The choice is yours."

The girl's expression was completely neutral. I flushed, conscious suddenly of how eccentric I must have looked, brandishing a gas lighter, hair flecked with paint, in an old stained t-shirt and shorts held up with a piece of string. I hadn't bothered about my appearance since being at the château.

"Nothing to do with me," I said, laughing to hide my embarrassment. "The people before left everything. I haven't been here that long. Do you like sugar? Greg does. Seven spoons. He needs the energy."

I talked as if she understood English, with lots of finger pointing and hand gesticulation in case she didn't follow my meaning.

In the end, as she didn't express a preference, I gave my uninvited guest filtered coffee from a cafetière. She pulled the croissant apart with long fingers and spread it with jam and margarine. She ate hungrily and seriously. All her concentration was on the food. I became more concerned for her. Her shoulder blades jutted out too much. Her bra line sagged, as if she has recently lost weight. I didn't know what more I could do for other than give her breakfast before she went on her way.

"Would you like a lift somewhere?" I asked, when she had finished. She looked up at me, her eyes completely unfathomable.

"How about seeing the house before you go?" I assumed she was interested in old houses, as she'd seemed genuinely interested in the salon. Besides, in the two months that I'd been at the château I hadn't shown the house to anyone.

I took her up the stairs and into the dining hall. "You should have seen it before." I pointed to the best piece of furniture in the house; the fine eighteenth century table which could sit twenty. "That was covered in junk. You name it, it was there: old curtains, newspapers, boxes of broken crockery." I didn't tell her that the sideboards were still overflowing: crammed with everything and anything. Her fingers skimmed over the back of one of the grey plastic office chairs which provide the seating for the grandiose centerpiece. She gazed solemnly at the seventies replica of a glass candelabra.

In the salon, she sat on one of the sofas as I told her that the beautiful paneled ceiling above her head had been hidden by aertex tiles. She examined it closely. "You know," I confided, "when I first came in here, it was like the previous owners had just popped out. Pretty creepy." She picked up an ornament, a small stuffed donkey with panniers and the inscription 'A gift from Portugal'. She turned it over to look at its belly. "They were funny people, though, the people before," I told her, "you know, odd, the sort of oddness that you don't really want to know more, especially when you're living here on your own." She looked at me so studiously that I thought I should stop talking.

She returned the donkey and opened a marquetry box. She spent so long gazing into it that my curiosity was piqued. I looked over her shoulder. The box contained what looked like shrivelled crescents of nail; toenail clippings. Nothing surprised me about the house anymore.

"You see what I mean?" I smiled. "Yuck."

She snapped the lid shut.

*

At a window, I made her look out on the glorious far-reaching view of the hills of Provence.

I showed her the library, the smallest room in the house with its heavy executive desk and five-foot tall bookcases, the thin glass doors protecting gold-tooled leather volumes. One of the bookcases I'd emptied. She stretched out her hand to feel its smooth wood and I warned her to watch out — the bookcase was very unsteady, not attached to the wall. I caught our reflection on the thin glass doors. She was a good head taller than me. She could easily have been a model. I told her how it took almost two days to prise every sweet wrapper stuffed into every keyhole in the house, showing her exactly what I meant. She gave a little shudder. "Yes," I said, "I know exactly how you feel. Who would want to do that? I mean, I am certain that no children have lived here for an awfully long time..." I stopped because I felt so foolish. I didn't know whether she understood anything more than intonation and gesture and even if she did, why should a stranger want to know anything about me or the château?

Chapter 5

We returned to the hall and my visitor, without my invitation, started up the main flight of stairs. I was perplexed that she seemed to be so intent on the house but everything about her was so odd, it was just another oddity. For all I knew, she could have been a student of architecture. I was concerned that she would be disappointed in the upper parts; two floors, each with a corridor of still, almost empty rooms divided by a wide landing. There were still no beds. Greg and I had found a delivery of beds — the flat-pack variety — in the original packaging in the stables, but they were too damaged to be of any use.

Greg and I had worked very hard. Except for one room, there were no longer any wires protruding from the walls, holes in the lath and plaster, or rotten floorboards. The plumbing had been fixed — which, in the event, was easy enough to do as the pipes were attached to the walls. Most importantly though, there was no sense of the dereliction which used to pervade the house. No rush of dust to settle like a second skin every time I opened a door.

As I thought, the girl wasn't interested in the upper floors. She seemed to withdraw further and further into herself, shutting herself off from me and her surroundings. It was as if she was disappointed and I was disappointed for her. I was so proud of what Greg and I had achieved. I wanted though, to show her the gym on the second floor. I could remember the real start of surprise when I first saw it. It was so incongruous.

The girl didn't react to the gym. She hardly gave it a glance. She seemed suddenly exhausted, drooping on her feet.

I led the way to the first of the tower's two rooms. She sat on the bottom rung of the spiral staircase while I drew back the four sets of curtains covering the four windows. Unlike me, when I first saw the grisaille panels, there was no gasp of delight.

"These," I said grandly, "are absolutely the most precious part of the château."

Her expression was blank, totally bored. I gave up then trying to placate her disinterest. I redrew the curtains, plunging the room back into a sunlit twilight. I didn't take her up to the upper room, my bedroom. I'd exposed enough of myself.

I stopped to turn round and to look up at her as she followed me down the stairs.

"Please, if you're in trouble, let me help."

She flinched at the suddenness of my movement but her eyes held mine before looking away towards the front door.

"Why have you come?"

A shadow flitted across her eyes.

"Are you escaping from someone or something?"

I took her lack of reaction as a 'no'.

I expected her to go at that point, to take her suitcase from the bedroom and to take her leave of me, with a slight wave of her hand. She didn't. She disappeared straight out the front door. I watched her back, ramrod straight again, descend the front steps with some amusement. I couldn't quite believe the cheek of her but, at the same time, I admired it. I didn't call out 'Your suitcase!', because I knew, in that moment, that she had absolutely no intention of leaving just then.

I was also relieved. I would have hated for her to walk out the gates with nowhere to go. She reminded me of myself when I first arrived at the château. I didn't know if she was heartsick but whatever had happened for her to land up at the château gates, meant that she needed respite. It was such a small act of kindness to allow someone some respite. Besides, the house needed kindness. I just knew it needed that.

Chapter 6

After my father died, my mother went off the rails. She was only thirty, fourteen years younger than I am today. Home life, for Tom and me, was punctuated by a bewildering series of 'uncles'. She partied until the small hours and we never knew what strange man was behind our mother's bedroom door. She would leave a tie or a sock on the door knob as a signal for us not to enter. At first she would still put on her bobbly white dressing gown and make our breakfasts. She gave up by the time I was ten. For a while I made boiled eggs and soldiers for myself and Tom, but soon we just stopped off at the bakery on our way to school. The 'uncles' always left us money under the pot plant in the hall.

The men came in all shapes and sizes. Tom and I poured salt in their tea, placed pins in their shoes, filled the pockets of the suit jackets they left hanging off the backs of chairs full of sneezing powder, but most didn't even look at us — their shiny eyes only reflecting images of our mother darting around the room, pouring them a drink, smoothing down her skirt, snapping on the standard lamp. She had a beautiful mouth which she painted red and she used to pucker kisses at us like a goldfish gasping for air. Tom tried to cling on to her. She brushed him off. 'Darling you're creasing my skirt.' 'Off you get sweetie, you're messing Mummy's makeup.' It was 'How lovely darling!', when he presented her with something he had made at school, only to find it chucked in the wastepaper basket a couple of days later. I held him in my arms, his face against my skinny chest, his shoulders shaking. I hated her then.

*

Tom called again, early in the afternoon. "Has our visitor left?"

I bristled at his easy assumption, sitting at his desk with a backdrop of the gleaming citadels of Canary Wharf. I was the one dealing with the situation, not him.

"Not yet."

"Why not?"

"I think she is exhausted. Isn't lack of speech a sign of trauma?"

"It's very sweet of you and all that, Sis, but seriously, she can't stay. I'll worry myself silly."

Despite my misgivings, I had to respect Tom's wishes with regard to his property. So I went in search of my visitor and I found her sitting on the grass under the lee of the terrace. She didn't look as if she was enjoying the sunshine. Her bruised arms hugged bony knees. As I approached she lifted her head and, all over again, I was struck by the loveliness of her face but she looked tired and miserable. I stood in front of her.

"You can't stay here," I spoke quite clearly and slowly. I pointed up in the direction of the house so that she had to understand. "This isn't my house. It's my brother's." I pointed to her. Both my hands made a 'no'. "He says you must go. Do you understand?"

For a second, her eyes weren't blank. I could see deep into the heart of her. She was like me, as I was when I arrived at the château, totally at a loss and full of heartache.

The rigidity of her face shifted. She buried her face in her knees. I thought she cried, but she didn't make any sound. Loneliness reeked from her.

I sat on the grass a few feet away. I didn't offer any comfort. She wouldn't have wanted a stranger embracing her any more than I would.

For a long time we just sat there. I watched a lizard sunning itself on a stone. I thought about how I came to be at the château, about how I drove like the wind to get away from London. I made a decision.

"Why don't you stay a couple of days? Get your strength back?"

She raised her face, her eyes questioning mine.

"It'll be okay," I said, getting up from the grass. "I'll sort it with my brother." I brushed her hair lightly. "Everything will be okay."

The lizard darted between two stones. I watched for a while to see if it would reappear.

"But, if you're going to stay here," I continued, "I have to call you something. I can't go round saying 'oi' every time we're to have a conversation." Even as I said it, it sounded a little ambitious.

"Then can I call you Eveline? It's one of my favourite names."

I had always been entranced by the name Eveline. It was the name of a character in my father's first novel. I wanted to be that character when I grew up — or failing that, to call one of my daughters by that name. I had always thought that I would have four daughters and two sons — the younger, of course, I would have called Tom; the elder, by my father's name.

That evening, I became as sure as I could be that Eveline understood English. I was in the cellar, lying on my back

41

in three inches of water, trying to stop a leak from underneath the old washbasin and shouting for Greg. I must have left the tap on, the last time I had been there. Not ever staying long enough to find out, I hadn't realised that the sink leaked.

The cellar wasn't a place I liked but it was where the washing machine and drier were housed. It was lit by one low energy light bulb and was full of junk and superfluous items like rusty chest freezers, rolls of carpet, and the ten ironing boards which were haphazardly propped against broken tables and chairs. A couple were still in shop plastic, covered, like the others, in sticky spider web. There could have been others in the nether regions of the cellar. At the time I hadn't explored. The excessive number of ironing boards gave me the creeps — conjuring up images of batty housewives and me in particular, back in London where I ironed everything, including Philip's socks.

I'd brought a torch and, shining it up, saw that an old washer had slipped. A trickle of water was dripping onto my face. It was just a matter of tightening the washer back into place. I heard footsteps near me.

"Greg," I said, "on the table by the door, there's a monkey wrench. Can I have it?" There was no point in him getting as wet as I was for a job I could do myself. The rusting spanner was handed to me and with a couple of cranks, the washer was back in place.

"Give us a hand," I stretched out my arm to be pulled out of the dark space. I had barely time to register that the grip wasn't Greg's horny old paw before Eveline's luminous eyes smiled down at me.

"You!" I was so surprised that I let go and toppled back, knocking my head. When the stars cleared, she was still

42

standing there, still offering me her hand. She hauled me up, with a strength which belied her slender frame. The expression in her eyes was blank, like she was looking and not seeing. Like she had shut herself away.

Chapter 7

My lack of French was a serious embarrassment. I did try to ask the impassive Madame la Boulangère had she seen a young foreign girl wandering around the village a couple of days before. Somehow she thought that I was asking for a jar of her raspberry jam which she gave me and then realising that maybe it wasn't exactly what I wanted, gave it to me for free. Even then she had to forcibly stuff my wallet back into my pocket before I understood.

Tom called just as I arrived back from the boulangerie for the third time in less than twenty-four hours.

"Before you say anything," I told him, "I've told the girl she can stay a couple of days."

"I've never heard of anything so stupid." His anger exploded down the line. "Why put yourself at risk?"

"Please Tom, I can't just chuck her out on the streets."

I could tell from the silence which followed that he was softening.

"She could be a terrorist."

"She's not. I'm sure of it. The gendarme was here, remember? She'd have made a run for it."

"Take a photograph and send it to me."

"Of her?"

"No. Donald Duck. Seriously Sis, I sometimes wonder…"

"Shut up," I said. "Okay."

"I've got a contact in the police — they could send it through to Interpol…"

"She wouldn't be here if…" I gave up trying to argue. Tom was talking sense. "Okay. It will be some sort of security I suppose."

I didn't think to take my camera when I left London so I asked Greg if I could borrow his. He liked to record our work on the château.

Eveline was sitting on the balustrade of the terrace. She had her back to the view: ancient roofs of village houses tumbling down to the lake, glinting in the sun, which the locals used as a lido. I hadn't yet been there. I really had been locking myself away.

She was shy of the lens, turning her head. I panicked then, thinking that maybe she did have something to hide — what could be better proof than not wanting your photograph taken?

"Please," I said to her. "It's for my brother. He wants to help you."

She put an arm up, half obscuring her face.

"If you want to stay, you must let me take a photograph of you." She must have heard the urgency in my voice because it was as if she were a model. She threw back her shoulders and tilted her chin — just so, in that disdainful way you see in magazines. I took a photo of a very beautiful woman without a voice, without a name — and I was both puzzled and flattered that she would want to stay with me.

My brother was right. Eveline had to be at the château for a reason. We were too far up a hill for her to have arrived by chance. There wasn't a train station for the village and the buses, Greg told me, were very infrequent.

I did think that perhaps she had arranged to meet someone and that someone had failed to materialise. But then I noticed that she kept her eyes on the ground. Eveline wasn't waiting for anyone.

She spent a lot of time drifting around the house and if not the house, the grounds. I tried to keep watch over her as best I could, whilst still working on the château.

Greg was sure that she wasn't going to do anything silly. "Walking about the bloody place as if she owns it." He was as exasperated as Tom that I hadn't asked her to leave.

"Don't you like her?"

"What is there to like?"

"I saw you two yesterday," I teased him. "By the stables."

He was embarrassed. "I didn't see you."

"I was inside. I looked out when I heard her laughing."

"Yes," he says. "She could be almost normal if she spoke."

"She's beautiful."

He gave me a sceptical look. "She's alright."

"More than alright, surely."

"She's got no warmth about her."

He'd been flexing his biceps for Eveline, making her laugh out loud, peals and peals of girlish laughter. It had made my heart lift. She'd been so miserable earlier on, until I'd told her she could stay. Greg had a tattoo of a mermaid on his arm and when he crunched the muscle, the mermaid's tail flicked. It was a party trick of his.

"But you know," Greg looked at me wonderingly, "as soon as she caught herself laughing, she stopped. Put on her zombie expression again. Nice girl and all that, but I don't know how you sleep easy at night."

I slept better at night, with Eveline there. There was no longer any need to keep the lights blazing all night to keep the shadows at bay. It honestly had never occurred to me that she might creep up the stairs to the tower, and stand over me, ready to plunge a knife which she had found lying about in the kitchen, straight into my heart. I am sure had I thought her remotely capable of such an action, I wouldn't have slept at all.

I was only ever seriously frightened once — and that was very early on in my stay. I walked into the kitchen and was confronted by a wizened old hag, doubled over a stick, standing as bold as brass in the middle of the room, ranting at me. She could have popped out of the cellars — or worse still, not be real, though I didn't believe in ghosts. If I'd believed in ghosts, I wouldn't have been staying at the château. I grabbed the broom and shook it at her fiery eyes, screaming to drown out whatever incantation she was spouting. I followed her halfway down the avenue; she hobbling, still hurtling back at me God knows what. When I asked Greg about my visitor, he was very noncommittal.

"It sounds like Claudine," he said. "Don't worry, she's the local mad woman."

With Eveline around, I started to make lunch. I'd been making myself a well-balanced evening meal from tins of vegetables and meat left by the previous occupants — not that I had bothered much before Eveline came.

Greg and I talked about what we were planning for the afternoon. It was stilted conversation, both of us very aware of the little pockets of silence between three people when only two of them talk. Eveline kept her head down, studiously avoiding eye contact. Greg started to tell silly jokes with silly gestures, looking mischievously at

Eveline, willing her to laugh. "Why did the turkey cross the road?" It was one of his better ones. "Because he wasn't chicken!"

Eveline disappeared up the backstairs while I washed up. Greg went back out to the stables. He was in the process of replacing floorboards on the second floor and needed to sort through the planking. I'd told him that I would stay in the cool of the house restacking the empty shelves of the bookcase in the library.

I love the smell of old books. I like the way they offer a direct continuum with the past — although our father has all but been forgotten except by universities. I can't find him even in London charity shops anymore. I used to like buying second-hand copies of his novels. I liked the roughness of the pages that had been in baths, planes, trains. I found a rasher of bacon once, five pages from the end. I wondered what had interrupted the person reading. Had someone come to the door? Were they taken from behind in a bout of impulsive sex? I liked the fact that my father had been alive in somebody else's head — even if, in the end, the last five pages were five too far.

There was a tranquillity about the house in the afternoon — a quietness, like a membrane through which I could hear other sounds, like the faint hum of the antediluvian refrigerator in the kitchen. The whir of Greg's saw lifted and faded on the air. I sorted through the pile of books I'd deposited on the threadbare carpet. For the first time in months I realised that I was happy. It was a lovely, liberating feeling of well-being.

I reached up to open the glass doors to the bookcase and caught the shimmer of movement as it toppled towards me. I broke its fall but I was holding books in my left hand, so that hand smashed through one of the glass panels and hit the back of the bookcase. I was crouched, contorted at an excruciating angle. A steady stream of blood ran down my arm. If I let go, my head would punch through the glass, giving me a necklace of unthinkable consequences.

"Greg! Come quick!"

I listened to the staccato of the saw.

"Help!" The sweat was pouring off my face.

I saw Eveline's feet first: long and slender bones with bare, strong toes. I could feel the warmth of her body as she leant across me. Gently, she pushed the bookcase back against the wall. I scrambled to my feet clumsily, holding my cut hand.

"Thank God, you heard me."

She smiled back at me, the smile lifting her face and there was this wonderful feeling — that we were partners, a sisterhood, allies together against this old house. Down in the kitchen, she helped me wash and bind the cut, her face full of concentration, her cool fingers pressing against my skin.

Greg wasn't pleased. He was cross. Guilty that he didn't hear me calling. "There could have been a bloody awful accident. One slip with a piece of that glass…"

"I know. My jugular."

He marched off to inspect. "I don't understand. I fixed the bookcase to the wall yesterday. The braces have been unscrewed."

"Well I didn't touch them."

He looked at me steadily.

"Oh come off it," I said with a laugh, "you don't seriously think that that girl… why would she?"

"You tell me."

"There's got to be a simple explanation, like the braces being faulty."

He looked around. "Where is she now?"

"In her room?"

"Floating about like a bloody ghost."

I ignored my prickle of unease about Eveline staying at the house. I was beginning to realise how much more comfortable I felt at the château, with another woman around, albeit for a few days. I was no longer scuttling up to my room in the turret before night fell.

Chapter 8

The phone rang that evening, on the extension in the salon. It had to be either Tom or Philip. My friends had long given up calling as I refused to tell them why I'd left London — although surely they must have guessed. The reason was as old as Adam and Eve. I hoped it was Tom, so that I could tell him how Eveline had saved me from a very nasty accident. "You see?" I could have said, " she has already repaid us tenfold."

It was Philip. My heart clenched when I hear his first, tentative "hello?" as if he felt he had no business in calling. He was right. He hadn't. I could have put the phone down on him but I didn't. I never had. Not once.

"How are you?" Philip began.

"Fine. And you?"

"Missing you. Pepper's pining."

"Poor Pepper."

"How's it going?"

"I have a guest."

"Who?"

"Eveline." Eveline looked up. She was sitting with me. She was looking at a large picture book of châteaux on the Loire. I couldn't tell whether she was reading the text or not. I thought not; she was turning the pages so listlessly. All the animation of the afternoon was gone.

"Who's she?"

"I don't know, she just turned up. She's going soon." I glanced at Eveline. Her face was bent right over the book.

"Where's she from?"

"Do you know, I don't know?"

"I don't understand,"

"How's London?" I changed the subject.

"Much the same. I'm thinking of visiting."

"Where?"

"You. The château."

"I might be going away." It was a lie. I really didn't want to see him.

"Going away? Haven't you gone far enough?"

Half of me wanted to cut the connection, the other half of me said brightly "I miss the sea." It was true. I did miss a long, straight horizon and my toes curling into impacted, soggy sand.

"So do I," Philip said softly. "I'm so sorry."

I was sorry too. In the end, he caught me unawares. I had known. Of course I'd known, but I thought the danger had passed — and the pity of it was, from what he told me, that I had been right; the danger had passed.

"Here is nowhere near the sea," I said.

We'd lost our deposit in Norfolk. It didn't matter that we'd been loyal customers for years: same cottage, same two weeks in August.

"What about Pepper?"

"What about her?"

"She'd need a rabies vaccination."

"I thought I'd book her into kennels. So if I get some dates…"

"We'll see. I'll have to check with Tom, see if he's coming down."

"If Tom's there…"

"I know. You'd rather not." I was aware that Eveline was watching me, all pretence of reading gone. She must have heard the tension in my voice.

Eventually Philip began again. "Say hello to Pepper."

"Hello Pepper," I said brightly. "Are you being a good girl?"

"Talking about Tom, there's a lot in the press at the moment."

"Is there?"

"They might be on to something this time," Philip hesitated. "In fact — "

"There is no internet here," I cut him off. There were day-old English newspapers at the tobacconists, but I didn't read them, not even the headlines. England was the last place I wanted reminding about.

"Something to do with pension pots," Philip said portentously. I didn't care. As far as I was concerned my husband was jealous of my brother's business success. Philip was a backroom boy, an accountant, and totally risk-averse.

"I'm sure Tom's not bothered. People are always sniping at his success. He'll face them down as he's done before."

And, in the long silence which followed that silly jibe, I recalled the last evening in London.

I'd been sitting out on the patio with Philip, enjoying a glass of wine on a lovely early June evening, revelling in the promise of the summer to come after a long, dark winter.

"There's something I have to tell you," he'd said, breaking the silence between us. There had been a lot of silences over the past months which I'd done my best to ignore. I hadn't wanted confrontation. I'd told myself that if I paid no heed to the dead weight of suspicion which was dragging me down — making me feel that I was living life underwater — that eventually it would disappear and I'd be free again.

"There is something I should tell you." Only the once, should a woman hear that from her partner.

"Did you sleep with her?" I'd asked stupidly, because his words hung in front of my eyes and I was having difficulty in linking them, to give them meaning.

He told me. I could never have been prepared. Everything, utterly betrayed. I'd wanted to beat myself insensible, beating him. He wouldn't fight back, enraging me even more. In the end, I picked up the vegetable knife lying on the draining board. I managed to stab him in the arm before he wrested the knife from me, dragged Pepper into the hall and left me, locking me in the kitchen.

It was Pepper's anguished howling which brought me to my senses — that, and the sight of Philip's blood on my dress.

Past midnight, to calm the dog, Philip took her for a walk in the park. My keys were in my handbag on the kitchen island. I let myself out by the back door, went around the side alley and re-entered the house through the front.

By the time Philip had returned, I'd gone. I had packed a suitcase and left for France.

*

There was a click on the other end of the line as Philip hung up.

"I'm fine," I told Eveline who had got up off the sofa and was standing by it, looking at me as if she didn't know whether to approach or stay away. She was looking at my hand. I looked down to see that I'd been clenching the handset so tightly that the cuts on my hand had opened again and beads of blood were dripping onto the floor.

Chapter 9

Our mother met Uncle Mani about five years after our father's death. She started cooking properly again and she didn't leave us to go out to her drinking club. She actually — almost — sought my permission before Uncle Mani came to live with us. Tom wasn't yet back from school. He was going through a phase of having evening detention almost every day. School rules, as far as Tom was concerned, were there to be broken.

"You know it's been very lonely for me since Daddy died." We had a large wooden peppermill which appeared during the short time Tom and I had had an Italian 'uncle', and she was twisting it over a chicken she was preparing for our supper. The peppermill made a curious creaking sound which always made me want to laugh. She was looking at me, showering the white chicken in a red casserole with black pepper.

I thought of my father and the thrilling sensation of being lifted high above his head with his big hands and twirled around and around. Had he been alive then, needless to say, he couldn't have picked me up. I'd reached the grand old age of thirteen, far too big and heavy.

"How much pepper does Uncle Mani like?"

"Lots," she said, popping the casserole into the oven. "No one could ever replace your father. He was the love of my life. Not a day goes by that I don't think of our loss…"

"I know," I said, though I couldn't have begun to know. My mother was embarrassing me.

"I like Uncle Mani," I said carefully, "but I don't want you to marry him. Neither does Tom."

"Oh Tom," I remember my mother's dismissive shake of the head. "I am not going to marry Manfred, darling, but he would very much like to live with us. What do you think?"

Then, before I could answer, she asked why I didn't want her to marry. "Is it Manfred or any man?"

"Anyone." Tom and I had rehearsed the reason why. "It would make Daddy even further away."

"Oh for goodness sakes," our mother said. "He's just up the road."

Despite her protestations to the contrary, we very rarely visited the cemetery. It never occurred to me that perhaps it was just too much for our mother to bear.

*

My mother was a social butterfly. I am not. Before Eveline, as I've said, I hardly ventured out of the château. Plenty of English lived in and around the village and its surroundings. A few made it up the avenue to introduce themselves and I rebuffed them politely. Greg was different. I trusted him. He asked no questions of me and I, none of him. It was a perfect relationship in many ways. After a few weeks though, I needed a little more by way of conversation.

I found the drinks party invitation in the letterbox at the end of the avenue.

I showed it to Greg, who was on his knees in the downstairs cloakroom, replacing cracked tiles.

"Why didn't they just come up the avenue and say hello?"

He wiped the grouting off his fingers with a rag. Normally, he wasn't so fastidious.

"It's Babs and Dora, their annual do. Everyone's invited."

"It would have been nice if they'd dropped by." I must have sounded wistful.

"After the way you've sent your few callers packing, it's a wonder you've got an invite at all."

I laughed.

"You're not going to go are you? To be honest," he looked at me so speculatively that, standing in the doorway in such close proximity, I blushed. "I wouldn't have thought that the ex-pat scene was for you."

"I can't hide away forever," I said, which was true and I was lonely.

Greg insisted on accompanying me. On the appointed evening, he trekked back up to the château in his inordinately long and shiny winkle-pickers. I had little choice in what I was to wear: jeans, shorts, or the only dress I had brought to France. For the first time ever, I'd ironed. Like ironing boards, there was an excess of irons in the house: seventeen in total, all found in nooks and crannies. All filthy. I spent a good half-hour scraping black sticky stuff off a flat plate before ironing my white linen dress.

The party was held in a garden which ran down to the river. "Difficult to get away from eh?" Greg nudged me with his elbow, as we went through the gate. He nodded at the silhouette of the château high on the hill with the tower like the stump of a periscope, scanning the horizon.

Babs and Dora were two octogenarian sisters.

People were very kind, welcoming me to France. "How are you finding it?"

"Wonderful." It was wonderful, but the château was peculiar — which I was too bloody-minded to admit to myself, let alone anyone else.

Greg hovered by my side. "What plans do you have for the château?" I don't know how many times I was asked that question with varying degrees of intensity. In the end, Greg started answering for me. "She's just doing it up for her brother."

"Tom Braid, isn't it? I do hope," a floral dress with fake pearl earrings touched me earnestly on the arm, "that the renovations will be sympathetic?"

"Just because he is in business," I tried to make the point light-heartedly, "doesn't mean he has no taste."

I was surrounded by a good-humoured crowd. Greg was in his element, revelling in the attention, as he filled in details of exactly what we had been doing with the château. A large man with a ruddy face asked me if Tom was feeling the heat back in London. People stiffened, as if he were guilty of gross bad manners.

I diffused the moment easily. I answered truthfully. "No I am. I'm the one who's here after all." A sausage fell off my fork. Greg picked it off the grass and made a great show of eating it, much to everyone else's laughing consternation.

Someone wanted to know when I would be replacing the gates. When would the pillars be repaired? I was congratulated on having had all the rubbish removed from the grounds. Heads shook, teeth tsked, eyes glanced up, up at the darkening bulk high on the hill, darker than the darkening sky. "Bloody disgrace it was, the way it was left." The conversation moved on to someone's bid for planning permission at the other end of the village.

So when Valerie introduced herself, she was a welcome relief. Greg shot off which was also welcome. I'd been like a prized possession of his all evening. Valerie raised an eyebrow at his departing back, but made no comment. She talked about herself, about how difficult it was to make ends meet as a single woman in this particular part of France. Finally she did ask a direct question.

"What did you do with all the stuff they left behind?"

I presumed she meant at the château, but before I could answer, we were interrupted.

The woman was thin and small. "Are you going to have a party in the grounds soon? That would be so much fun and a chance to…"

She was drunk, red wine sloshing around in her glass as she waved her hands because she couldn't recall what else it was that she'd wanted to say. Valerie gave me a look and slipped away.

A man appeared by her side, looking so embarrassed he had to be her husband. He put a hand on her elbow ready to steer her away.

"Home time, Sandra." He was firm.

"You!" Without warning, she was cross. "You're such a spoil-sport!" She chucked her wine at him half in fun, missed, and instead got me on my dress.

It was mayhem. Her husband had to literally pull her away from me as she frantically tried to dab at the stain with the end of her scarf.

I did not want the fuss. I definitely did not want to wear one of Babs' or Dora's frocks. Greg insisted on driving me back in his socks as his winkle pickers were too long for him to manage the clutch and brake.

"I knew it," he said furiously. "I shouldn't have left you alone. You're like a lamb among wolves with that lot."

I thought he was going a little too far but something the drunk woman had said worried me far more than the ruination of my dress. "Do they expect me to give a garden party?"

"Don't be daft, you're not the Queen."

Chapter 10

It was Greg who pointed it out. "The circus arrives and hey presto, you have a visitor. Two and two make four."

"Or they might make five," I said. "You did send the photo off?" I had deliberately left my laptop in London — not that it mattered with no internet access.

"I used the computer at the caff. You owe me five euros."

"Tom hasn't called."

"Give him a chance. It was only yesterday."

Greg was making coffee, which involved a palaver with a cafetière. He was very insistent on explaining to me, the first morning he started working at the château, that since being in France, he couldn't abide instant. I then discovered that he couldn't abide my coffee either, so he made his own.

"Where is Little Ms Stray anyway?"

"Outside last seen making her way in the direction of the chapel."

The chapel was not far from the house, across what must have been once a lovely lawn, in a dip of the land. It was a ruin, with only a few grey stones left scattered about — the rest must have been carted off centuries ago — but someone, sometime in the last fifty years, had tried to rebuild one wall with a space for a door and a niche for St James of Compostela. At least, I assumed it was St James. He was high up and the weather had worn away all the detail on the stone, but I could just about make out a carving of a shell dangling from his waist.

"Are you sure about her roaming about?"

"What is there to steal?"

He shrugged. "It's not that, but how can you be sure?" He twisted his index finger into his forehead, looking quite mad himself with his wide eyes and bits of paint and straw in his hair.

"For such a nice man," I teased him, "you're not very empathetic."

"All I know is that she is all over the house. I've seen her opening doors and drawers when she thinks no one's around."

"Your imagination's running away with you."

"Yeah, you're probably right." He looked at me sheepishly then suddenly got serious. "But you should try to find out where she's from. Someone must be looking for her."

"And what if they're not?"

"Then," he said, "something is very wrong."

*

Much later on that afternoon, I saw her sitting on the swing hooked up into the massive oak, staring into the long grass which almost came up to her knees. It was a patch of the grounds I hadn't yet cleared, thinking that there was no use for the swing, not until Tom's children visited. She looked so alone, so hopeless, that my heart went out to her.

"Wait!" I shouted and her head came up and she watched me as I scurried off to the stables as fast as I could in the blistering heat. It took some time, but I found the scythe while she waited. She watched as I scythed a path through the grass to reach her. She held up her feet

63

when bidden as I cut a swathe a few metres square around her. I felt I owed her an explanation.

"I hate snakes. Even the idea of them." I told her how Greg had laughed when he saw me scouting for snakes in the château. They rarely, if ever, came indoors. "I've haven't even seen one outside yet," I said. "Lucky me." As soon as I said it, I saw a movement in the long grass nearer the avenue — just the tips, the seed heads moving. I couldn't help myself. I screamed. Eveline jumped off the swing in panic.

Greg came running up the avenue, red-faced with the exertion, a lathe in his hand. "What's going on?" He looked at Eveline as if somehow, she was to blame. I willed myself to stop trembling. It was a mouse, I told myself. I'd disturbed a mouse. Greg returned to the château, stopping every so often to check back on us.

Bees buzzed, attracted by the scent of the freshly cut grass. I flapped my arms energetically to ward them off and made Eveline sit back on the swing from where she gazed at me with her solemn eyes. She made me feel very conscious of the enormous damp patches underneath my armpits. I hadn't bothered much about personal hygiene at the château.

"Shall I give you a push?"

Needless to say, Eveline didn't answer. She didn't have to; the silence she engendered was so powerful that it quelled any questions.

She wasn't squeamish about nature, I could tell. She didn't flinch as a bee grazed her cropped hair. It was a brutal cut, which had me wondering if she'd had longer hair and hacked it off herself. Given her taste in designer clothes, her haircut was out of keeping. Nothing though, could have taken away from the sense of perfection about her lovely face: the brow, the high cheek bones, the chin below the beautiful mouth which occasionally displayed a faint smile.

She remained sitting on the swing, so I went round behind her and gave a first tentative push, the way you do a child, with both hands on her back, pressing my thumbs into the knobbles on her spine beneath the thin cotton t-shirt. She used her legs to power the swing higher, and we fell into a rhythm of sending the swing and Eveline soaring into the branches of the tree. In total silence, but it didn't matter. I could tell that she was enjoying herself as much as I was, and I was: with the swish of air from the movement of the swing, the heady scent of the cut grass under my feet, and the feeling of being totally at peace with another human being. I didn't need to know her, nor she, me. We were women together, that was all that mattered. It didn't last of course. It stopped as soon as she slipped off the swing, spots of perspiration peppering the cloth between her shoulder blades.

In the evening, I took Eveline to the circus and she came unquestioningly, without a flicker of interest, as if it was quite normal to accompany someone she didn't know downhill to an evening's entertainment. It had been so hot that the tarmac smelt molten. Eveline walked a couple of paces behind me, like she was my shadow, so that I had to keep looking round to make sure that she was following. It was beginning to grow dark and her eyes were very large in her face.

The ticket lady paid us no attention whatsoever. She banged down our tickets and my change and we were ushered through heavy tarpaulin drapes.

*

It was the smell which brings back memories of the only time that I have been to a circus. It's that mixture of straw, earth and tarpaulin. Tom and I had gone with our father on that last summer holiday before he died. I remember burying my head in my father's lap as the trapeze artists swung high above our heads. "Don't be silly," my father said, curling my hair into ringlets with his fingers. Tom had been transfixed by the acrobats' display. Days after the circus, he was still spending hours up a tree trying to make himself fly from branch to branch. I taunted him that his arms were too short and he was too stupid, making him cry with frustration.

Eveline and I were shown to seats by the ringside. We had arrived just as the lights dimmed. As far as I could tell no one behind us was pointing, no one was saying 'Look! There she is! There's Eveline! She has come back!' Eveline didn't belong there anymore than she did at the château. A spotlight swept across a suddenly silent audience and caught the solitary ringmaster in its beam. The show began. Eveline's eyes danced. Strongmen built human pyramids. Dogs jumped through hoops. Acrobats flew above us. A fire-eater swallowed a plume of flame. Eveline gasped like the children around us, open-mouthed with wonder. It was as if she had forgotten who she was and whatever was troubling her.

Then, with a drum-roll, 'El Caballero' appeared. He had a smile as white as a dollop of toothpaste. He cracked a whip, and the sound rolled round the Big Top like a volley of thunder. Unconsciously, Eveline leant into me.

The cowboy bowed towards his assistant, a tiny lady in a glittering red bikini who was standing still, a few metres away, waiting for him. With theatrical deliberation, El Caballero removed a pistol from the holder slung around his waist. He spun the gun dramatically to the sound of a drum-roll — not just one roll of the drums, but three — and with the last drum-roll, Eveline hurtled to her feet. She stood transfixed, staring at El Caballero. I tugged on her jacket. I tried to pull her back into her seat. She didn't respond. The little boy sitting on the other side of me, started to cry. I wondered if it was my fault that the ice-cream which he had been enjoying so much, was now in his lap. The people behind murmured their disapproval. Eveline was blocking their view.

El Caballero realised that something was amiss. Slowly he turned to face Eveline. He had a thin cruel mouth when he wasn't showing his teeth. For a moment, it looked as if he is going to abandon the act and then he smiled a slow, taunting smile, and turned towards his assistant again who had placed an apple on top of her yellow hair. El Caballero pointed his pistol. He steadied his arm in readiness. Another roll of the drums started slowly, then picked up pace.

Eveline bolted like a startled racehorse. She trampled over my feet, and over the feet and possessions of everyone else in our row. She was out of the tent. She had gone. After a moment's stunned silence, the noise from the audience started to swell.

I came to my senses. I rushed after Eveline, alternating "sorry, sorry," with "*excusez-moi*." When I had reached the exit, I looked back. Every face, every chattering mouth, was turned towards me. El Caballero was watching me, motionless, his crooked shadow looming large behind him. Then with a heart-rending crack of his whip, the audience was silenced, and I was out of the tent into a chill, starry night.

I was so frightened by what might have been, that I wanted to grab Eveline and shake her by the shoulders and shout right into her face, 'What the hell do you think you were doing? One slip and that man could have shot the woman in the head.'

It was deserted outside the Big Top, an empty expanse of scuffed ground. Multi-coloured lights blinked feebly around the vacant window of the box office booth. A scraggy moggie appeared from nowhere and threaded itself between my ankles.

I could have gone up the hill to the château on my own, and left her there, just as I should have left her at the gates, three evenings before. The clowns were on; the Big Top rocked with silly noises and gusts of laughter.

I followed the perimeter of the tent, towards the back.

I saw Eveline in the distance, with someone else. When I got nearer, I saw it was a girl with her hair pulled back tightly into a ponytail. She was holding Eveline's arm and gesturing animatedly. I could tell that Eveline wasn't responding. As I hurried towards them, across the faint wash of light, the girl turned to greet me. I recognised her as one the acrobats. She had pulled on a dressing gown, but she was still in stage make-up, a white face with glittering eyes heavily outlined in swoops of black eyeliner.

"*Elle parle francais?*" she asked, indicating Eveline, smiling sympathetically.

"No — *non.*"

"*Et vous? Anglaise?*"

"I'm English. Do you speak English?"

"Leetle. Very leetle. *Amie?*"

I hesitated. "Yes," I said.

"She… *Quel horreur*!" She stood rigid, like Eveline had. She cupped her face in her hands and contorted her face. My heart lurched. The make-up made her face a horrific parody of wide-eyed terror. Eveline looked at me. She held out her hand. I ignored it. The lights caught the tracks of her tears and I caught my breath. The acrobat pressed Eveline close to her, with Eveline about as responsive as a ragdoll.

"Eveline, I'm going back to the château. Are you going to come with me or not?"

Eveline started to disengage herself. The girl held her back, gripping her arm. "*Le château*? *Non*!" Her eyes were wide with urgency. She refused to relinquish her hold on Eveline, launching into a torrent of words which could have come from Russia, Hungary, Poland. She broke off when she realised that it was no use. We didn't understand. She shrugged her shoulders, releasing Eveline. "Bad," she said, puckering her mouth at me "Bad, bad, bad."

I felt cold with anger. "How dare you?" I said stiffly. "I'm just trying to do my best by this girl."

She shook her head with Eveline watching me, standing by her side.

I'd had enough. I wasn't going to allow strangers to judge me. I turned my back on both of them.

People were still inside the Big Top, still having a jolly time. There were hoots and squawks and squeals of trumpet. The ringmaster bellowed. The audience shouted back. Eveline had to run to catch up. I looked back and the acrobat girl was standing motionless, watching us, her white face hanging like a moon beneath the tree.

Chapter 11

I found it difficult to get to sleep that night. 'Bad! Bad! Bad!' The circus girl's cry was a drumbeat for my heart. I did feel bad: I felt bad for Eveline, I felt bad for myself. I regretted bitterly my offer for Eveline to stay for a few days. Her silence was a mirror, and I hated my reflection. I had noted the occasional flicker of derision in her eyes, and had pretended not to notice. I was the silly woman who had invited a stranger into her house.

I was sure I heard crying once from the floor below but when I listened, all I could hear was silence thudding against my ears, with little bits and pieces of sound like flotsam. Suddenly Eveline's bullet popped into my mind, a glistening fully formed image cradled in the pink of her palm. I had completely forgotten about the silver bullet. She was frightened of El Caballero's bullet. I must have drifted off to sleep then, focusing on her bullet.

Eveline washed her cup and plate, splashing water over the dirty crockery sitting in the sink which she chose to ignore — which annoyed me. I had allowed her to eat her breakfast in peace, and then I couldn't find the right moment.

"Eveline!" I called her back as she slipped out of the kitchen and into the archway.

She turned around quickly, as if she knew what I was going to say. She lingered in the doorway, looking at me, waiting.

"Last night was very upsetting," I said. "I think it is time for you to think about moving on? You have been here four nights now. Long enough." I made a batting movement with my hand.

She gave no indication that she understood me. She dipped her head and smiled — so unexpectedly that I smiled back — and disappeared into the archway, out of my sight.

When it came to it, I just couldn't confront her head-on. My words were too weak in the face of her silence.

The archway, which split the basement of the château into two, was a very inconvenient architectural detail. It belonged to another age, designed I think, for a carriage and horses. The stables, four walls and half a roof, were behind the house, quite a distance away.

On one side of the arch, were the kitchen and cellars and on the other — more rooms, I presumed. The massive studded door which gave access to that side was locked. I had looked for the key which would have been as enormous as the one for the front door. I couldn't find it, like I couldn't find any keys to the interior doors. Greg wanted to try to open the door in the archway, but I hadn't let him loose on it. I was mindful that the château was Tom's and he hadn't given me any instructions with regard to the archway.

I waited until Eveline was down by the pool, dipping her feet in the water, leaning back on her hands, chest and face to the sun. Then I went up to her room in search of the bullet. Already, it had a smell of her, a light, indefinable fragrance which I caught sometimes, in other parts of the house.

The room was untidy. Her bed was a rumpus of sheets and blanket, her dirty clothes tossed into a corner. An ironing board was in the middle of the room. I picked up the iron The flat plate was so sticky and black, she had obviously abandoned all notion of ironing. I looked around the room — the little stuffed donkey from the salon, 'A present from Portugal' was on the bedside table. There was a Pink Floyd album which I knew also to have been in the salon, on the dressing table. 'She's a little magpie' I thought indulgently and then I noticed the heavy gold chain draped over the top left hand corner of the dressing table's mirror. I thought I recognised that as well. I had to stifle the feeling of panic — that Greg's not so subtle suggestions that she was casing the house were correct — but then I thought, if that were true would she not try to hide what she had taken?

I checked anyway. I ran up the two flights of stairs to a room on the second floor, where Greg and I had found a leather box on the uppermost shelf of an otherwise empty wardrobe. I'd left it where we found it. The leather box was still at the back of the shelf and it was still full of trinkets — gold chains, pendants, a couple of odd cufflinks and a bracelet or two. I couldn't be sure that the gold chain had been amongst them.

"What are you doing?" Eveline's sponge bag, full of expensive unguents in glass jars, nearly slipped from my fingers. It was Greg, taking a break from plastering over large cracks in one of ceilings upstairs. He was covered in chalky dust.

"Looking for that bullet she had. And look what I've found." I showed him the chain still draped on the mirror.

"I told you she's been snooping around."

"But why leave it out in full view if she were stealing?"

"Search me," Greg shrugged. "She's weird."

"She could have taken the entire box... I don't know what to do."

"You do. Tell her to get her skates on. Vamoose." He looked around the room. "Did you get any joy at the circus?"

I told him about El Caballero.

"Crazy."

"Frightened. It was the pistol and the apple on top of the assistant's head."

"Listen," Greg said. "She's not your problem. Your only problem is that she is here." He nodded towards the suitcase I'd left open on the table. "No I.D. I suppose?"

I rechecked the suitcase's contents. "Nothing." I fingered a cashmere top. "They're good clothes, these."

"You'd wonder how she could afford it."

"Daddy," I said.

Greg snorted. "Sugar daddy more like. She's a looker."

Like a mirage then, I saw Eveline lying on the bed in front of me like Matisse's Blue Nude, hands behind her head, elbows akimbo, her small breasts (bra size only 70A) with nipples like little slivers of almond and a taunting smile on her lips, inviting me. The vision reverberated and vanished. The view from the window quivered with heat. Greg looked at me, as if he was going to step across the room and envelope me in his powdery arms. I was so tired that, just for a second, I could have rested my head on his narrow shoulder.

"Here," he said, making for the bed, not for me. "Have you looked under her pillow?"

"Hang on Greg!" He stopped dead in his tracks midway between the door and the bed.

"I'm sorry. Look at the floor. I don't want her to know that I've been in here."

He looked at me levelly. "It doesn't matter if she does."

I looked back.

"Okay then." He pulled a rag from the bib on his overalls and retreated, rubbing out the white footprints his trainers had left.

There were a couple of damp, crumpled tissues under the pillow.

"Have you looked in her shoes?" Greg asked from the door. "It's where I keep my grandfather's fob watch."

Eveline's canvas lace-ups were by the bed. There had been a pair of extraordinary stilettos in the suitcase which were there no longer. The shoes were at the bottom of the empty wardrobe, neatly arranged side by side amidst the dust and fluff. They were green satin with a large pink rose detail. I could feel a small, hard object at the tip of the left shoe. I tipped it out. The bullet winked up at me. It had been polished, and it had a mark, a small zigzag across a triangle, scratched onto its surface. Greg hung off the doorpost, waiting.

"What's that there?" he asked, pointing into the wardrobe's interior.

There was a piece of paper inserted, half-hidden, between the frame and a side panel. Slowly, I unfolded it, hoping against hope that it would solve the question of Eveline's identity. It was a photograph — an A4 photocopy of a head and shoulders shot — of a bespectacled smiling young black man. His smile was spliced by a deep crease running down his head. The other fold practically decapitated him.

"Let's see," Greg says, practically falling into my chest for a closer look. "He's a bit young for a sugar daddy."

Underneath us, a door creaked open and closed. Eveline was back in the house.

"You don't keep cash hanging around?" Greg asked, knowing full well that I did.

Chapter 12

Greg's wages were still intact under my mattress but that didn't stop me from growing more and more resentful and angry with the girl I called Eveline. Her very presence was jeopardising the precarious peace I'd found at the château. I didn't want it broken. I was still too fragile after London.

I didn't trust myself to speak to her. For the rest of the day, I worked furiously in one of the first floor rooms, preparing the walls for paint. I didn't make lunch, and Greg didn't come looking for it. Nor did Eveline.

Passing through the hall in the mid-afternoon, I caught sight of Eveline in the salon. Again she had been rummaging around — and so openly, I didn't think that Greg was right to call it snooping. Certainly I couldn't detect any guile in a girl who squinted at her reflection in the Venetian mirror, trying on the prescription glasses that I'd been keeping for charity. She was so engrossed that she didn't notice me. There must have been twelve or so pairs of glasses and Eveline, it seemed, was going to try them all. 'Good,' I thought, softening a little because she looked so like a child playing innocently. 'She's bored. Maybe she won't need the push from me.'

I stopped work only when Greg shouted up the stairs that he'd see me in the morning.

For supper, I made rice with tinned green beans and tomatoes. I boiled a tin of frankfurters. I called Eveline and she hovered shyly, in the doorway. I didn't welcome her. I didn't encourage her to enter with expansive hand gestures in case she didn't understand me — when we both knew full well that she did. I was sick and tired of playing silly games and being made to feel like an idiot.

I banged the plates of food down on the table. We ate in a tense silence because I wasn't talking — me, who was no good at small talk and yet had spent hours those last few days spouting light pleasantries in the face of silence. I could feel her eyes travelling across my face, watching. She pushed the salt towards me. I took it without acknowledgement. She offered me water by picking up the jug. I nodded. I wouldn't catch her eyes. I focussed on the hollow in her neck with its two delicate bones. The silence between us magnified every move she made. I hardly touched my meal because suddenly I was aware of the sounds I made as I ate. As I started to clear away the plates, Eveline's hand brushed against mine. It was very slight, but it was a blandishment. It gave me courage.

"Why did you take the gold chain?"

For a second, her eyes registered shock — quickly erased and replaced with the familiar blank look of incomprehension. I couldn't be bothered to argue with her. I took the back stairs up to the ground floor and her room. I snatched the chain still draped on the mirror. I was surprised to see Eveline still in the kitchen waiting for me. I'd half expected her to go.

"This," I said.

Her hand reached out to take the chain and I hid it behind my back. Our eyes locked together. Hers were full of despair.

"Tomorrow, first thing," I said, "You have got to go. I can't deal with you anymore. You are doing my head in — literally. This not speaking, pretending not to understand

English…" It gave me great satisfaction to see her eyes flash with anger.

Then the eyes switched into their non-communicative mode and her face realigned itself so that it was absolutely expressionless, the mouth immobile. She took a plate and let it clatter into the sink. The sullen sound resounded around the room.

"I'll take you wherever you want to go," I said, enjoying my moment of triumph as she retreated from the kitchen.

I swam that evening. I was desperate to reinstate the routine I had had before Eveline arrived. It had become such a ritual for me to peel off my sticky clothes after Greg had left for the working day and to slip into the pool. I passed Eveline on the terrace. She was sitting in my chair, staring out at the view. She could have been meditating, she was so still. I said nothing as I passed by. I had nothing more to say.

The water was lovely. It was like slipping into a warm scented bath except that the perfume was of lavender and pine, cracked by the heat of a long day in the sun. I struck out. It was bliss. I could feel the tension leaving my body and my mind settling.

When I got out of the pool, it was almost dark. Eveline was no longer on the terrace but I thought I could see her silhouette, head bent, walking near the chapel.

Tom rang that evening. I wonder sometimes if he had a sixth sense.

"How's tricks?"

He was out on a street, raising his voice above the traffic.

"I've asked her to leave. I should have taken your advice in the first place…"

A siren screeched past.

Tom only heard the first part of what I said.

He gave a great sigh of relief. "Definitely?"

"Have you…" Another siren. I gave up trying to ask if he had circulated my photo of Eveline.

"Great. Just going into a meeting."

"What? This late? It must be ten o'clock your end…" Another siren.

"Catch you later!" He cut the connection.

I had a wonderful dream that night. Tom and I were in Devon and it was as if our father had never died. We were playing on the beach, with our mother not far off, sitting reading, shaded by a long finger of shadow from one of the pines which fringed the bay. Tom was laughing, throwing back his head, showing all his pearly little baby teeth while I was trying to pull him down to the shore line where the waves lapped and the light sparkled like little diamonds caught in the sea. I woke once, disturbed by a creaking sound, but I managed to submerge myself back into the same dream except that time all four of us were sitting at the kitchen table eating fish fingers doused in tomato ketchup while our father's hand lay on our mother's lightly freckled arm and he looked lovingly at us, a true pater familias.

*

I woke hungry, immediately thinking of what I should buy at the boulangerie. Pains au chocolat. Maybe Eveline would like a little chocolate to set her up for her journey but then my heart sank at the thought of facing the girl, if she didn't speak how the hell would I know where to drive her?

The kitchen was particularly gloomy in the frail, early morning light. I was puzzled to see the door to the archway wide open. I was sure I had locked it the night

79

before, but then I hoped against hope that it was Eveline's way of telling me that she had actually left. That she had gone.

I saw it then. Coiled on the floor. The head raised. The jaws open. The tongue flicking. Hissing. I opened my mouth to scream — but I couldn't. I was facing a snake, not the terrifying prospect of death and I still couldn't. A few choked sounds emerged from my throat. I was on the verge of blacking out.

Eveline appeared. She just arrived in the middle of the kitchen. I saw her disappear in the direction of the range and reappear with a pair of tongs. She wasn't cowed by the hissing. She crouched down and caught the snake with a swift pincer movement. Pinioned, it thrashed in the air. She held it at arm's length and disappeared out into the archway. I sank into a chair.

She must have been gone five minutes at least. By then I had calmed down but was still shaking uncontrollably. Eveline leant over me, wrapping her arms around my shoulders. Her strong body was a source of strength and I held her tight, listening to the rhythmic beating of her heart until the trembling subsided.

"Thank God you were here," I kept saying over and over again.

Gently she disengaged from me. She moved towards the kitchen door. It was then that I noticed the suitcase and panicked at the idea of being left alone.

"Please don't go," I begged. "Stay a little longer."

Greg snorted when I told him. "Ain't that a coincidence."

"What?"

He glared. "She knows how frightened of snakes you are."

I shook my head disbelieving.

"I don't trust her," he said softly, "as far as I could throw her. What about the gold chain she nicked?"

"She didn't steal it. I'm not even sure that it is ours. Maybe we're doing her an injustice."

"You should be careful. Before you know it, she'll have squatters' rights."

Chapter 13

After that dreadful morning, there was a feeling of happiness, like a shadow had been lifted, about the place. Eveline stopped drifting around the house and started to help. She still looked through cupboards, but this time to empty them of their contents, sort through the junk and to clean the shelves as I had shown her, with a bowl of warm water and a cloth. Only once she seemed troubled, when she showed me a plastic bag full of what looked like little plastic stirrups. I knew I knew what they were, but I had to think hard. "They're nose clips," I told her, "for swimming." I felt like a mother, handing down domestic traditions to a daughter. She became quite the model guest. When I looked into her room her bed was made without a crease on the counterpane.

Tom didn't call to tell me that he had received and had circulated Eveline's photograph. He didn't even call to check that Eveline had left, like I'd promised. I tried a couple of times to phone him to tell him that Eveline was, after all, going to stay on for a while. All I got was his P.A. who gave me to understand that my pleas for him to return my calls were not of high importance. I tried his mobile. Again, no response. I started to worry that I was putting Tom in an invidious position — that, in allowing her to stay, I had overstepped my authority and Eveline could have some arcane squatter's right over the property like Greg suggested.

So a couple of days later, first thing in the morning, I told Greg that I was going into the main town. I wanted to ask the British Consul's advice about what to do with a person who turns up, about whom you know nothing, who doesn't speak, seems to be very nice and seems to be quite happy to stay and doesn't seem to have anywhere else to go. Even as I was saying it, I knew it was an excuse to escape the château for a while and to be on my own.

Greg was making thick coffee with an inchful of grounds at the bottom of the mug.

"Why bother going into town?" he asked. "All you have to do is get her things, take her firmly by the arm, march her down the avenue, dump her suitcase by the gates and point in any direction but backwards. She'll know what you mean."

"You know I've told her that she can stay a while."

"You're as mad as she is." He made that awful twisting motion with his finger again.

"Will you stay until I get back?"

"Yep. I'll make sure she doesn't burn down the house," he said cheerfully. "Have a good trip."

By the time I reached the Consulate, it was lunch time and the offices were shut. I took myself off to the first available café. There was a vague sense of the sea being nearby, but it was the wrong sort of sea for me. It had no smell. Besides, I like my seas flecked with grey and with strong, white waves. I sat outside on the terrace and a waiter weaved in and out of the tables. I asked for the menu du jour.

"*Une personne*?" he held up his index finger.

"*Oui.*"

"English. I thought so." He wiped the table with three quick smears of a cloth, and deposited one placemat, one glass, one knife and one fork as if by magic from the tray he twirled above my head. "Where are you from?"

I hesitated. "London."

"I used to live in Wolverhampton."

"That's nice," I said.

The people on the next table were English. A man and woman and their two teenage children. The man and woman were chatting, the man's hand resting on the woman's freckled arm, but the girl and boy, slack in their chairs, wires dangling from their ears, took no part in the conversation. The parents didn't seem to mind. The man talked very animatedly about a property he wanted his wife to view.

"Half an hour to get there, half an hour back. What do you say?"

"No," the woman said wearily, "No more wild goose chases. I've had enough. So have these two. We're supposed to be on holiday." The woman glanced at me. She knew I was listening. I averted my eyes.

*

I was recalling being fifteen on a family holiday in France, although with one parent instead of two. For some reason, Uncle Mani wasn't with us. I could see myself, long-limbed and bony, sitting self-consciously with my mother. She wasn't aware of the surreptitious glances men gave her. Tom was supposed to be with us, but he had sloped off somewhere. It was night-time and a fête was swirling around us, a band belting out Beatles' songs in broken English. Couples and children were dancing under the coloured bulbs strung up around the square. It was our first holiday since the death of our father. He had been dead for seven years. I didn't think about him all the time anymore, but when I did, there was still a big hollow in my chest.

My mother was trying to talk to me, shouting over the music.

"Do you know where Tom is getting all this pocket money?"

She had noticed how independent he was — paying for pedalos, ice-creams and clandestine beers.

"He's been selling stuff at school."

She looked alarmed. "Drugs?"

"He doesn't do drugs," I said, which was true.

"Then what?"

"Stuff from his room." That was a lie. He had been dealing drugs.

I'd made him stop under pain of death and threatening to tell his headmaster and Uncle Mani.

"You will tell me if he does anything untoward…" She was interrupted by a man, leaning over her shoulder and asking her for a dance. She glanced at me and I gave an ungracious nod of consent. She was whirled away, her peep-toed sandals matching every move of his clumpy French farmer's boots. It was the first and last time my mother and I had any meaningful conversation about Tom.

*

The sun bore down on my neck and shoulders. I was half-in, half-out of the shade of the parasol. The waiter brought me steak and chips and a small carafe of rosé wine. From the first sip, I realised how much I'd missed the glass or two of wine of an evening when Philip came home. I hadn't found any wine at the château which, given that everything else had been provided — or abandoned — by the former occupants, was odd. You would have thought that there would be mountains of Château Lafitte

85

or Dom Pérignon. Perhaps, I thought light-headily, I'd explore further into the cellar. The English lady was frowning at me, I must have been staring although I wasn't listening anymore. If I'd been listening, I wouldn't have been looking at them. I concentrated on the steak and thought about what to do about Eveline.

The waiter brought me a bowl of two scoops of vanilla ice-cream which were as tightly moulded as the little buttocks in the shiny seat of his black waiter trousers. He knew he was handsome. When he bent to ask me if there was anything else I desired, he left a trace of perfume so tangible I could have stuck out my tongue and licked the air.

"More wine," I said, and called him back, "and an espresso."

I spent two hours in the town. The Consulate reopened. People went in and out. I moved my chair around to let the sun beat on my chest. The English family were long gone and I was surrounded by the French language, which made a pleasing background murmur, a bit like the sea. I didn't go into the Consulate to discuss Eveline. It had never really been my intention. I would have been too embarrassed by their incredulity; to have taken in a stranger knowing nothing whatsoever about her.

Chapter 14

Out on the open road again, my car flew by terraces of gnarled olive trees. I caught myself speeding. I pressed less heavily on the accelerator. Sunlight flooded across my hands and arms, the steering wheel warm to the touch. Both windows were down. The breeze brushed my hair off the nape of my neck. My heart lifted. I was enjoying travelling through a landscape pulsating with heat, so different from the pastel tones of a summertime in England.

Eveline owed me an explanation, I told myself giddily. As soon as I got back, I would call her into the salon. I would sit on the sofa to the side of the fireplace and she would sit facing me. I would watch her cross and uncross her shapely legs and would wait, as she would wait. Then I would ask her, point blank, who she was, what had happened for her to arrive at the château, and how long she intended to stay. I wouldn't take 'No', or silence, for an answer. Together we would watch the shadows slide across the parquet floor and, if needed be, dissolve into the darkness before the moon rose. I would have a reply.

A young couple by the roadside jumped up and down, waving. I whizzed past. Then, in my rear-view mirror, I noticed their car with its bonnet up. No one, on my way down through France, had bothered to stop for me when I'd run out petrol. I put on the

*brakes, and shunted the gear into reverse. Their car
was small like mine, but considerably more battered.*

*The youngsters tossed their rucksacks in first, then
bundled themselves into the back. They were both
sporting trilbies. He had a wispy goatee beard and
she, a fat yellow plait resting on her shoulder. I just
knew they were British before they opened their
mouths.*

*"Thanks," he said. "We were just thinking that we'd
better start walking."*

"I'll take you to the nearest garage." We moved off.

*"It just wouldn't start," the girl said, taking her hat
off her head and mopping her forehead. Her cheeks
were flushed with the sun. She glanced at her man.
"Isn't this nice, Harry?"*

"The bloody battery's flat," Harry complained.

*They looked so wholesome — like scones with
clotted cream and strawberry jam just asking to be
eaten on a Saturday afternoon in Devon.*

*"The next village is about ten kilometres away," I
said.*

*They glanced meaningfully at each other. It was
easy to see that they were lovers. They reminded me of
Philip and I, when we were around the same age;
when* our skin too was taut and unblemished. I recalled
how Philip's light touch used to stir up an ache, a physical
ache, of desire in me. Even now, I can conjure up an echo
of what I felt then, all those years ago.

*I had had one too many glasses of wine. A car horn
blared. I righted the car, which was instinctively
making towards the left. My passengers were too busy
looking out of the open windows to notice. The road
was taking us alongside a narrow river bordered by*

meadows full of wild flowers and the occasional tumbledown shack.

"You could paint this," the girl said.

"It is so good of you," Harry leaned forward, "I do hope that Serena and I aren't taking you out of your way."

"I'm just happy to help. Do you have to be anywhere for any particular time?"

"No," Serena said, "we don't have to be anywhere for any time." They caught my smile in the mirror and laughed at themselves, at me, and at the wind as I pressed down on the accelerator, lifting the young man's hat to reveal an impossibly high forehead and receding hairline. We started to climb up a steep hill, leaving a gloriously hazy valley behind.

"Are you on holiday here?" Harry asked.

"Not exactly. I'm renovating a property." The car's engine panted up the incline. I changed into first gear.

"Near here?"

"Not far," and I told him the name of the village. His girlfriend was content to look out of the window.

"I've heard of it," he said.

"Surely not. It's very small."

"I have," he insisted.

"Do you know someone there?"

"No," he said. "I can't think why..."

"I know what you're thinking," Serena said, her eyes catching mine via the rear-view mirror.

"Innocence Kumono had a house there."

"Innocence Kumono." It was a name so out of context I couldn't place it for a moment and then it came to me: a ravaged face with bulging eyes below a

89

peaked, fringed cap of khaki green. I remembered the stories of what was found when the rebels finally gained access to his palaces — the walk-in fridges full of body parts; the skulls at the bottom of the crocodile enclosures; the dungeons full of resuscitation equipment.

He was a man who traumatised his nation for the best part of twenty years. A tyrant who killed for the most inconsequential, indiscriminate of reasons.

"What on earth," I started to say, "makes you think that a dead despot has anything to do with…" I didn't need to finish the question. I remembered the passport I'd found in one of the chests of drawers. My brain froze. I felt cold all over.

The car's front wheel hit something — a stone amongst the row of stones which provided the only physical barrier between my car and the valley below. My car was almost over the edge of the narrow road. There wasn't a sound except the 'click click' of the hazard lights. I looked up and caught sight of my passengers. They were clutching each other, ashen-faced. They looked as if they were too frightened to say anything — anything at all — in case the weight of their words caused the car to fall over the precipice.

A bird floated across the blue sky, directly in my line of vision.

"Sorry," I said, "a momentary lapse of concentration."

I'd thought of the passport as just another oddity in a houseful of oddities — the excessive amount of food stored, the ironing boards, the bottles of bleach, the tongue scrapers. I'd mentioned it to Tom in passing but I hadn't questioned why it was in the house in the first place — but then again, why shouldn't it have been? Why should everything need an explanation?

Harry cleared his throat. "I can drive, if that would help."

"No thank you." I switched off the hazard lights. I felt very tired suddenly.

Serena cleared her throat. "What if a car comes? I mean if it hits us then…" There was a note of rising panic in her voice.

If I'd been in their place, I would have got out of the car there and then and taken my chances on an empty road high up in the hills of Provence, but they didn't. We continued the journey after I managed to unhook the car from the stone with their help. We didn't speak for a while.

The car reached the crest of the hill. For a moment, we had a 360° view of the glories of Provence and a line of sea shimmering below the horizon.

I still couldn't quite believe what I knew to be true.

"It's a dull little village," I argued. "It wouldn't have been flashy enough for him. He was a showman, wasn't he? The Riviera's more likely."

"There was a house there too," Serena said softly, "he had properties all over the world…"

"But he did have a place in that village. Didn't he Serena?" Harry didn't take kindly to being challenged.

"We're members of the uni lobby group…" Serena explained.

"We've been trying to get sanctions they've still got in place, lifted," Harry added pompously.

Serena shook her head, eyes full of sorrow. "Babies and children."

"But he's gone now," Harry said. "Thank God."

For a moment, all I could see, as I'm sure the others did as well, was the mournful eyes of matchstick children with bloated bellies.

"Harry's going to stand for the Conservatives," Serena announced brightly. "Aren't you Harry?"

"Shush," Harry had the grace to look slightly embarrassed. "Actually," he says, "in a couple of years..."

I couldn't give a damn about what he would be doing in a couple of years.

"Okay," I said, "just supposing you're right about Kumono's house being in my village — where exactly is it?"

"That's easy." Harry sniggered. "It'll be the biggest!"

High up in the sky, the sun disappeared behind a cloud and the landscape darkened momentarily with fleeting shadow. I was full of foreboding, certain that I'd been taken for a fool — only I wasn't sure by whom, which made me feel even more foolish.

Chapter 15

That afternoon, all anomalies at the château slotted into place. There was a taint to the place, and that taint was Kumono to which I'd been wilfully oblivious — not wanting to risk, quite literally, turning back the carpet to find something nasty beneath. I started to laugh at the irony of my situation and then caught sight of my passengers' faces in the rear-view mirror. They looked frightened. I was behaving like a mad woman. I stopped laughing and concentrated on driving.

The château had been left the way I'd found it, because the owners expected to return. They hadn't bargained on being executed back in their own country.

Harry tapped me on the shoulder. "Where is your house?"

"But the château," I said, instead of answering him directly, "if you're saying it's the one for that village, it looks too run-down — "

"It would have been the sons who used it." Serena's eyes, like Harry's, regarded me solemnly.

Like everyone else who picked up a newspaper or watched the news, I knew that the two sons were, if such a thing could be at all possible, more terrible than the father.

"I can't believe you didn't know about the Kumonos." Harry shook his head.

"Of course I know about the Kumonos," I snapped. "You'd have to be a bloody ostrich not to have heard of them."

I had to change the subject. "Tell me," I say lightly, "which university do you go to?"

My passengers couldn't wait to get out of the car at the first garage we came to after our drive over the hills.

"Shall I wait for you?" I offered weakly. Harry had already marched into the workshop, leaving Serena tussling with both rucksacks wedged in the foot well.

"It's okay," she said. "I expect the garage will drive us back."

"Thanks," Harry shouted back at me, tilting his trilby.

Serena smiled. It was an apology for his lack of manners, one woman to another. She leant into my window and laid her right hand on my left hand which was resting on the steering wheel.

"Have we offended you somehow? If we did, it wasn't intended..."

"Don't be silly," I smiled and turned the ignition. "Good luck with the car."

"It's just that you seem so upset..." She was a witch, that girl, in her swirly tattered skirt.

"I'm fine."

She withdrew her hand. There was an awful lot of space suddenly between us.

"Was it Harry's talk about General Kumono?"

"Your boyfriend's very sure about his facts, isn't he?"

"Yes," she said, "sometimes he can come across as a bit arrogant."

"You can say that again." I was doing my best to sound jolly.

"I'm sorry," she said softly, her large blue eyes gleaming with empathy.

When I looked back, through the dust cloud caused by my sudden acceleration of the car, Serena was standing by a petrol pump, upright, a hand shading her eyes, as she watched me disappear. Her legs were sturdy, like milk bottles. She was so unlike Eveline. I'd forgotten about Eveline, arguing with Harry about the Kumonos. Was she connected to the Kumonos? Was that the reason why she was at the château? Tears pricked my eyes. It didn't matter that she had made no promises — hadn't in fact spoken a word — I still felt completely betrayed. My trust broken.

I had to get back to the château and confront her. My car zipped along at a breakneck speed, past flat fields with lines of vines. I needed facts.

Chapter 16

I had spent my life shying away from unpleasant truths and now, ironically, I was living within the mediaeval walls of one. With a shock, I realised something else; I'd told myself that it was the oppressive masculinity which I found distasteful. It wasn't. There was an atmosphere of cruelty about the château, which I'd been unwilling to acknowledge. It was the real reason why I had allowed Eveline to stay.

I had been so stupid, so bound up in my own thoughts — living out, and not even happily, my own version of reality. It wasn't a comfortable drive back to the village.

It was too much of a coincidence that, out of all the châteaux in France, Eveline turned up at the former Kumono château.

As soon I thought that, I chastised myself. I was being stupid and ignorant. I was guilty of racism, judging simply on appearance. On what grounds could I link her to a dissolute dictatorship? The answer was none.

I was desperate for a drink. I wanted to buy a bottle of wine, a deep, dark, red wine and to drink myself into an insensate stupor and then I wanted to wake up and find myself back in London, with everything normal as it had been two months before, except that nothing then had been normal. I had been wracked with suspicion just as I was now, in France.

I imagined Philip sitting on his side of the bed, bending to tie his shoelaces. I could see myself in my bra and pants, in the en-suite, face pressed up against the glass, rubbing away the mist my breath was making I tried to apply mascara. "Another cup of tea?" he'd offer and I'd say yes and as soon as I'd hear his footsteps descend the stairs, I'd rush to his suit jacket and delve through his pockets looking for something — anything — to prove that he was having an affair. I hated myself then. If I could have sloughed off my skin, I'd have done so.

I pulled up in front of the mini-supermarket a little further along the main road into the village. Despite the bottle crates piled up beneath the awning and the out-of-date posters on the door, it looked as deserted — abandoned even — as ever.

If General Kumono had sons, he could have had a daughter.

It took a while for my eyes to adjust to the cool dark space. I stood in front of the delicatessen counter with a fluorescent light flickering and humming over a range of palely pink, chunky hams. I don't know why I was standing there. I don't buy delicatessen ham. I don't like the way a thin slice slithers away from your hand and thick slices are too reminiscent of the pig they came from.

"Are you alright?" Someone touched me lightly on the arm. It was a woman, small and lank-haired, whom I recognised but couldn't immediately place.

"I'm Valerie. We were at that party when — " Her beady eyes were frank in their curiosity. "You're very pale."

"I remember. I'm fine, thank you."

"You were swaying." She looked almost accusing. "I thought you were about to faint."

"It's coming out of the sun. I'm looking for the wine."

"Are you sure?" Her eyes continued to assess me. She had a shallow basket at her feet, full of salad with hairy roots. Her toes, which hooked over the edge of her sandals, were like a marsupial's.

I had the chance then to admit that I had just found out who the former owners of the château were — but I didn't. I didn't like how she was looking at me.

Anyway, right at that moment, I wanted to buy some wine.

"It's over there," Valerie pointed to the back of the shop.

I picked up four bottles of red wine and two litres of still water. She was still standing by the delicatessen counter, waiting for the assistant to finish with me and serve her. I could feel her eyes watching as I paid for my goods and left.

Back at the château, no one came out to greet me as the car crunched to a halt on the gravel. The house was shut, except for a salon window which I couldn't remember opening. Even the huge archway doors were closed.

"Greg! Greg!" The words bounced back off impenetrable walls. Sky and clouds were jumbled together on the ancient panes. A fortress. The château's shadow stretched past me, blanking out the sun's warmth. I tried the front door. Locked. I hammered.

"Eveline! Eveline!" The words danced in the air. I panicked, gripped with the fear that something dreadful had happened behind those thick walls. I remember my heart thudding and the sudden weakening of my legs as all my energy drained away. I remember sitting down on the steps leading up to the front door. They had gone for a walk, I reasoned, and quite properly, Greg had locked up. They hadn't left me alone. They wouldn't. They couldn't.

I managed to quell the tidal wave of panic threatening to engulf me.

I had four bottles of wine, two lukewarm bottles of water and no corkscrew. In the end, I successfully used a long thin nail I found lying on the terrace. I sat out of reach of the château's shadow on the other side of the ornamental pond. I swallowed mouthfuls of warm wine and waited for Greg and Eveline.

I distracted myself by looking for the dull gold of Greg's carp flickering beneath water lilies. I couldn't see them. "A pond without fish is a sad thing," I'd said to Greg, months before, when we were both up to our knees in water, clearing the pond of weed. Then the morning after Dora and Babs' disastrous party, he appeared carrying a plastic bag full of water with the two fish. "Sorry," he'd said gruffly, "that your dress was ruined.

I was touched. "You don't have to apologise for your friends."

"I'm not," he said, decanting the fish unceremoniously into the water. "Those people are acquaintances, not friends."

"So what am I then?"

He'd turned his head towards me. "The boss," he'd said, grinning. Even that wasn't quite true.

A youngster burnt up and down the hill on his moped. A dog barked. The air was heavy and sweet with the fragrance of late roses run wild. I was hungry.

And while I sat waiting for Greg and Eveline that evening, I couldn't get out of my head one lurid detail about the dictator's sons which I had read years before, sitting with the newspapers and the bacon and eggs which Philip always made on a Sunday. Everything else I'd read about the Kumonos I had forgotten, in the way you do when events don't actually impinge on your own life. The horror of the image of young men, with their right feet cut off, trying to play football in a prison yard, still churns my stomach. Those young men were the national football team who had lost a prestigious football match. Execution was, mercifully, their final punishment.

By the time Greg and Eveline appeared from the direction of the woods, I was so relieved that I could have cried — but I was also stiff and cold, cross and a little drunk.

"Sorry," Greg smiled sheepishly, "we got lost. Went round and round for bloody ages." Eveline looked like one half of a couple standing beside him, her eyes warm and happy. She also looked as if she could be a Kumono. I saw an in-built arrogance about her — an assumption that everyone would do her bidding, as I had done over the last few days.

"Do you know what time it is?"

"Late." Greg was all gangly arms and legs. He looked so inappropriate as the escort of a beautiful woman. "I thought it best to shut the place up as it's not my gaff…"

"And on whose time did you go on your little excursion?"

The smile was wiped off his face.

"I pay you to help me renovate this place, not to go traipsing around the woods. What do you think I thought when I saw the place empty? For all I knew, you could have upped sticks and left."

"I'm not listening to this shit," Greg turned on his heel. "You asked me to look after little Miss Madam here. Which I did. I've worked ten hour days for you and charged for eight and you give me grief about one fucking afternoon when I'm still doing what you want me to do but not with my nose to the grindstone. Fuck off. I don't need your money — your brother's money," he shouted back as he marches off down the avenue at a lolloping pace, so furious that he forgot his bicycle.

Eveline and I looked at each other. Her eyes were unflinching. She, who was the cause of all the trouble, made me feel ashamed of my outburst.

I wanted to slap her, scream at her 'who the hell are you?', and shake her till she answered but I didn't, because I wasn't sure if she wouldn't hit me back harder. She made me feel weak, impotent and a little fearful. I was the first to drop my gaze.

So Eveline and I stood there, beside the pond and watched Greg about to disappear out of our lives.

Chapter 17

"Greg!" He kept walking, his back resolutely turned. I ran after him. "Greg! Please." My breath caught at the back of my throat. "Greg." I hooked my fingers into the back of his overalls. "What about your bicycle?"

"I'll pick it up some other time." He propelled me along with him, not deigning to look at me.

"We can't get into the house."

"Funny that. The key is in the urn."

"Please Greg." We were almost at the front gates where we found Eveline, eight days and a world away. "I'm sorry."

Finally, reluctantly, he stopped and turned to face me.

"I thought it might do her some good." There was no warmth in his voice.

I glanced back. Eveline was still standing where I left her.

"She was doing my head in — drifting around the house like a lost soul without you around. I thought if I got her out, it might help. You know?" He took a step towards me, his anger fizzing in my face. "Look, I don't need this crap. What do you think I left England for? I'm a free man. All I need is a place to sleep, something to eat. I don't need this shit. She's a problem and you're not dealing with it."

He flung up his arm so abruptly, he nearly knocked me off my feet. "I'm sorry I didn't mean…"

He caught my arm, righted me. There couldn't have been more than a couple of inches between us. We were standing much too close.

"Why didn't you tell me, Greg?"

He took a step back. He knew exactly what I meant.

"I tried. You wouldn't even talk to me in the beginning, remember?"

"I'm sorry."

"So am I. I gave up trying. Thought you'd find out eventually."

We walked back together, with the sun setting behind the château. He nodded towards the still figure of Eveline, wreathed in shadow, standing by a pool of liquid gold.

"But when you saw her at the gates, didn't you think that she maybe had something to do with them?" My voice was so low, the words couldn't carry.

"Yes," he said, "but like you said, she's just a young girl."

The kitchen felt different. It felt cold and shut-up and damp after a long afternoon of incubating shadows which flapped against my face, like wet washing on a line, making it difficult to breathe. Greg marched through the them and snapped on the light. The shadows drew back, becoming flat planes of darkness, pooling in the corners, normal. Greg gave me a funny look. "Are you okay?"

"Of course."

Eveline disappeared straight upstairs. The kitchen looked almost homely in the artificial light. Greg retrieved the bottle I'd been drinking by the pond and the rest of the wine from the car. I asked him to stay for supper. He accepted, decanting what remained of the open bottle into a large tumbler. He lounged against the dresser, watching while I rummaged through the cupboard looking for something to eat. I regretted buying just wine and water at the supermarket. He finished the wine in a couple of gulps and waved his empty glass at me.

"Oh go on then, Greg, open another." I couldn't say anything more because Eveline had started to run herself a bath and when the ancient plumbing system cranked into motion, it could have been the gates of hell opening. I decided on foie gras, courtesy of the château's stocks of the stuff, on hard little slices of pre-toasted bread, and a bouillabaisse soup which smelt revolting as soon as the can opener touched the tin. Greg, meanwhile, crashed open drawers shouting obscenities over the thunderous clatter from the pipes. He shook me on the shoulder, making a pumping movement with his hand, holding up a bottle.

"A corkscrew," he bellowed. "When is she going to turn off that bloody water?"

In the end, he found a skewer with a curlicued end into which he threaded a knife sharpener, the sort fathers in TV advertisements use before ceremoniously carving the Christmas turkey, and winched the cork from bottle. I found three crystal glasses, green with age, at the back of a high shelf.

The noise stopped. Eveline had evidently run out of hot water.

"How did you find out about the Kumonos?" Greg broached the subject, while his back was turned, intent on opening a second bottle of wine.

"A couple of kids whose car had broken down. I took them to a garage. They knew about the château."

"Did they now," he said jokingly, plonking the bottle on the table. "Clever clogs. Is Ms Mystery coming or what? I'm starving."

At which point, Eveline glided in smelling expensively luscious.

Eveline put her thin, elegant hand over the rim of her glass before Greg could pour her some wine. She sat with her back to the window, her shadow truncated by the windowsill behind her. Headless. As far as I could remember, the Kumono sons had been hung. Greg was sitting at one end of the table and I was at the other. His shadow was elongated and pointed, just like him.

Greg ate with gusto, lips smacking, soup flying off his spoon, crunching through the foie gras toasts. Our shadows shifted places, a breeze slipped through the window. I straightened my shoulders.

Greg smiled over at me. "What do you call an Irishman..."

"Not now, Greg, please."

I took a deep breath. "Eveline, you know I want to help you."

Her head was bent over the bowl, hair still damp from the bath.

"It's just that it's a bit difficult..."

Greg snorted.

"Please, Greg," I glared at him.

Without looking up, she pulled the plate of foie gras nearer.

Four dainty bites and Eveline polished off a toast.

"Please look at me."

Finally, she looked up at me with her unfathomable eyes and perfect face, dabbing her mouth with a piece of paper towel. I took another deep breath before I launched into the unknown.

"Did you know General Innocence Kumono or his sons?"

It's amazing what reverberations names have. Just think of the name 'Hitler'. Both Eveline and Greg looked at me: he, worried and anxious, and she, frozen, huge eyes above the makeshift napkin pressed to her lips. The shadows hung motionless in the middle of the room. They were waiting. I was waiting. Greg was waiting.

"You're not related to them by any chance are you?"

Eveline pushed the table back with such force, our half-full bottle of wine spilt across the table. With a flash of pure torment from her great eyes, she ran out of the room. She clattered up the stairs. A door slammed.

We listened to the wine drip onto the floor.

Greg righted the empty bottle, and bent down to mop up.

"That's that then," I said, breaking the silence. "We're no nearer knowing who she is or what she's doing here."

Greg squeezed his wine-red paper towel, filling his plate with liquid.

"Well, she's heard of the Kumonos."

"All this time," I said wonderingly. "How come you never said?"

He shrugged. "It was no secret. Want another?" Greg opened our third bottle of heavy red wine. I pushed my glass over to him. I was like a lake, an unruffled surface deep with red wine.

"Was it just the sons here?"

"As far as I know," he said. "Look, I only came to France three years ago. I don't know much. Nobody talks about them."

"You could have told me."

"Look," he said, "you were so uptight when you came you were bloody impossible. You're lucky I didn't walk out." He scraped back his chair. "Thanks for dinner. I'll see you tomorrow."

I sat at the head of the table with the detritus of our meal in front of me and started on the rest of the bottle, trying to ignore the mass of darkness banked up against the weak, watery light from the low energy bulb. I drank steadily, watching the shadows change form when I wasn't directly looking at them.

I decided against phoning Tom: one, it would mean leaving the kitchen and two, it was past midnight and he would think me drunk. I was drunk, deliberately drunk. It was liberating to feel so detachedly drunk. When I had enough Dutch courage, I made a break for the stairs.

In the dining hall, I stopped in front of the telephone. So what if I was inebriated? It took a while because my fingers kept missing the holes for the digits on the old-fashioned, circular dial. The shadows seemed to have solidified into the corners of the room. I kept a watchful eye on them.

"Hallo!" Philip said welcomingly as if I had just walked into our house in London. It couldn't have escaped him that I had never called him from the château before.

"Listen," I enunciated very clearly and slowly. "Can you find out if General Innocence Kumono had a daughter?"

"Excuse me?"

"Innocence Kumono. The dictator executed about four years ago. Daughter."

"What's going on? Darling, are you by any chance…?"

A shadow seemed to have detached itself from the others and is starting to slip across the floor towards me.

I slammed down the phone, but not before I said "Africa", "Don't darling me", and "Call me tomorrow."

Chapter 18

When I woke, the early morning light was filling up the window behind the curtains. For a moment I thought that I was back with Philip. I'd had one of those delicious dreams in which you surrender yourself to a lover's caress and your body floats away on a cloud of well-being and happiness, and you think to yourself I must keep this dream going, and why don't I get this drunk more often, if this is the effect? Then I remembered that my room in the tower didn't have curtains and Philip and I hadn't made love for months. With horror I realised that the arm flung over my chest was Eveline's and it was her knees pressing against my thigh. I was in Eveline's bed. She was asleep beside me. A hangover drummed on my brain. For a moment, I thought I was going to be sick.

I'd checked on Eveline on my way up to my bed. As I pressed down the handle to her door, a shadow loomed over me, drowning me in its darkness and I'd made a dash for the safety of her bed and had been too frightened to leave it.

Something bumpy bit into the small of my back. Carefully, infinitesimally slowly, I moved Eveline's arm back to her side. I hoped that she was sleeping so deeply that she wasn't aware of me at all. Gently, I rolled off the bed onto my knees. I could see what had hurt me, lying in the middle of the rumpled sheet: a little drawstring pouch, silk, oyster pink and slightly soiled. I stayed absolutely rigid, my hand outstretched. A soft little sound had escaped from Eveline's lips. Then she shifted onto her side, ragged hair in tufts around a tranquil face which was even more beautiful sleeping.

They looked like bits of glass, cupped in my hand, but so sharply faceted and so heavy with light even in a semi-dark room, that they couldn't have been anything other than diamonds. There were five, and the largest was half the size of my little fingernail.

I put them back in the pouch and placed the pouch just under the edge of Eveline's pillow. She hadn't heard my gasp or seen the look of disbelief as I made the connection between what was in my palm and the girl I'd assumed was some sort of defenceless waif, who'd arrived at the château because she had nowhere else to go — even if she were a Kumono. This girl hadn't needed to be found at the château gates. She definitely hadn't had to rely on the kindness of strangers.

Innocence Kumono presided over a country famed for its diamond mines, I knew that much. I also remembered some sort of international embargo against that country's diamond trade, because of the dictator's régime. It was the sort of information you could pick up from any of the broadsheets, your eyes irresistibly drawn to the lurid headline of 'Blood Diamonds'.

For a while, I knelt beside the bed and looked at the girl, as if she were a baby sleeping, trying to work out what I felt about discovering her with diamonds — and I found that I couldn't think with a hangover drilling into the front of my brain.

I picked up my shirt, shorts and underwear. I dislodged something and it rolled away beneath the bed until it stopped. I stayed absolutely still. She didn't wake. I retrieved the small hard object. I placed the bullet back under Eveline's pillow. I crept out of the bedroom, pulled the door to, and in the dark corridor, scrambled into my clothes which were covered in fluff and reeked of sweat.

*

I had seen a bag of diamonds before. Years before I'd been with Tom when he had paid a visit to a Hatton Garden jeweller. He decanted a dozen diamonds onto the rectangle of black velvet which the jeweller had placed on the glass counter. "Where did you get those from? Are they real?" I was so surprised I couldn't contain myself. The jeweller laughed. Tom laughed and tapped the side of his nose. "Finders keepers," he said facetiously.

That was the only time — apart from when he acquired the château — that he actually swore me to secrecy. Not that it was necessary. He never mentioned the diamonds again and I never saw them, as I thought I might, around Samantha's slender throat.

*

It was going to be a very hot day. Already, there was a cloud of flies buzzing over the remnants of last night's meal on the kitchen table. I made myself a coffee, slowly, because my brain was sluggish and was trying to grapple with thoughts of diamonds, Kumono, and the girl upstairs. I took the cup out to the ruins of the chapel and sat, with my back to the château, on a lump of fallen masonry.

There was a church on the hill opposite the château, with a tall steeple and a roof like a witch's hat. When the sun's rays were long and low, it floated on a sea of light. It took me a while to work out why: the church was surrounded by graves, mostly made of granite and the majority with photos inset into the headstone. The French favour glass domes, the sort you find with a cheese platter, to preserve their wreaths and everlasting flowers so when the light

110

struck the mica in the granite, the glass fronts of the photos and the protective bowls sparkled with dazzling intensity.

I could feel eyes watching me. I could hear footsteps behind me, rustling over the gravel. I stayed quite still, wondering if Eveline would be able to hear me if I screamed.

Greg wished me "good morning". He smelt stale and boozy even from a couple of metres away.

"You gave me a fright."

"Sorry." He grinned. "I didn't get home after all. I bunked down in the stables." He slumped on the grass beside me, not caring about the heavy dew. We waited while the sun burnt off the last of the early morning mist in the valley. Greg rubbed the stubble on his chin.

"The coffee smells good."

I smiled. "You must be as hungover as I am. What do you know about diamonds?"

He laughed. "Me? Nothing. Why?"

I would tell him later. It was all too complicated with a hangover.

"Do you know what they were like, Greg, the sons? Was there a girl with them? A little girl?"

"I wasn't here, remember?" I wondered if my eyes were as bloodshot as his. We must have looked a pretty pair.

"But…" I encouraged him.

"But…" he repeated. "The sons used this place three or four times a year. They'd bring friends down. I never heard of a sister."

"It doesn't make sense if there was a house on the Riviera."

"Yes and no," Greg said. "This place is high on a hill, and the village is off the beaten track… The Kumonos were pretty paranoid about security from what I've heard."

111

"The General himself never came?"

"That's what they say."

"What did the locals feel about their château being owned by the Kumonos?"

"I don't rightly know," Greg shifted uncomfortably. "No one wants to talk about the General's connection to the village. And after he had gone, when there was talk, it was about the state the château was in…"

A piece of stone fell off the chapel wall, startling us both.

"It wasn't right. Your brother didn't want you to know about the Kumonos."

For a second I thought that I had misheard him.

"I beg your pardon?"

"Like I said, I didn't think it right."

I laughed. "Tom wouldn't do that."

Greg broke the silence. "And I needed the job."

Slowly, the world reinstated itself — the prickly grass, a yellow butterfly, my still warm mug of coffee.

"When did he tell you not to tell me?"

"The second time — when he phoned to say that you'd be over in a couple of days."

It took a minute or so for me to assimilate this piece of information.

"Well that's not possible," I said with relief. "I didn't know I was coming until an hour or so before I left London."

"Maybe," Greg allowed himself to look at me. "He knows you better than you think." He smiled, anxious to dispel the tension between us. Greg caught my elbow to steady me as I stood up.

"No one at Babs' and Dora's mentioned Innocence Kumono and his sons," I said as casually as I could.

Greg stood up as well. He looked me straight in the eyes.

"I told them," he said levelly, "that if you knew who had owned the château there'd be a good chance you'd leave."

"But why would they care?" I was completely baffled.

"This place was becoming an eyesore. The locals were petitioning central government to do something…"

"So?"

"Property prices," Greg said lamely.

"They were worried about house prices." The idea was so absurd I laughed.

Greg looked relieved.

"You've done the local property owners a huge favour."

"So have you," it hurt my head when I laughed, "and you're the one who lives in a caravan." As soon as I said it, I was sorry. "Let's go up to the château. I'll find us some breakfast."

Greg helped to clear the kitchen table. "I don't suppose the Kumonos ever had to do domestic."

"I suppose not," I said. I took a deep breath. "I spent last night in Eveline's bed. I was drunk and got spooked and before you ask, I'm not."

Greg looked as if he was struggling not to laugh.

"It's not funny. I found diamonds in her bed. A pouch of diamonds. Big ones."

"You're joking?" Suddenly he was no longer amused.

I shook my head.

"Hells bells. You have to give it to her — there you are with your charity case and there she is, possibly a Kumono, richer than you, taking everything you've got to offer…" He whistled with disbelief.

"Diamonds," he said. "That's serious stuff. Where are they from?"

"I don't know. She must keep them on her person."

113

"Do you think she could have nicked them?"

"I don't think she's a thief," I said slowly, thinking.

"What about the gold chain," he snorted.

"She was keeping it. Not stealing it."

"How do you know?" he asked. "I mean, how can we know?"

My head began to throb again.

"Seriously," Greg said, "the sooner she goes the better. The house hasn't been right since she's been here."

"It's never been right."

"Beats me why you stayed if it gives you the creeps."

"Do you know," I said laughing, "that apart from anything else, I wouldn't ever let my brother down."

I did though. I would fail to protect Tom. I would let him down.

Chapter 19

Six months before, when Tom had asked me to supervise the renovation of his recently acquired château, I distinctly remember asking him how long it had lain empty. "Years. Five years at least." That's all he had said. It never occurred to me to ask who had owned it previously. You don't when someone shows you a photo of their new house, but I was puzzled. He had never shown any interest in France before, not even for a family holiday. He brushed aside my reservations. "It fell into my lap. An offer I couldn't refuse. Don't you think Mum would have loved it?"

"Yes," I said. "She would have gloried in it." She always had said that she and our father had intended, one day, to live in France. With him being an author, it didn't matter where they lived. Then our father died and Uncle Mani never had enough money to buy our mother her 'little place in France'. For our mother in her congested little flat in Maida Vale, the château would have represented glorious quintessential France, the sort of France about which she could only have dreamed.

*

I tried to phone Tom. I was certain that had he known that the château had belonged to the Kumonos, he would never have bought it, never in a million years — but I needed to hear the consternation in his voice when I told him. Greg's assertions about Tom had unsettled me. Greg didn't always tell the truth but he didn't lie. My brother's relationship with the truth, I knew, was more based on expediency. As a child, he had told whoppers. He always told you what you wanted to hear for the most altruistic of reasons; he didn't want to disappoint.

After numerous attempts to reach him directly, I had to beg Tom's P.A. to ask him to return my call. As soon as I replaced the handset in its cradle, it rang.

I picked up immediately. "Tom?"

There was a silence at the other end of the line. "Philip?" I had a faint recollection of phoning him the night before.

"I think," a vaguely familiar voice replied, "that maybe I have the wrong number."

"Who are you looking for?"

"My name's Valerie. I was," she said with a tinkling laugh, "looking for you. We met yesterday, in the supermarket... and you seemed so unwell I thought I'd ring today to see how you are."

"That's sweet of you." I felt guilty that I had ever thought her an inquisitive busybody.

"Look," she said, "I'm an old hand at France. If you ever need anything, anything at all..."

"I'm sorry I can't chat. I'm waiting for a call." Just as I was about to put down the phone, a thought occurred to me.

"Do you mind me asking how you know this phone number?"

"I looked it up in the book. One would have thought that he'd have been ex-directory."

"Who?"

"Why, General Kumono of course."

In the silence which followed, Valerie gave another little laugh.

"Oh dear," she said. "I hope I haven't let the cat out of the bag? You were bound to find out anyway."

I put down the phone. The rush of rage I felt was quite startling.

I waited for Tom to return my call. I waited for Philip to phone. They didn't. I was angry with everyone — Philip, Tom, Greg, Eveline and all the English I had met in France — I felt so foolish with only myself, really, to blame.

Eveline was by the swimming pool. When she saw me, she rose like a startled fawn and scurried through the archway into the house. Maybe she was still upset by the scene at the dinner table or — worse — embarrassed that I ended up in bed with her. Either way, I didn't have the energy to embark on an awkward conversation beginning with 'when I was getting out of your bed this morning', and ending with 'by the way I found the bag of diamonds.' Just thinking of trying to have that conversation made me smile and my anger dissipated. It was too hot to be furious.

Part of me wanted to peel off my clammy t-shirt and shorts and feel cool water eddying against my skin, but even the thought of doing that required too much effort. Eventually, I wandered round to the front — in through the shade of the archway, past the two doors — one open and giving onto the kitchen and the other locked, on the opposite side, denying access to a room or rooms — who knew? "Leave it," Tom had said airily, when I asked him whether I should try to open the door, "I'm sure you have enough to do elsewhere in the house."

In the afternoon, the front of the château took the brunt of the sun. Only the ground floor was in shadow, dug out at a lower level. All the windows on the lower level were protected by iron grilles with sharp spikes and, unlike the rest of the house, the windows of the room or rooms behind the locked door were shuttered. Ivy grew in behind them.

The sun beat on my head. I could hear Greg in one of the upstairs rooms. He was humping something about and every time there was a thud, a belligerent profanity followed. I wondered if Eveline was in her room, lying on her bed, fingering her diamonds. She kept three things hidden: her bag of diamonds, the bullet, and the photocopy of a photograph of a young man.

Then everything stopped. My brain stood still. No Greg. No Eveline. No Tom. No hum from the cicadas. No doves. No traffic noise from the village. No noise at all. No nothing except the château shimmering in the sunlight as if it was about to lift off and float away like a helium balloon in a depthless sky. Then I blinked, and my heart took a beat, and I was conscious of being rooted to the spot and everything reverting to normal. My hangover had miraculously disappeared. I decided in that small moment of clarity to open the locked door. No more secrets.

Greg swore he would rather lug bags of plaster about.

"Please, it's now or never."

"How about never," he snorted but he reappeared with his tool-box. "Are you sure about this?"

"You're the one who's been gagging to have a go at this door."

"Yes," he said reluctantly. "But that was then and this is now."

"Look," I said, "this door is locked and we're going to open it — damn the consequences."

"You're sure?"

He could see the determination on my face.

He rummaged through his box and picked out a screwdriver. "I'll go and get the mallet."

I could see why, when confronted by the door, Greg was apprehensive. It was small and wide, like the rest of the doors in the château, and studded its length and breadth with little black knobs. It had three hinges, implacably wrought in iron. It had an enormous keyhole through which I'd peered and into which I peered again and saw only blackness. When Greg returned with the mallet, he was still uncertain.

"Look," I say, "Tom owes me big time anyway, for not telling me about Kumono."

Greg didn't look convinced.

"Maybe it's where they kept their wine," I said in a moment of inspiration, "I mean there are wine glasses… Let me have a go." The sillier the reason, the better. I made a grab for the mallet. Smilingly, Greg hoisted it out of my reach.

With twenty strokes, Greg heaving and me counting, the door splintered across the lock. Greg leant against it wiping the sweat from his forehead.

"You want to go on?"

I nodded, my heart in my mouth. Leaves and the odd bit of paper swirled about our feet. I'd been concentrating so hard that I hadn't noticed that the wind had risen and the archway, when the wind did blow, turned into a wind tunnel. Greg pressed his back into the hard oak. "Okay?"

He gave it a hefty push, and it creaked ajar. Greg kicked. The door opened with a heart-rending crack. It was the stuffy smell I noticed first, a rush of dust and heat. Then, as my eyes focussed, I saw an enormous grey space with streaks of light filtering through cracks in the shutters and at its centre, a mass of bulky shapes. Greg strode across to the nearest window, levered the bar off its latch and wrenched the shutters apart, tendrils of ivy ripping off the wall as he did so.

"There you are Madame" he said, flourishing a hand and bending into a mock bow.

I hear the faint sound of the phone ringing, upstairs in the dining hall.

Chapter 20

I reached the phone just as the outgoing message flowed serenely into the room. Philip was saying "Hello?" over the machine. We waited, both of us, for the 'beep'.

"There were only the two sons," he said over the whirring of the tape. "I've checked and rechecked. No daughters."

I was so happy I could have cried.

"Has this got anything to do with the girl staying with you?"

"I've got to go. Call you later."

"Please," he said. "I've no idea what's going on — but please, take care."

I ran back down the stairs, through the kitchen and through the archway. Greg was busy opening the last of the shutters — the room was the width of the château with windows on both sides.

The jumble of shapes under dust cloths looked like furniture. I hadn't given any thought to what the room contained, if anything. I had just wanted it unlocked.

"She's not a Kumono."

"How do you know?" Greg wrested with the heavy bar across a pair of shutters.

I told him. He staggered backwards as the bar suddenly gave.

I looked around the room. Against the furthermost wall was a pointed triangular shape, draped in a dustsheet, the height of a small man or woman. I yanked off the cover. It hid an ironing board and an iron, the iron on the floor.

"They sure liked their ironing boards," Greg said with a chuckle.

We pulled the dustsheets off heavy old armoires, chests of drawers, lots of bedsteads, bedside tables, chairs — all stacked around an enormous bit of furniture which could be either a wardrobe or a cupboard. We coughed and we sneezed. Our eyes watered horribly.

I took a rest for a couple of minutes and unlatched a window. The rush of fresh air was wonderful against my face. The light outside was tinged a sultry yellow and the topmost branches of the trees — which was the only bit of tree you could see from that low down in the château — were swaying.

Meanwhile Greg unhooked the rockers of a bamboo rocking chair from a chest of drawers and flopped into it, choking on another cloud of dust.

"Idiot," I laughed.

"I'll have to get some men in. To get all this upstairs."

I crossed back over to the furniture and pulled open the top drawer of a chest of drawers. "Do you think all the keys that are missing for upstairs might be here, in a drawer?"

"Why? Who do you want to lock up? Eveline?" He tried to laugh which turned into a cough.

I was glad that Greg was sitting down. He wasn't getting any younger. Nor was I for that matter, but he looked like a radish with his red face and shock of dusty hair. Greg gestured at the mountain of furniture.

"Who'd want to get rid of all this?"

"They didn't. They stored it. They don't seem to have ever got rid of anything."

"When you think of the crap upstairs…" He shook his head.

Suddenly I understood why the bedrooms were left so bare. "They were going to renovate the place."

Greg creaked merrily on the rocker, backwards and forwards, humming away to himself, something in his tune made me stop and listen. I dredged it up out of my memory: 'Hickory, dickory, dock.'

"What do you think you'll do with this room?" Greg asked.

The nursery rhyme had given me a brilliant idea. I should have thought of it earlier. I squinted, through the gloom.

"Playroom for Tom's kids? If you painted these walls a primrose yellow and got rid of those lights…"

The lights were iron sconces with fake candles.

Greg heaved himself to his feet and, with a heavy tread, went to the switch beside the door. Half the room was immediately illuminated with a weak yellow light.

"Better?"

*

Like eavesdropping on someone else's conversation, nothing good can come from opening the effects of others. I remember Philip's mother, after we had been married ten years or so, asking me to fetch her cardigan from their bedroom. The four of us were in the sitting room, having the obligatory pre-dinner drinks. Philip's mother, who had just had a hip replacement, had her leg stretched out across the chintz-covered sofa. I didn't listen to her precise instructions as to which drawer exactly to open and pulled them all open in succession and found packed away in the bottom drawer, baby clothes — little matinée jackets, bootees, leggings — beautifully knitted little reproaches from a mother of an only child to the barren daughter-in-law.

"What took you so long?" Philip asked when I eventually made it downstairs again. I didn't tell him. And I'd forgotten his mother's cardigan. We started on a second round of IVF treatment a couple of days later. I wouldn't look Philip's mother in the eyes, not once, for the rest of that weekend. She knew. She never liked me. Not even Tom's successes in business counted for much in mitigation.

*

We were like children, Greg and I, playing at finding treasure.

Greg played the game with gusto.

"You never know," he winks at me, wrenching back a drawer. "Friend of mine found a diamond brooch once in the back of a desk he'd picked up in a job lot."

"So did your friend sell it?"

"For a fortune." There was more than a hint of disapproval in Greg's tone.

I leant across the chest of drawers. I could see the top of his head and his little bald spot because he was squatting, investigating the bottommost drawer. I flicked his hair.

"You're not telling me..." I teased.

Greg stood up. He grinned.

"I am actually. I would have done my best to find the owner. Otherwise it's stealing, plain and simple. Why? What would you have done?"

"Kept it," I said with a laugh. "Like I'll keep anything we find here — although — " Greg knew I was just fooling around, "I might, just might, split it with you."

He had a lovely smile, Greg.

We arrived at the enormous wardrobe. Greg and I had shunted and sorted what furniture we could move — all the bedside tables in one place, chairs in another, tables in one corner, etc. It was all of very good quality, much better than a lot of the stuff upstairs.

We contemplated the wardrobe in silence. I caught my breath after all the heaving. The air smelt like burnt biscuit from crisped-up dust on the illuminated light bulbs. My hair was plastered against my scalp; like Greg's, it was lank with sweat. The heat in a room which has been shut up, can bake you.

"How we will ever get this upstairs…" Greg shook his head.

It was a beautiful piece of walnut, with a curlicued top and curlicued legs. It had two doors and a deep drawer beneath.

"Never mind that now," I said. "Let's see what's inside — if anything."

So far we had found nothing of any interest — only dead insects and discarded clouds of hair, the sort which comes off a comb. We had both forgotten that we set out looking for keys for the doors upstairs. We were on the hunt for a pot of gold.

Greg twisted a gilt handle. Nothing. He tried the two together.

"Locked?"

"It's the doors, they're stuck. Let's leave it."

"Let's just see what's inside. Go on Greg."

He struck a pose and flexed his biceps, making the mermaid tattoo flick her tail.

"Superman himself to the rescue. What do you think's in here?"

"I don't know — a body?" I was giggling like a schoolgirl.

He staggered with the effort of yanking back the doors. I just managed to avoid being hit on the nose.

"Hells bells," Greg was totally bemused. "Why would you…"

I rushed round to take a look.

Chapter 21

"Clothes. Just clothes." I laughed with relief.

"Why down here and not up there?" Greg jerked his head towards the ceiling.

We were looking at a cupboard with shelves: eight shelves laden with clothing — neatly arranged into piles for underwear, t-shirts, shirts, and trousers.

How I wish we had just left the cupboard, as he'd suggested. All I can think is that the intuition — my intuition — which I'd deliberately kept dampened down because I didn't want to know, I didn't want to think — had finally sparked into life.

We started with the bottom shelf, intending to work our way upwards. At first we just tossed the clothes onto the floor but by the second shelf — maybe because they had been so beautifully pressed — we shook out the clothes and laid them carefully on the heap we had made on the floor.

They didn't have the sickly sweet scent of the clothes that I had cleared from the cupboards upstairs. They smelt of mothballs.

The clothes came in all shapes and sizes. Their storage puzzled me. It seemed so frugal and so different to the excesses we had found upstairs. Still though, old underwear was as repulsive as old underwear always is.

Greg tried on a particularly florid shirt of red roses on a blue striped background. He pranced about, the sleeves flapping over his wrists, making me laugh.

"For a much taller man than you, you nit."

He stopped short, as if struck by a thunderbolt. "It's all men's have you noticed?"

Of course I'd noticed. I'd noticed by the third pair of y-fronts. In fact I would have been very surprised if any of the clothing had been female.

So we went on. Greg stood on a chair and started to clear the second shelf from the top. He handed me one folded item at a time. We were caught up in a cycle of sound and silence: the rasp of Greg's rough fingers on the cloth; the flap it made as I shook it out; the soft flop as it hit the heap. It was soothing, mindless activity.

"Hallo Princess," Greg said softly.

Eveline was standing in the doorway, quite still.

"Look what we've found," I said inanely. She was holding herself with a rigidity that I found disturbing. The expression on her face was unreadable.

I braced myself as she hurtled towards me, arms outstretched. For a moment I thought that she wanted to give me a hug.

She came to a halt in front of the pile of clothes. She dropped to her knees and she buried her face in them. She looked as if she was praying and so mad, that I laughed — that horrible involuntary laughter which comes from fright. Greg caught my eyes, rolled his, lifted his index finger to his forehead and started to twist it, pretending that what we were witnessing wasn't alarming.

The laughter died in my throat. Greg remained rooted, standing on the chair. Eveline started to scrabble through the shirts and trousers with such an urgency, it was as if she thought that someone might be suffocating under the weight of the clothes.

Greg didn't exist. I didn't exist.

I didn't know what to do. I didn't know what to do for the best. I was totally and utterly panicked, staring at her burrowing through the mound.

"Eveline," I said, but nothing came out of my mouth. I cleared my throat. I looked at Greg. He looked at me, looking as helpless as I felt.

"Eveline."

She didn't hear me.

I took a step towards the kneeling figure with the flailing arms. I was close enough to smell her light, sweet fragrance, so utterly different to the miasma of mothball around us. I put out my hand tentatively. I grasped an arm as it moved upwards. I held it down. She shook me off and launched across the carpet.

Greg jumped off the chair.

She picked up the blue striped shirt that Greg had been fooling around with earlier. She fell forward, clutching it to her breast. A low keening rose out of her crouched form. The sound brought tears to my eyes.

I bent over her. I wanted to hug her, hold her, tell her that everything would be okay — that we could sort out whatever it was, no matter what it was.

She started upwards, crashing her head against my jaw. The impact was so unexpected, I cried out. Tears that I'd been keeping at bay, ran down my face. Greg started forward, hand out to grab her.

"No, Greg. Don't."

She laid the shirt on the floor. She arranged the sleeves so that they stretched out, across the carpet. She smoothed out the material, like she was trying to get rid of the creases. The shirt had loose cuffs with buttonholes instead of buttons. Eveline aligned the buttonholes. All she needed was cufflinks.

I realised then — or I had a glimmer of understanding. I couldn't think further than that, so I acted.

I moved away from Greg. I stepped out across the short distance between me and Eveline.

"That's enough now," I said, kneeling in front of her. I folded my arms around her shoulders and bend her head to my chest. It was her sweat and my sweat. My tears dropped on her hair. I felt her breath on my skin and her heart beating against mine. For a moment, her head leant against my breast.

Carefully, she folded the shirt. She stood up, the shirt pressed to her chest. Greg and I watched her walk out the door, head erect, totally poised — leaving in her wake a tumult of clothes.

I started to follow.

"Leave her be." Greg righted the chair.

"Why? I can't just let…"

"It's not you she needs."

"No. It's her mother, her parents, her family."

"We don't know if she has any family." Greg was back on the chair and peering into the topmost shelf.

"I thought I saw…" he started, pulling out sweatshirts. "Here we are."

He drew out a plain white cardboard box, long and low, the sort that shirts come in. The contents slipped and rattled inside.

It was a set of house keys with a car key and a pair of black, heavy-rimmed glasses with prescription lens.

Greg shoved the box back in the wardrobe. "Christ," he said, "this place."

The possible connection — the explanation for Eveline's behaviour — suddenly came to me.

"The young man in Eveline's photograph. Wasn't he wearing glasses just like those?"

Greg wiped the sweat from his forehead. He started to laugh. "This is completely bloody bonkers. We're going mad."

Chapter 22

Down in the furniture repository, we'd started out looking for the keys to the doors in the rest of the château. We hadn't found them. I'd discovered something far more important; the key to Eveline. And it was the photograph of the young man. I was certain of it.

While Greg stayed in the kitchen, slumped in a chair and silent, I went up the stairs. There was a sense of desolation in Eveline's room, but no Eveline. I sat down on her bed.

I cried. The first proper tears I'd shed in France. What had happened for them to be apart?

Eventually I dried my eyes and shut the door to her room. I looked in the salon and library. I opened the front door and stood on the steps and shouted "Eveline!" I tossed the name out, with all my strength. The air was empty of sound except for a woman shouting down in the village and when I listened harder, I heard a few dead leaves scratching across the gravel and a rose stem scraping against a windowpane. As I passed through the dining room I noticed the red light blinking on the answering machine. I ignored it, thinking that it was Philip, earlier.

Greg was standing in front of the range, the kettle in his hand when I got back to the kitchen. He had a confidence about him, which he hadn't had half-an-hour before.

"You can't find her?"

I shook my head.

He handed me a lukewarm mug of tea. "She's mad," he said dismissively.

I told him what I thought; that Eveline was looking for the man whose shirt we found. That the keys and glasses were his. That the passport I discovered was his.

"He was here," I said firmly. "And she never heard from him again."

"So?" Greg shrugged his shoulders. "He did a runner. Didn't want to tell her to her face that it was over."

"She wouldn't pursue someone who'd dumped her like that. It's just not her style."

"How do you know? I mean, seriously, what do you know?"

I sipped my tea. Greg was right. I knew very little about Eveline and very little about the château — but I could find out about the house. She had offered to help, after all.

Greg tried to dissuade me from going to Valerie's.

"You're crazy to go now. Look at the sky."

A storm was rising. "I'm not waiting a moment longer."

"She's a two-faced busybody."

"Good. Then she'll be able to tell me what it was like here with the Kumono sons."

Greg followed me to the hall. "So you're off to see Mrs Nosy. Her second name is Parker. Valerie Parker." His shout of laughter was forced.

"Did anyone ever tell you about your jokes?" I tried to be equally as light-hearted.

He offered to come with me.

"No. Stay and look after Eveline. Please."

"What if I can't find her?"

"Please. I'm worried for her."

"So am I," he said softly. "Poor little girl."

Eveline was sitting waiting for me in the car. No, she wasn't. It was a shadow and a rather portly one at that and when I got a little nearer, I realised that it was the shape of the laurel next to the car. Black clouds were banking up behind the woods.

I got to Valerie's just in time. There was a streak of lightening and a rumble of thunder as I arrived. Through her glass front door, I could see right through the house and into the garden where Valerie was standing with her back to the house and her head upturned to the sky. She was quite still. She could have been a statue. She was like the rest of the world, holding its breath, waiting for rain. She turned around as soon as I rat-a-tat-tatted.

"I thought it might be you," she said, as she let me in. "The door's always open by the way. There was something in your voice this morning…" She had an irritating habit of letting her sentences trail away.

I thought I'd been terribly matter-of-fact.

"There was a sense of…" and she paused and her eyes glanced over me. I felt very uncomfortable. "of unease." She had a brilliant, welcoming smile. "Come in."

Valerie was so small and light, she made me feel very ungainly, ducking under the bunches of herbs hanging from the ceiling.

"As you can see," she said. "I live very simply."

She caught my look of incomprehension.

"I live to nature's rhythm. Radio, TV, internet — they get in the way."

She was a Luddite. "I miss the telly," I told her.

I squeezed myself between table and chair and sat down. Valerie cleared the table of baskets of yet more cut herbs and offered me peppermint, apple, rosehip, lemon balm.

"Just 'builders', if you have it."

She darted out into the alien light in the garden, and returned with a large bunch of leaves.

"Verbena," she said pouring boiling water onto the leaves. "Don't worry: for me, not you."

She reached up for a very battered pale green Fortnum and Mason tea caddy which was so reminiscent of England it brought a pang to my heart.

Fortnum's was where Tom introduced me to Samantha. I hadn't seen him for a while as he had started travelling all over the world on business by then.

As soon as I saw my brother weaving through the tables, smiling broadly, leading a very young, shy Samantha in his wake, I knew. She was exactly what Tom needed at the time; instant access to the establishment through his prospective father-in-law. Samantha's father was a hereditary peer. Had he not given consent, Samantha would have married Tom regardless. Whether Tom would have married Samantha, I'm not so sure. In any event, Samantha stayed with her man, despite his numerous affairs in the early years. Those stopped about six years ago, Tom actually telling me, with a straight face, that he had 'turned over a new leaf'.

"What do you think?" Tom asked me anxiously when we were on our own outside Fortnum's. It was one of those rain-sodden blustery November days in London — just as it is today, twenty years later. I was trying to flag down a taxi with Tom helping. Samantha was still inside the shop, buying a particular brand of marmalade for her mother. She had talked of little except the forthcoming wedding — wistfully mentioning how she wished she had a brother to be close to, like Tom with me. She had sought out Tom's hand at every opportunity and he'd kept giving me soppy, embarrassed little smiles.

"Sam was so nervous about meeting you." A fleet of taxis sailed by, all occupied. Tom was waiting for my answer. "She knows how important you are."

"You must be very much in love. That's an enormous diamond you've got her."

"Jealous are we?" He grinned. A taxi splashed to a halt beside us. "Cost me an arm and a leg. You could say," he said suddenly serious as he leant into the interior to kiss me goodbye, "that it's a mortgage on my future."

"You do love her Tom?"

He brushed his lips on my cheek. "I adore her."

I wasn't jealous. I was simply frightened of another woman having more claim on him. I didn't exactly encourage the affairs but I did provide Tom with alibis when needed. Philip hated my connivance and Samantha, knowing full well what was going on, hated me. I didn't care. I loved my brother.

*

Valerie said very little. She busied herself with the paraphernalia of making proper tea. There were lots of photographs and cards interspersed with the herbs on the dresser.

"Family?" I asked.

"Some," she smiled, "But mostly people I've helped." She smoothed wisps of hair off her face. The rest hung down her back in a ponytail. My fingernails, like Valerie's, had crescents of dirt. Eveline had so many baths there was never enough hot water for me.

"Sugar?" Valerie asked. "I've bought you milk," she added waving a carton of milk from the fridge at me. She put the milk in first.

Valerie slipped into the seat opposite. Every time she moved there was a whiff of something pungent and earthy.

I pressed my arms tightly into my sides. Valerie observed without comment. She cupped her hands around her tea. It smelt heavenly. She was right to drink a tea which doesn't need milk. French milk sits on top of tea.

"Is everything okay?"

I was suddenly gripped with anxiety that I was about to betray Tom in some way.

"What can I do for you?" Valerie asked, with a pleasant, knowing smile.

Chapter 23

Valerie liked power over people.

"The thing is, Valerie," I began carefully, "that my brother didn't know about Innocence Kumono when he acquired the château…"

Valerie raised an eyebrow. "Difficult," she murmured.

I had my answer. "No," I said. "In the circles he moves in, property is often in the name of a company so the owners can remain anonymous and I — " I rushed on with what I knew to be the truth, which was so much easier, " — didn't know myself until very recently."

"The General never stayed there you know," Valerie sounded defensive. "It was just the sons and they weren't there that often."

"But nevertheless they were…"

"You'd be surprised at how many people don't know what they're buying into," Valerie interrupted forcefully. "Coming over here, not knowing the language, not knowing the history. Some people are very foolish."

She meant me, even though she knew that the château wasn't mine. The last of the light was retreating from the garden. We were sitting in darkening gloom with a strange metallic glint to it — sharp-edged like the taste of Valerie's tea.

Valerie withdrew a box of matches from a drawer under her side of the table. "I don't know why," she said slowly, "people think that they can just buy a place and take it over, as it were." She carefully lit the candle on the table between us. The sweet scent of beeswax permeated the air.

"People," Valerie shook her head, "have no sense." She busied herself with placing the dead match back in the box and back in the drawer. "You do know," she sipped her tea, "that the château dates back to mediaeval times?"

I wasn't there for a history lesson.

"But why have a château you hardly ever use? It doesn't make sense."

Valerie shrugged, expressing her lack of interest. "What does anyone do in a holiday home?"

I was getting nowhere. I tried a change of subject. I asked how she came to be in France?

She laughed. She was embarrassed. "The usual story I'm afraid."

When I didn't say anything, she continued. "I met a man. He happened to be French, and I ended up here. This was his parents' property. When we split, he didn't want to be in the sticks so I bought him out. I couldn't afford to return to England…" she smiled brightly, refocusing on me. "Are you married?"

I told her that my husband would be coming over.

"Soon?"

"I hope so." There was an ache, a very lonely ache, in the pit of my stomach.

The garden flashed up against the window. As we waited for the roll of thunder to recede, a splash of rain hit the pane and then another and another. A river of water coursed down the other side of the glass, catching in the candlelight's reflection. Rain drummed on the roof.

Valerie smiled, the angularity of her face softened by the light. "Nice isn't it? Nice and cosy."

I hoped that Greg had found Eveline; that she wasn't outside, wandering around in the deluge.

"So many English," Valerie said softly, "come over here to buy the property of their dreams at a fraction of the price they would pay back in the UK... I wonder if they would bother if they could afford to buy the equivalent at home?"

"You know," she continued, "there's even a stall at the market selling English produce: HP sauce, baked beans, Colman's mustard. I mean, if you want all that, why don't you just go home? What's the point in living in France? I mean, living in France isn't like choosing from your high street Tesco's confectionery counter..."

I tried to imagine the General's sons in my local Tesco back in London, squabbling over lemon sherbets and chocolate éclairs with a couple of heavies squaring up menacingly to anyone who even so much as glanced in their direction. Unfortunately, I knew their taste in sweets, given the amount of sweet wrappers at the château, but I couldn't picture them at all. I thought of the smiling, bespectacled young man in Eveline's photograph.

"I mean, don't get me wrong," Valerie was in full flow. "Some of my best friends are English even though I prefer my French friends nowadays... I do wish the English would make more of an effort, you know? Learn the language for starters. I give French classes... herbal therapy doesn't give me enough to live on — there are a few spaces, if you ever feel the need to brush up..."

"My French is practically non-existent I'm afraid."

"Even better. A clean sheet."

Outside, it was pitch black. The flame on the candle between us faltered and Valerie's shadow swung alarmingly on the wall behind her. Another flash of lightening illuminated her face.

I was beginning to feel completely claustrophobic. "Could we have the light on?"

"You know," she said as she returned to the table, "you look a bit peaky. I've just the thing." She opened a cupboard door. "Elderberry wine," she flourished a bottle. "It's not as expensive as some of my other products."

"What you have to understand," Valerie announced when she has poured out two glasses and I had taken my first appreciative, hypocritical sip, "is that the château is very ancient. It's got a long, long history. It has survived and will survive anyone who occupies it. For ancient buildings," she intoned softly, "are entities in themselves with layers of energy and memory which we displace at our peril."

She fixed her eyes on the candle flame. "Tell me, have you found any names?"

I was puzzled, wary of the direction in which the conversation was going. "What sort of names?"

"I've heard that there are names scratched into the walls with the invocation: '*Mon Dieu, sauvez-nous*'."

At that moment the bulb in the overhead light pinged. Valerie paid no attention to the fact that we were almost in darkness again. She beckoned me closer. I leant my face further into the warmth of the candle flame.

"Save us my God," she whispered dramatically, grasping my hand with both of hers.

I pulled my hand away. Valerie leant back in her chair, satisfied with my reaction. "It was during the French Revolution. The château was pillaged and the family executed but before they were carted off they managed to scratch their names into the walls. You haven't come across them? The names, I mean?"

"No," I say. "Nothing like that. Just a lot of really weird things and now we've found clothes, modern clothes, in a locked room off the archway. They definitely didn't belong to the Kumono sons and so I was wondering," I say in a rush, "would you know whose they could be?"

Valerie looks at me speculatively. "Friends? The General never came himself. Just the sons and their friends would come to your château…"

"My brother's château."

Valerie ignored my interruption. "We'd know when the sons were coming because they'd send a housekeeper a few days before to air the place. A nice chap, jolly. He spent so much money shopping in the village, he was very popular with the locals. The sons would come down in the dead of night, in a convoy of black limousines. I saw them once when I was out in the woods. They'd stay two weeks max. We always knew when they'd arrived because they liked their music loud. Heavy bass. You could hear it from one end of the village to the other but no one dared…" She stopped talking, lost in reminiscence.

"Dared what?"

"To ask them to turn their music down. Daft, isn't it? They weren't friendly. Not at all in fact. They had army types patrolling the grounds. Louts more like."

In a way, I was relieved. "So that's all it was; a party house."

"Yes," Valerie agreed, "but you always have to remember who they were."

She shifted back in her seat, remembering. Her face brightened with recollection. "There was an incident once.

A couple of locals found a man up a tree, in the woods. You know where I mean?"

I had an awful feeling of foreboding. "Behind the château?"

"They had wild parties up at the house, hence the music, if you could call it music, pumping out… Anyway this man, hardly more than a boy, he was completely non compos mentis. Stoned out of his head… The Kumonos wanted it all hushed up — drug taking wasn't good for the image…" Valerie snorted. "I mean to say when we know now what they got up to in their own country…"

"So what happened?"

Valerie looked at me vaguely. "The couple managed to coax him down from the tree and wrap a coat around him because he was so cold. He had been terrified out of his wits by something — the boar hunters, probably. He kept on saying that he wouldn't go back to the château."

"He spoke French?"

"Yes. And English apparently. Highly educated, I expect — well, you would be wouldn't you, if you're hob-nobbing with the likes of the Kumonos. Weren't the sons educated in England? Anyway, they had to practically frogmarch him up the avenue… what else could they do? They couldn't be responsible."

"No," I said.

"September is the start of the hunting season here. It was so warm that year that the butler bloke gave a garden party, after the sons had gone back home…"

I remembered talk of a garden party. The drunk woman at Babs' and Dora's party.

"How long ago?"

Valerie thought. "Well, the Kumonos have been gone — is it five years?" She nodded. "A year or so before that?

143

But I haven't told you the funny thing about the man in the tree..." She stopped and looked at me speculatively.

"Go on."

"The couple who came across him must have had a fright. I mean, you're walking along and you hear someone whimpering, starkers up a tree. Can you imagine?"

"No clothes?" I felt sick.

"Not a stitch," Valerie giggled. "Poor chap. I tell you what, you're as white as a sheet, even in this light. I'll run you back. We can sort out your car in the morning."

Chapter 24

I didn't feel well. I hadn't eaten all day and hunger was making me light-headed — that feeling of dislocation as if the centre of gravity has moved to the moon, except there wasn't a moon that night. Valerie drove slowly, pressed up against the steering wheel. The rain pounded against the car and the wipers wheezed backwards and forwards. "I'm sure you're going down with something. You weren't well yesterday in the supermarket, remember?"

I'd got drenched from running the short distance from the house to Valerie's car. I couldn't stop shivering. As we drove through the village, Valerie swerved sharply to avoid a plastic bin lid bouncing across the beam from the headlights. No one was on the streets.

"How did the villagers know that the young man came from the château?"

She gave me the answer I had been expecting. Dreading. "There aren't exactly many foreigners around here."

I couldn't stop thinking of the shirt which Eveline had so carefully smoothed out on the dusty carpet, as if she was trying to conjure up the man to whom it had belonged — or boy, I thought with a sickening lurch. She was so young herself.

The car strained up the hill to the château. I could see patches of light between the flailing branches of the trees. Valerie shifted down a gear. "Which reminds me," she said, "your visitor caused quite a commotion at the circus."

"She's not a visitor as such."

Valerie gave me a sideways glance. "Is she your maid?"

I laughed. "Good Lord, no."

From the gates, except that there were no gates, the château looked crazy, like the prow of an ocean liner ploughing through a stormy sea. Every window was ablaze. Valerie swung the car into a rectangle of light beside the front steps.

"So she's a friend helping out?"

"Not exactly. She turned up at the gates with a silver bullet in her hand. No explanations. None at all."

Valerie's eyes shone with ill-concealed curiosity. I was sorry for offering that nugget of information. I wasn't thinking. It just came out.

"Anyway, she's gone," I lied, shutting the door firmly so that Valerie couldn't ask me any more questions.

Valerie shrugged her shoulders and sent the car into reverse.

I stood in the driving rain and watched as the red eyes of her tail-lights flickered down the avenue and disappeared.

A finger of light slanted across the darkness in the archway. I was certain that we had shut the door to the furniture store and almost as sure that we switched off the lights. I called for Greg and Eveline, straining my ears to hear above the wind and the rain. Nothing. No one. Fear sparked up, somewhere deep inside me but I couldn't cross the sliver of light, not without knowing what was behind the door. A retreat back into the elements wasn't possible.

I summoned every ounce of courage I had. Slowly, the door yawned on its hinges. The furniture was there, just as Greg and I left it. So were the dust-cloths, pooled on the floor: like the Hoover, ironing board, and iron — still there, undisturbed. Just the pile of clothes, scattered by Eveline, had gone. The room with its acres of empty space looked ordered and peaceful. It was as if we — me, Greg and Eveline — had never been in the room. That I'd imagined it all.

Greg had scrawled a note, 'Gone to find Eveline', and left it on the kitchen table. I towelled myself down with some kitchen paper. I needed to eat. There was foie gras in the fridge, growing a crust because it had been shoved onto a shelf without being covered, and a few bits of stale baguette. I wolfed them, and took a slug from the remnants of wine in the bottom of a bottle which somehow Greg and I missed the evening before and I felt warmer, less light-headed — and definitely more brave. I went back out into the archway.

I stepped into the room, very conscious that the only exit was behind me.

The doors to the enormous cupboard were closed. I put my hands on the handles, twisted them, closed my eyes, and pulled. It was such a relief to see the eight shelves of shirts, t-shirts, trousers and underwear refolded into neat piles. No wonder I couldn't find Eveline earlier. Then I saw a shadow move and for one wild moment, I thought it was the man who Valerie said had been found in a tree, returning to reclaim his clothes. I rushed out of the room, dashed through the archway. When I slammed the kitchen door behind me, I told myself that I was being ridiculous, that it was my shadow moving in that desolate room — but when I think back, sitting here in London, it couldn't have been. I'd been in between two open cupboard doors so couldn't have cast any shadow.

I walked through the hall, the sound of my steps purposeful and confident which almost made me believe that I wasn't in the slightest bit frightened. I ascended both flights of stairs. I walked down the four corridors. I opened every door. Every room was already lit up because Greg, I assumed, had already paced the house, looking for Eveline. I kept my eyes trained on what was in front of me and when I dared to look around I was relieved to find that I only had my shadow for company.

I went into Eveline's room. Nothing suggested that she had done a bunk. Her suitcase was still in the corner. The bed was rumpled, like she had been lying on it. The silver bullet had gone from underneath her pillow. I opened the wardrobe and delved into her fancy shoes. Nothing. Hidden under a couple of t-shirts in the suitcase was the photo of the young man. It was a little crumpled and damp and I knew, with a heavy heart, that Eveline hadn't stop crying for a long time after she left the room off the archway.

The phone rang and I ran, clattering down the stairs, two at a time. It was Tom, his voice so clear despite the storm that he could have been talking to me from the kitchen. I was disappointed. I'd wanted him to be Greg, to tell me that he had found Eveline and that she was okay.

"How's tricks? I tried to call earlier. Did you get the message?"

"No."

"The photo you sent of the girl? I had it circulated. No joy. Not that it matters now."

"I don't know where she is…"

"I thought she had gone?" His tone was sharp.

"Who is it you said you'd bought this place from?" I was just as sharp.

"What's got into you?"

"You haven't answered my question."

"Why do you need to know?"

"You could have had the decency to tell me."

I knew he was using the silence which followed my outburst to test which variation of the truth would placate me.

"The rumours are that it belonged to Innocence Kumono," he said eventually.

"Fact," I said. "I can't believe that when I told you about the passport you still didn't tell me."

"I didn't think it mattered. Past history, you know? Anyway I didn't buy the château. It was given to me."

There was a crack of lightening which turned everything white for a second. I waited for the rumble of thunder to roll over.

"Come off it." I shouted down the crackling line. "Why would anyone want to give you a château?"

"In lieu of debt," I could tell from the strain in his voice that he was shouting too. "I took it as a favour."

"What sort of debt gives you a château?"

I could hear someone calling my name outside. Greg.

There was no more interference on the line between Tom and me.

"I thought it would be a nice place for Sam and the kids — " Tom continued more calmly.

"The girl you are so anxious I get rid of," I said sweetly, "turned up because she looking for someone. It makes me wonder what went on here."

"For God's sakes!"

Finally I'd got to him. Him and his château.

Chapter 25

Although the storm had passed, the wind was still up. The dark swirled with moonlight and swaying shadow. Greg lurched towards me, half-carrying Eveline. Her head was slumped against his shoulder, both arms around his neck.

"Get us some tea, will you?" He wouldn't allow me to take Eveline or help carry her. "And towels!" he shouted after me.

The phone rang upstairs: shrill and insistent. Eveline sat folded over, hiding her face, clutching a rag on her lap. Her clothes were sodden, limp against her body. Greg stood over her, arms crossed, droplets of water falling onto her bowed head. I gave them towels but Eveline was too miserable to move and Greg too tense with anger. I pressed tea bags against the sides of mugs, squeezing the last ounce of brown out of them. The phone stopped ringing and Greg rounded on Eveline.

"What the hell do you think you were doing? You could have got yourself killed."

He looked at me, his eyes flashing with anger. "Do you know where I found her? By the chapel. Out in the open. Totally exposed to the elements. Meanwhile I've trekked through the woods, calling out for Little Ms Silence here. There's no point in calling you Eveline, is there?" He jabbed a finger into her shoulder, making her look up at him with eyes swimming with tears, "Because that's not your name is it?"

"There's no point in shouting," I said, handing him his tea. "That'll get us nowhere."

"Nowhere," he repeated sourly.

He cupped the mug in his hands and blew on his tea, in and out like a bellows. The tip of his nose looked red and sore. I pressed Eveline's icy fingers around her mug.

"Please drink."

Dutifully, she began to sip the tea.

"I found her with that shirt," Greg nodded at Eveline's rag. "Would have walked past her if it hadn't been for a bolt of lightning which missed her by a few feet — and me for that matter." He gave a bitter little laugh. "Completely bloody stupid. I'm starving. Any chance of something to eat?"

I opened a can of confit de canard and spooned the glutinous mess into a saucepan. Greg sniffed the empty tin. "Duck. Can't get anything else to eat in this bloody country."

"Then why do you bloody well live here?"

He was right beside me at that point, both of us standing by the range. He stared at me and I stared at him, until I dropped my gaze. The thin, trilling sound of the phone upstairs started up again. It stopped before the answering machine clicked on. I lit the gas for Greg's duck. The flame took at the first try.

Then someone cleared their throat. Not me. Not Greg.

"I am sorry," a small light voice, a voice I had never heard before, announced from the other end of the room.

Greg and I looked at each other, not quite believing what we had just heard.

Eveline was smiling, ever so slightly, sitting on the chair, as if embarrassed by our reaction.

"Fuck me," Greg said. "What was that you said?"

151

"I am sorry," she said again, the voice stronger. She had a slight trace of an American accent.

Unlike Greg, I was not angry. I just felt overwhelming relief: that she could speak, that finally we would have some answers. I crossed the kitchen. I took both her ice-cold hands and warmed them in mine.

"You are with friends."

Greg threw his mug into the sink with such force, it shattered. The sound made me jump, Eveline jump.

"I don't believe it," he shook his head. "She speaks. After all this, she speaks." He advanced towards us, with slow, deliberate steps. "You've led us a pretty dance, haven't you?"

He stopped short like he was on a leash, like his anger had jerked him backwards.

"I speak English." She flattened the curve of her back into the chair, away from him.

"And I just thought you were dumb," he jeered.

She let go of my hands. She wiped away the tears. There was a spark of defiance in those great eyes.

"And French, German, a little Italian and…"

"You turn up: no explanation, no money, and a bag of diamonds." His voice rode over hers. Shock registered on her face.

She started to her feet, almost knocking me backwards. She pulled at the sodden waistband of her skirt, pulling it outwards like she was checking it, like she checked the clothes from the cupboard. She collapsed back into the chair, clutching her head in her hands.

"Who the hell are you?" Greg's voice rang around the kitchen.

In the silence which followed, I could see the three of us: Eveline sitting, chair askew, at one end of the kitchen table, slumped forward, face hidden; me crouched beside her, an arm perched awkwardly across her bowed shoulders, anxiety written all over my face; and Greg standing, one foot thrust forward, fists clenched, quite still, his stance reflected in the blackness of the windowpane, looking at Eveline with a mixture of pity and anger.

There was a smell of burning and a plume of smoke rose from the hob. Greg rushed to switch off the gas.

He turned to look back at me, still with my arm around Eveline. His body, suddenly, seemed slack with weariness.

"I've had it," he announced. "Stuff the bloody duck. I'm having a bath."

So Greg left us: me and my poor, uninvited, and impossible guest. She shook her head when I offered her another tea. I made myself one. I watched the steam spout out of the kettle. I poured the scalding water into a stained mug. I poured in the thick, UHT milk. I ignored the carbonised mess in the saucepan. All the time she sat with her arms wrapped around her, shivering.

Greg started to run a bath, the pipes beginning to clatter.

I raised my voice. "Where do you think you lost the diamonds?"

"In the woods."

"You should come over to the range." I set the little tongues of blue flame dancing at the back of the oven. I coaxed her onto her feet, and made her sit on a chair in front of the open oven door.

I busied myself by picking up pieces of Greg's mug.

"At last you can tell me your name," I said lightly, jokingly.

Somehow, I knew she wouldn't. She stared into the oven. She had stopped juddering with the cold.

"Okay," I say. "So what you are doing here? At the château? I mean — why?"

Her lips parted. "My husband left me." She told this to the oven.

"Husband?" I was so surprised that all the bits of broken mug drop back into the sink.

"At the beginning of the avenue."

The pipes stopped knocking and the phone started to ring.

"And where is he, your husband?"

She started to weep again, slow silent tears, dripping into her lap.

The phone rang off and in the sudden silence, I tried to marshal my thoughts and think about what best to do. Then the phone started again. Tom. It could only be Tom. Philip would never be so insistent — or selfish. Furious, I left Eveline and bounded up the stairs.

"Can't you pick up the phone?" Tom bellowed. "I've been calling for the last hour and a bit."

"Why can't you leave a message?" I yelled back.

"I have. I've left several. You're really worrying me, Sis."

"Sorry. I've just left a girl in front of an open oven door and I'm not sure if she's suicidal or not. By the way, she's just lost a bag of diamonds. There's a lot going on here."

The sarcasm was lost on Tom. He picked up on one word. "Diamonds?"

"It'll take too long to explain. And she speaks. And she's married."

"But diamonds?" he asked. "Where are they from?"

"I haven't had a chance to ask her!"

"Calm down, Sis," he said. "I know it's difficult…"

"Like hell you do!"

154

"Look," he said, "I didn't tell you about Kumono. I thought it might put you off — "

"You're damn right."

"But he never stayed there — "

"His sons did."

"You can't believe everything you hear."

"You didn't even check the place out before I came."

"I meant to, but something blew up over here."

"Business?"

"Yes," he sighed.

"Did you know Kumono?"

"I had to meet him a couple of times. All part of a marketing initiative…"

"You never told me that you'd gone over there."

"If you knew the half…" He changed the subject. "So do you think the girl is associated with the old régime?"

I told Tom about the locked room off the archway and Eveline's reaction to the clothes.

"I told you," his voice was hard, "to get rid of her."

"Philip says that she isn't a Kumono."

"So Philip's in on this? That's just bloody brilliant."

"Of course he bloody knows."

"I didn't think you and he were in contact?"

"And where did you get that idea from?" I asked stiffly.

Tom laughed. "Come off it, Sis, I know you better than that! Anyway, apart from anything else," he continued, "the girl sounds mad. I'll phone the embassy in the morning."

"No you won't. That's too cruel."

"I'm phoning and she's going."

"You're not. She's not."

"It's my house."

It was my turn to laugh. "Is it? Just because you've got a piece of paper to prove ownership. Or have you?"

"You have it then. Good riddance." He slammed down the phone.

"And fuck off to you too." Us — who never rowed, had rowed twice in a matter of hours. I didn't care. He deserved it.

"What?" Greg had come into the dining hall He looked better, having had a bath. He had found a man's dressing gown from somewhere.

"'Not you. Tom. My bloody brother."

Greg wandered off — to find a bed I presumed. I went back down to the kitchen and roused Eveline, who had fallen asleep, lulled by the warmth of the range. I took her by the hand and led her wordlessly up the stairs, and into the bathroom opposite her bedroom. She sat on the toilet lid and watched me as I ran a bath. Miraculously, there was still enough hot water. The racket from the pipes was so great that we couldn't have talked, had she been capable. I helped her to undress. Her limbs were stiff. She had to hold onto me. I steadied her as she climbed into the steam. I cupped water, slippery with bath oil, over her chest. I handed over a flannel for her face. I watched as she slipped her head and shoulders beneath the water to wash her hair. Her body looked too virginal for a husband. I held the hand-shower so that she could rinse off the suds. I towelled her down like you would a child, quite roughly, to keep the warm blood coursing through her veins. I found her nightdress under her pillow. The soft silk stuck to the still damp skin. I pulled the bedclothes up so that I could only see the tip of an ear and a portion of forehead. I switched off the light, returned to the bathroom and gave my own aching body up to the wonderfully warm water, which carried a faint scent.

I thought of my four babies who never made it to fruition, two too small to have been much more than a rush of blood. They would all be teenagers now, not much younger than the young woman I had just helped to bed. I remember thinking about her mother, wondering if she was as beautiful as her daughter. I tried to imagine the woman's sense of loss, her daughter gone — gone to a husband who presumably didn't care enough to find her. I couldn't imagine it. I didn't have the resources. My loss is for what never happened.

Philip and I, we had so much hope once, so much innocent hope: the rush of delight when the pregnancy indicator turned blue and the castles in the air we built with a myriad of nurseries — only to have them cruelly crash at nine weeks, thirteen weeks, twenty two weeks and, last of all, seven months, which almost broke me and us. All a long time ago. Thirteen years to be precise: since the last raging against fate, the final hopeless weeping in Philip's arms.

I wrapped the damp towel around my wet body. I slipped my clean feet into sandals gritty with dirt. I pressed open the bedroom door, just to make sure that she was okay. There was a bank of shadows between the window and the bed. I listened to the rhythm of breathing and shut the door. I crossed the hall and went up the stairs, two flights and a spiral, up to my bed and, for the first time since Eveline arrived at the château, I left all the lights blazing, behind me, warding off the darkness which was pressing against the windows.

And lying on my mattress, the naked man pitched out from the wall, faceless. "*Mon Dieu*," he intoned from the cavernous slash where his mouth should have been, "*sauvez nous…*"

"Pleasc," I whispered. "Leave me alone." The shadows on the walls shook, like trees in a gale. I buried my face in my pillow. It was no use. Two floors down, the telephone rang, and I couldn't sleep.

Chapter 26

I loved my father's novel 'Eveline'. I reread it when I was eighteen. It was a very precious experience; that particular book at that particular time gave me a very real sense of the man my father had been. His absence had become part of who I was — or rather, who I understood myself to be. The tempestuous relationship between the two principal characters was, I decided, my parents' love story.

*

Hardly surprisingly, I got up late, woken by a sun high up in a clear blue, sparkling sky over a world which felt washed and refreshed. I managed to buy the last few croissants at the boulangerie — I wasn't sure if Madame la Boulangère kept them back for me, because I'd become such a regular, so I smiled anyway to show my appreciation.

The girl I called Eveline greeted me with a shy "good morning" when she appeared.

I was suddenly wary at the prospect of having a conversation with her. She was quite capable of snubbing me, I knew.

"Come in, come in," I said, welcoming her with my plateful of croissants.

She sat down in front of the window which had become her place at the table and ate so hungrily, I felt guilty. I hadn't offered her any of Greg's confit de canard last night, before it burnt in the saucepan.

"Did you sleep?"

She looked at me with tired eyes. "Not well," she whispered, dipping her head back to the croissants.

I drew out a chair and sat beside her. "I'd like to call you by your real name — the name your parents gave you."

Her knife layered jam onto flakes of croissant.

It was if I hadn't spoken.

"Or shall I just call you Eveline?"

"I don't care what you call me." She whispered, her head bent. I could feel the heat of the blush rising from my neck. She might as well have slapped me across the face.

Anyone sensible would have stood up, drawn herself up to her full height and told her if that was the way she felt she should leave immediately. I wish I had. I missed another opportunity to stop us hurtling full-pelt towards disaster. It would have been kinder to Eveline but I was only thinking of myself.

"Eveline it is then," I said cheerfully. "It's a special name, for me, at least."

When he was little, my brother shortened my name 'Sis' – he couldn't cope with the other syllables — and has never called me anything else since. My father had a myriad of pet names for me: 'Smiley', 'So-so', 'Twinkle-toes'. I used to call Philip all sorts of silly little endearments. Tom though, for me, has always been 'Tom'.

Eveline didn't say anything. Particles of dust swam in the sunshine spilling in over her head. The drip from the tap splashed into the saucepan I'd left soaking in the sink.

Greg strutted into the kitchen. He was back in his painter's overalls, his hair carefully slicked back. His ears were very large, quite goblinesque.

160

"How are we all today?" His eyes were full of concern. He sensed the tension emanating from me, watching Eveline who was still munching her way through croissant.

"I'm sorry," he addressed Eveline directly, "for shouting last night."

She lifted her face. "That's okay." Her voice was little stronger than before.

A ray of sunshine cut across the room with me and Eveline on one side and Greg on the other.

Greg's eyes lit on the croissants.

Eveline pushed the jam in Greg's direction.

"You've a visitor," Greg said between bites. "Valerie. Outside. She's wandering around the chapel or at least she was, five minutes ago."

Eveline started on another croissant.

"Where will you be later?" I asked him lightly. I wanted to tell him about Eveline's husband, but not in front of her.

*

"I've brought your car back," Valerie called. "I thought I'd save you the journey. Wonderful, isn't it?" she said when I got nearer. "So spiritual."

I stood with her as she paid homage to the view of the church on the opposite hill. The birdsong was extraordinary. The smell of the earth, pounded by the rain the previous night, was glorious. Down in the village, a horn blared. Someone shouted. Someone else shouted back, a man. Valerie lifted her face up to the sun, closed her eyes and drew in deep, deliberate breaths.

"The elixir of life," she pronounced. "So clean, so fresh after a storm. It must be so nice for you to breathe fresh, clean air after London." She opened her eyes and contemplated me solemnly. "You look better, rested."

I smiled, thinking of the night we had and then, before I knew it, I was laughing — horrible, involuntary laughter. Valerie giggled.

"Did I say something funny?"

"No. Sorry." I hiccupped, gulping down superior French air.

"Not much sleep?" She raised her eyebrows. "Greg stayed here last night, didn't he?"

The laughter stopped as suddenly as it started. "How do you know that?"

"I went by his caravan after I dropped you off. His roof leaks."

I watched a strip of cloud like a lamb's tail — the only cloud in the sky — drift past the church steeple.

"Just wonderful," Valerie murmured. "I've never seen the inside of the château, would you believe?"

"I couldn't help but notice," Valerie kept up with me as I strode across the gravel, "that your car clock is still on English time."

"It's only an hour earlier." I took her in through the front door rather than through the archway. I wanted to protect Eveline from Valerie's curiosity.

"You really," Valerie said sweetly, "have got to take living in France a little more seriously."

In fact, the car clock was the only clock which worked over there. I hadn't found the keys to rewind the clocks at the château. Anyway, I didn't mind going into different rooms and finding wildly varying times. I'd left my watch behind in London. It was a silly gesture — my way of confirming that our life together, had stopped, that last evening in London. Philip had given me the watch on our twentieth wedding anniversary.

"So this is it," Valerie said with an intake of breath as she stepped across the threshold. "This is living history." Her eyes scanned the great height of the hall. I could see that she liked, as I loved, the light falling from the stained glass window. "You are so lucky."

"You know," she says, "the château was once owned by my husband's — ex-husband's — family? Well, distant cousins thereof."

"I only know about the Kumonos and someone with the initials CH? At least, that's the monogram on some of the linen in the cupboards."

Valerie closes her eyes as she tries to recall the name. "Christophe Hallier," she pronounces. "My husband's grandfather."

"That's CA"

"We don't pronounce the 'H'."

"What happened to him?"

"He died," she said blithely. "He had a heart attack in his car by the entrance."

Despite everything that had happened, I couldn't help but feel a surge of pride as I gave Valerie a tour. The rooms were lit up by sunlight. There was no real sense of the darkness within the château — over the surface of which I had paddled for months — leaving me free to revert to my fantasy that the château would be a lovely, comfortable family home for my brother. Valerie, though, looked disappointed. I think she had expected the château's interior to be far more grand. She was definitely not interested in restoration.

In the library she gazed at her reflection in the mirror while I pointed out the corner in the ceiling where Greg and I managed to replace the cornicing. It was a difficult job.

"And it was out of this chimney," I told her, "that bees swarmed."

"Aren't you disappointed that there's no wallpaper?"

I was taken by surprise. "How do you know that I...?"

"I googled the name," she said. "At the café. You don't mind do you? Everyone does these days."

I'd almost forgotten I had a name, it seemed such a long time since I'd left London.

"No," I said. "I suppose not. I thought you didn't hold with computers?"

"Only in my own home." She gave me a sideways look. "I guessed you'd use your own name, not your husband's. There are pages and pages on your brother. It doesn't look too good for him does it?"

I wasn't going to give her the pleasure of telling me what she meant. Tom was always of the opinion that bad press was better than none.

"Oh Tom," I said dismissively. "He's always been controversial."

"There is wallpaper by the way," I added.

I didn't bother to show Valerie the rooms on the upper floors. I made an exception for the room full of gym equipment.

There was a mattress with a couple of blankets between the running machine and the cross-trainer. I remember wishing that Greg had put a sheet over the stained ticking. It looked repulsive.

Valerie shuddered at the sight of the equipment. "I hate the gym. Let's go."

She didn't want to look out the window, at the view of the chapel. She definitely didn't want to know that an entire wall has been re-plastered.

So I took Valerie up to the lower tower room. There was absolutely nothing in that room to detract from the wallpaper — even in the twilight of a curtained room, its monochrome glory blazed off the walls. Valerie didn't pause. She started up the spiral staircase to where I slept.

"Wait a sec." I drew back the curtains. The light flooded in. "Well?" I said triumphantly. "What do you think?"

She gave the panels a cursory examination. "They are hideous. Are they old?"

Her forthrightness completely took me aback. "You can't really mean," I began.

"I can," she said. "Remember beauty is in the eyes of the beholder. What are you going to do with them?"

I laughed. "Make sure they're preserved for posterity for starters." I pulled the curtains back across the windows.

With three turns of the stairs, we were up in my room. Valerie took in the unmade makeshift bed, the narrow chest of drawers which I'd brought up from the floor below and the original chair, draped with my dirty clothes. With nothing else to examine, she turned to view the vista from one of the windows.

"You're related to Richard Braid?"

"The writer?" It was years since anyone had asked. "I'm his daughter."

"I did wonder. Your father wrote wonderful books. I've got them all. He died young didn't he? You must have been terribly young yourself…"

"A child," I said, seeing a solemn little girl in white knee socks and a yellow frock with daisies around the hem, in front of a coffin and an oblong hole with earth banked up to one side. The smell of freshly turned earth always brings back the memory. Our mother hadn't wanted us in black. Tom wore his sailor suit. He clung to my hand. Our mother didn't have to tell him that he had killed his father. I didn't tell him. He just knew that it was all his fault and I was so sorry for him.

Valerie looked at me slyly. "It is such a coincidence that you have an Eveline staying with you."

I couldn't recall telling her the night before.

"Do you know," she continued, "I always wondered if that book was semi-autobiographical? It's such powerful portrait of the disintegration of a marriage…"

"I have never heard anything so ridiculous."

"But it's all in there," she started, "My husband ran off with someone else. I should know…" She didn't dare to say anything more. She could see the expression on my face.

I remember Tom and I scattering petals, one by one, over the coffin. Pink and purple, I remember their soft, fleshy feel between my fingers. Our mother made a posy. She threw it in last. I could tell that she was trying not to avoid Tom because sometimes, her eyes would flick away from him, before returning with an effort to contemplate his face.

Chapter 27

We went back down to the hall. Valerie's skirt swished across the treads of the stairs, amplifying the silence between us. We had run out of things to say.

I didn't show Valerie Eveline's room. I didn't want her in the house any longer. She had outstayed her welcome.

At the front door, Valerie looked expectantly at me. For a moment I thought she was waiting for me to offer of a cup of coffee and then I thought no, she was waiting for a lift. How else would she get home without a car?

I heard the click of a door shutting down the dark corridor off the hall leading to Eveline's room. For a moment, it looked as if a shadow was moving towards us, and my heart stopped for a second. It was Eveline. She stopped short when she saw Valerie. Valerie held out her hand. Eveline glanced at me, advanced, and shook Valerie's hand shyly.

"Nice to meet you." Valerie clasped Eveline's hand, giving me a sly glance. "I am sure your hostess told me that you had gone."

"I'm just dropping Valerie back," I told Eveline.

"Hold on," Valerie searched through her pockets. She had pockets everywhere: on her skirt, on her shirt and on her leather jerkin which looks like part of a hunter's paraphernalia.

"You know you said last night that your guest came with something? Well I found this in a ditch a couple of years ago…" She burnished a small object with the edge of her shirt. "It's always intrigued me. You see this mark?"

With a dirty nail, she pointed to the scratched symbol on tarnished silver. Eveline leant over Valerie's hand to see better. Her head brushed against mine. Without warning, she crumpled to the floor.

Greg must have heard me shouting "Eveline! Eveline!" because he dashed up from the kitchen and shoved me and Valerie out of the way. He swung Eveline into his arms in one easy movement. Thinking back now, why should she have recognised that name? It was never her name.

Eveline's head slumped against Greg's chest, eyes closed, skin ashen. Valerie and I followed him into her bedroom. He laid her tenderly on the unmade bed. I pulled off her shoes. She opened her eyes. She looked absolutely despairing — worse even, than the day before. She refused water but I brought the glass to her lips and insisted. The effort exhausted her. She closed her eyes again. Valerie remained by the door. I drew the curtains across both windows.

Greg and I stood by the bed. I covered Eveline with the counterpane, which was green and blue with threads of yellow silk.

"Is she ill?" Valerie asked in a stage whisper.

"What the hell happened?" Greg tucked her arm under the counterpane.

"Valerie has a bullet, identical to Eveline's. Same markings."

Greg gave me a sharp look. "The one in the shoe?"

"Couldn't she have an underlying heart condition or something?" Valerie's voice cut between us.

"It's just shock," I turned towards her, "at seeing your bullet."

168

"Shouldn't you call the doctor?"

"Maybe, if she isn't better within the hour."

For five minutes or so, the three of us watched Eveline — so still that she could have been taken for dead if it weren't for the slight rise and fall of her chest.

I told Greg that I would check on her in half an hour.

"Good idea," He sounded gruff. "I'm off. Things to do."

He brushed past Valerie, rudely, without acknowledging her. She ignored him.

"Tea?" she asked me. "I don't know about you, but I could do with a cup."

Valerie bustled about the kitchen. "Where do you keep your mugs? Teabags? Milk?"

I was too anxious about Eveline to bother about Valerie taking possession of the kitchen. She slipped a mug across the table to me and sat down herself. She had forgotten that she'd told me that she never drank normal tea. She helped herself liberally to our carton of long-life stuff and two spoons of sugar.

"What is wrong with the girl?"

"I don't know. She's had a bit of a hard time."

Valerie drank her tea in careful sips.

"How come?"

I laughed. "I don't even know her name."

Valerie nodded. "I thought it a bit of a coincidence, you calling her Eveline. What's she doing here?"

I shrugged. "Ask me another. That's why I was asking you about the Kumonos."

"What a nightmare. Poor you."

For a while she concentrated on drinking her tea, thinking, not looking at me.

"I knew she was here," she started again. "I saw her by the swimming pool yesterday."

169

"How come?"

"I was walking in the woods."

"I didn't know you could see the château from up there."

"You can't really, just the roof and water."

"Why didn't you say?"

"How could I? You told me that she was no longer with you."

There was a shadow on the floor. I blinked hard. It disappeared.

"Where did you find that bullet?"

"In the woods. I can take you to the spot if you like."

"The Kumonos…" Valerie broke the silence between us. "If you want to know more — there is someone who might be of help. Claudine. You might have seen her wandering around. She was a collaborator during the war — in Paris, I think. She's an ancient old crone now and quite mad by all accounts. I mean, no one speaks to her. God knows how the Kumonos found the only untouchable in the village to do their cleaning, but they did."

"I've met her." I told Valerie the bizarre incident of the old woman appearing out of nowhere and brandishing a broom at me very early on in my stay.

"It makes sense," I said with mounting excitement. "It must have been her. She would have known how to get into the kitchen from the archway."

"She must have wanted her old job back. She looks destitute."

"Will you come with me to see her?"

"I don't think so," Valerie said after careful consideration. "It's not what I'm about. Not my scene."

"I'd need a translator."

"*Tant pis*," she said, "as the French say. Listen," she sprang to her feet. "Don't worry about a lift. I'll cut back through the woods."

It wasn't not until five minutes after she had gone that I realised that she had taken the bullet with her. I hadn't asked her to leave it behind, nor had she offered.

Chapter 28

"Eveline."

Maybe the movement of light as I widened the crack in the curtains woke her. Or my fingers slipping beneath her pillow, searching. Maybe she was never asleep at all. She was more of a mystery than ever. The bullet, tarnished and greasy from too much handling, had an identical mark to the one Valerie found in the woods.

"How are you feeling?"

She blinked, her eyes not wavering from the bullet rolling stickily across my palm.

"You're worrying me."

She levered herself onto her elbows.

"Are you in trouble?"

She shook her head.

"You're quite sure?"

She nodded. Her fingers grazed my palm as she took back her bullet. She tucked it beneath her pillow. She sat up, the pillow behind her, almost as if she was guarding it from me.

"It's yours?"

There was a barely perceptible nod. I was desperate for her not to retreat into non-speaking mode.

"And the one Valerie has?"

She cleared her throat. "My brother's."

"And where is your brother?" I was talking to her like a child but she was a child, someone's child. She was young enough to be my child — if I'd lived on another continent and had another man.

She flung her arms around my neck. "I don't know but when that strange woman showed me his bullet I knew he was dead."

I held her steady while silent, racking grief coursed through her, I would have done anything, anything at all, to comfort her, but I was not her mother. I couldn't love her like a mother. Like how our mother should have loved Tom and me, instead of leaving us to fend for each other.

Eveline slipped her hand beneath the covers and brought out the photograph. There was just enough room between us for her to smooth it out on the mattress. In faded monochrome, the young man smiled — the deep creases obliterating some of his image.

"It's all my fault," Eveline whispered.

She wiped her eyes with another handful of the toilet roll that I had got from the bathroom. "His bullet proves he was here."

"At the château?"

She nodded. "Six years ago. It was the last time my parents heard from him."

"So was he — you — related to the Kumonos?"

Her eyes flashed with disdain. "Of course not."

Nothing, I realised with a heavy heart, was going to be easy.

Eveline looked about the room and I looked too, the beat of my heart pounding in my ears. I saw a heavy wardrobe, and a dressing table with an ornate gilt mirror so mottled with age it reflected nothing except the passage of time. An upright ironing board stood in front of the window which looked out over the woods. The door to the wardrobe was half-open. I could see a blue striped shirt with a red rose detail which had looked like a rag in Eveline's hands the night before. It hung neatly from a hanger. I looked down at Eveline's photo. I looked again at the wardrobe.

"You think that is his shirt?"

She nodded. "I cleaned the iron especially. The chain I found — that was his too. And now the bullet."

"Why didn't you tell me before?"

"I didn't know if I could trust you."

"You had better," I said with a calm I didn't feel, "start at the beginning."

Eveline looked directly at me. Her face was expressionless. When she eventually began to speak, her voice was devoid of emotion.

"I was sixteen and stupid. He was eight years older than me. He had no choice. He had to pretend to like them, but he hated them. We all did — well, I didn't so much. I didn't know. My parents protected me."

She sat absolutely upright, without the prop of the pillow. She took a deep breath and continued.

"He came home one night covered in blood. I saw him. But it wasn't serious. My parents told me later that it was just a bullet graze to the head. I was sworn to secrecy. The servants were sworn to secrecy. Next day, my parents heard that there had been an attempt on the General's life. The sons didn't come for him then, they invited him here, to the château a few weeks later."

"Why?"

A bead of sweat trickled between my shoulder blades. The silence in the room washed around us.

"Because," she said with great effort, "they would have lost face. My family were supposed to be part of what was called the inner circle."

I reached for her hand. She tucked both her hands under the covers.

"How can that be your fault?"

Her voice changed. It became hard and clear.

"I disobeyed my parents. I told my best friend how my brother came back one night covered in blood."

Her eyes full of misery, she looked as if she expected me to jump off the bed completely repulsed by what she had said. I didn't understand.

Eveline gave a hollow laugh. "Her father was Minister of the Interior. I forgot. I was too busy being best friends."

There was a tree in the middle of the room, and in the middle of the tree was a man, cowering. I shut my eyes and when I opened them, he was still there in the tree, except that that time, he was silently shaking the branches. Eveline was watching for my reaction. I didn't have the courage to take the leap from my world into theirs.

"If he hadn't gone with them," she whispered. "My parents, me, we'd all have been dead then."

"What happened to your parents?"

"When the new régime took over, they were executed as collaborators."

"How did you escape?"

"They made me marry — a fat old man who lived in Paris. He prefers boys but he liked my hair so I chopped it off... Eventually he lost patience and left me here..."

"You see," she said, her eyes swimming with tears, "I wanted to find my brother. If there was even a slight chance that he was alive, that he'd escaped, that maybe he'd left a message for me here..."

"I am sorry. So, so sorry." What else could I have said? And I was, my heart was breaking for her.

175

"The bullet," I said, after a while, watching the man in the tree, "it could have fallen out of his pocket. It doesn't mean necessarily that he is dead."

"No." She shook her head.

The man in the tree disappeared as suddenly as he appeared.

"I mean," I persisted, "this place wasn't a prison."

"You are stupid," Eveline cried, pushing me with such force that I fell onto the floor. She watched me scrabble to my feet. "You can never say no to people like that! He was trapped! Like I'm trapped here with you!"

Her words rung around the room. For a second she looked as horrified as I felt. Then she rearranged her expression so that it was both smooth and distant.

"I want to be alone now," she spat. "Get out."

I closed the door on her and stood shaking, my hand on the doorknob.

In the hall, the light from the stained glass window cut across somnolent shadows, stretched out like cats in the afternoon heat. There was an unmoving calmness about the house as if nothing ever changed and everything stayed the same. It was an illusion. Everything had changed. The house was polluted. It had always been polluted.

I unlocked the drawer of the desk in the library. It was where I kept my passport and also, despite Tom having told me to chuck it, the passport I'd found. I hadn't wanted the responsibility of junking it. Maybe I'd had an inkling even then, but I'd hardly given it a glance. I hadn't wanted to know.

The passport was underneath building insurance documents which Tom had sent.

The green cover with the embossed lion looked new. The passport had hardly been used.

It belonged to a young man with glasses. It was quite possible that it was Eveline's brother and also, conversely, not. Eveline's photograph was so indistinct. The man's name was Zachary. His surname I couldn't have begun to pronounce.

I knocked on Eveline's door, the passport in my hand.

"Leave me alone!" A shout.

I put the passport back. I locked the drawer and hid the key in a little cloisonné pot on the mantelpiece.

Greg came into the kitchen whilst I was rummaging around the back of the cupboard looking for something to make for supper. My emotions were in turmoil.

"How is she?"

I told him about the brother.

For a couple of minutes, Greg didn't say anything. He focussed on the dresser, looking at the stuff that was on it, as if he had never seen any of it before.

"I wouldn't show her the passport this evening," he said eventually. "She has had enough for one day."

He changed the subject. "I've been up in the woods, looking for her diamonds." He hesitated and then he said in rush: "Thing is, when the lightning struck I pulled her up so hard off the ground, that the bag could have fallen out then. I was that frightened. I feel so guilty now."

I wiped my eyes with the back of my hand. I was close to tears.

"I feel guilty too. Of course I am sorry about the brother but another part of me is angry — I don't want or need complications."

I surprised myself with my honesty.

Greg, thank God, didn't judge me. He gripped me roughly by the arms. "I understand," he said. "But you

can't hide from what is happening in the world outside."
He shook his head. "What that girl has been through…"

"I know," I said. "Of course I know."

He made coffee for both of us, hot and strong.

"Has she told you yet where the diamonds are from?" he
asked.

"Husband? I don't know, I'm just guessing."

"She's married?" He was incredulous. "That's a good
one. Well, I suppose anything is possible." He started to
laugh. I laughed with him, though tension had made all the
muscles in my back hurt.

Greg disappeared through the archway and I opened a
can of haricot beans and a jar of sauerkraut. I tossed them
in the saucepan together. The gas took five attempts to
light.

I persuaded Eveline to come downstairs. She came
because she could see that I wasn't in the mood to take any
nonsense. She sat at the table.

"There's some salami in the fridge, could you get it for
me?"

Eveline rose slowly from her seat. She didn't like even
the merest hint of being ordered around. No wonder her
husband had abandoned her, I remember thinking
viciously. She must have been completely impossible to
live with on a daily basis. She gave me the salami. She
watched me slice it with the one sharp kitchen knife.

She looked up as I handed her a plate of meat, sauerkraut
and heated beans. "I can't talk anymore," she whispered.
"I've done enough talking."

Greg came back into the kitchen.

"I'll stay the night again, if you don't mind," he said,
addressing me but with his eyes on Eveline, sitting at the
table, head bent over her plate and eating.

"There's really no need," I said.

"Just to be sure," he said, still watching Eveline.

I was glad that Greg was staying.

Chapter 29

Greg shook me by the shoulder, jolting me awake. I was having a hideous dream where a faceless, naked man was wandering through the corridors of the château, crying out for his clothes and searching for me. Every time I tried to call out to him, darkness rose in my throat.

Greg's eyes were bleary with sleep in the cold dawn light.

"You alright?" His breath smelt. "Tom's downstairs. Could've woken the bloody dead."

"Who?" I could taste bile in my mouth.

"Tom. Your brother. That's what he told me."

"Tom!" I was overjoyed. It was such a relief to see him. Despite our rows over the phone, it meant that he cared enough to come and see me. That my suspicions were groundless. That together, we could sort everything out.

He looked very small from two floors up, dwarfed by the hall. His face, with a huge smile, tilted upwards as I ran down the stairs.

"Thank God you're okay Sis. I came as soon as I could." He pressed me close to him. I could smell coffee and London on him, warm and fuggy.

"You could have told me you were coming."

"I didn't know." There was a twinkle in his eye. "I'd fully intended to go home and then, what the hell I thought, I'll go and see my sister and the cab driver was game. Seriously, Sis, I've been out of my mind with worry with that mad woman running around. Is she still here?"

"You took a taxi?" I was flabbergasted. "All the way? Wasn't the plane available?" His company had a private jet.

"Never you mind," he grinned. He stretched out his arms, folded me in again. "I'm here now."

"Eveline's not mad."

"Eveline?" Tom put his hands on my shoulders, searching my face. "That's a bit strange."

"I haven't found out her real name."

Tom cocked his head and laughed. "Honestly Sis, everything with you comes back to Dad."

It wasn't deliberate — her name simply hadn't come up when we had talked.

If it wasn't for the smile in his eyes, I'd have been worried. He looked grey: grey and drawn and crumpled after a long night sitting in the back of a taxi in a suit with a very bad case of dandruff, except that it was not dandruff. It was psoriasis.

"She's very troubled," I said eventually. "With good reason."

Tom was looking around, as if he couldn't quite comprehend his surroundings.

"It's a long old way, London to the South of France." Tired as he was and even with a sore, red skin, he was one of those extraordinarily attractive people with a face where nothing quite matched. Even Tom's eyes were different colours: one green, one brown. I thought he was one of the most handsome men alive.

"I thought you were going to New York."

He waved a hand airily. "Cancelled."

"And the cabbie?"

"Hightailing it back to London. His wife gave him an earful when she realised how long he was going to be."

"Have you brought anything with you?"

Tom gestured at the small valise by the door.

"How long can you stay?"

All his attention was focused on the window behind the stairs. He squeezed my hand. His hand felt flaky and tender. I took care not to squeeze back.

"It's fantastic."

"You should have seen the state it was in."

A single ray of light from the early morning sun spilt through the leaded glass, reaching almost to our feet across the black oak of the stairs and the stone flagged floor. The colours glistened, alive with the light. Tom shook his head.

"Magnificent," he murmured. "Quite magnificent."

"I mended it," I said. "That panel there."

He squeezed my hand again. My heart burst with pride.

It was difficult to be angry with someone who had rushed all the way from London just to make sure that I was okay.

"It's a gem, Sis," he kept shaking his head in disbelief, "an absolute gem."

I knew what he meant. The proportions were beautiful. The vistas from the windows — of a winding avenue, an ornamental lily pond, a ruin of a chapel beyond and blue hills in the distance — were idyllic. If you knew no better, it was an Englishman's dream of a château.

Tom was full of wonderment, like a little boy who had to reach out and touch, checking that what he was seeing was, indeed, real. He rubbed his finger along the window frames as I pointed out where they were treated for woodworm. His hands brushed over the carved detail on the architraves as I demonstrated how Greg and I rehung rickety doors. His fingers stroked the freshly painted walls as I extolled the particular brand of paint that we'd used.

"You've done a wonderful job." He gave me a quick hug, his unshaven cheek grazing mine.

He didn't mention the Kumonos. Neither did I. I was enjoying the moment; basking in his appreciation.

Tom strode ahead.

"That's Eveline's room," I warned, when he put his hand on the handle of her door, "she'll be asleep."

"Did she find the diamonds she lost?"

"No."

"And this is the bathroom," he pressed open the other door across from Eveline's room.

"How did you guess?

"Easy," he said blithely, taking a cursory look behind the door. "You sent over plans, remember?"

As Tom marched purposefully through the house, the tremulous morning light got stronger — but still, he retained his childhood habit of switching on every light and just like I did when we were children, I switched them off, always the older, more responsible sibling.

We went up to the second floor.

We looked in on the other bathroom. Tom roared with laughter at the avocado with shell-shaped gilt taps and handles.

"Where is Greg by the way?" He shaded his eyes, pretending to search the corridor.

"Back at the caravan, I expect."

But I knocked on the door to the gym just in case.

"Wow!" Tom's gasp of astonishment was just what I'd been expecting. The sleek, black, contoured shapes looked amazing in a wainscoted room. Greg's mattress, where he'd slept until rudely awoken by Tom, was by the exercise bike.

Tom walked amongst the equipment. You could pump your shoulders, arms, legs in every which way according to the instructions fixed to the sides of the machines. There were fifteen in total, all in a circle, facing each other.

"How are Samantha and the children?"

He didn't hear me. He was too preoccupied, fiddling with the chest press equipment.

"They must have been pretty serious on keeping fit." For the first time, he spoke of the Kumonos.

"The floor can bear the load. Greg checked."

Tom stepped up onto the treadmill. He used the back of his sleeve to wipe the dust off the console. I had never seen him so out of shape. Tom caught me looking critically at him.

"What?" he asked teasingly.

I bent to flick the switch. The treadmill rumbled into action, forcing Tom to stride along at a lolloping slow pace.

"You've had all summer to tell me about the Kumonos."

Tom fiddled with a control. His legs started to move faster.

"I wasn't going to tell you over the phone, was I?"

"Not even when I told you about the passport? Surely then was the right time?" I reached across him and turn the control almost to maximum. Tom had to concentrate to keep his feet from slipping off the rubber strip. His belly wobbled like blancmange, behind his pink shirt.

"What passport?" he grabbed hold of the rail. His face was bright red. "I can't do this, I'm sorry."

He turned the control anti-clockwise. Slowly his feet returned to a walking pace. "I'm too tired."

"The one I found at the back of a drawer. Don't tell me you've forgotten."

184

The machine came to a halt. Tom delved into a trouser pocket and wiped his face with a screwed-up tissue. "Honestly, I've had other stuff on my mind. Things have been pretty tough."

"You should have told me."

"I thought you wouldn't want to know about the Kumonos. It would spoil the house for you."

He stepped off the treadmill, unsteady for a second.

"Haven't you been happy here?" He sounded so wistful.

"There is something about…"

"The Kumonos are dead, buried and history," he interrupted me. "This house — thanks to you — lives on."

"It is precisely because of the Kumonos that that girl is here."

He smiled at me. "Yep, the one you call Eveline. Where are those wonderful Dufour panels?"

Tom stood beside the spiral staircase in the middle of the tower's lower room. He didn't say anything. He just turned slowly to look as I drew back the curtains from each of the four windows.

"No wonder you're delighted."

"I am." I sat on the bottom tread of the stairs better to appreciate the beauty. "It's a conservator's dream, a once-in-a-lifetime find."

Tom ruffled my hair. I looked up.

He held out his arms. "Am I forgiven?"

"You should have told me there is stuff going on here…" In my mind's eye, I suddenly saw a young man fall out of a tree in the woods behind the château.

"Are you okay Sis?" Tom asked. "Are you okay?"

When he saw my mattress in the upper room, a look of concern crossed his face.

"Aren't there any proper beds? I don't know if my back will take sleeping on the floor."

"Eveline's the only one with a bedstead."

"There aren't any others?"

"Down in that room I told you about. Remember?"

"Of course I remember. I wondered when you were going to show me."

So we descended into the nether regions of the château.

Chapter 30

Tom surveyed the rudimentary kitchen. "It's more basic than I thought."

"You could have an in-built area for here for cooking." I showed him where I meant, where the sink and range were.

"Later, I've run out of the old spondoolies at the moment."

It had been difficult to get Tom to transfer funds for the château but the idea that he had run out of money was too ridiculous to contemplate.

"You? Never. What have you spent it on? Another château?"

He laughed. "Well, the state of this kitchen obviously hasn't bothered you. You don't look as if you've spent much time cooking."

"You know me. I haven't cooked properly for years."

Back at home, Philip cooked. It was his way of relaxing after a day at the office. I liked to grow the vegetables at the bottom of our garden: carrots, parsnips, cabbage, peas, beans… In very small quantities because there were only the two of us.

Thinking about the garden, I realised how much I longed to bite into a fresh green English pea. I'd eaten too many tinned petits-pois.

"You're a bit thin."

I could see myself through Tom's eyes almost as well as I could see him standing in front of me. I knew I was scraggy and unkempt.

"Thanks." I led him out through the open door and onto the cobblestones of the archway.

He pushed the door open, not commenting on the shattered lock. I watched Tom pick his way over the discarded dustsheets.

"Aren't you coming?" He asked, over his shoulder.

He spied the bed bases almost immediately. "It shouldn't be too difficult to get one up to the first floor."

Absentmindedly, he tilted the rocking chair and the empty chair creaked in the stillness, making me think of the man with no clothes.

"Stop."

Tom steadied the rocker.

He looked at the cupboard. He gave me a questioning glance.

I nodded. "Eight shelves of clothes."

He flung open the doors. "Is this what all the fuss is about?"

He picked out a white shirt. It fell out of its folds, and hung in his hands.

"This is crazy Sis. These are just old clothes."

"One of those shirts belonged to Eveline's brother."

"So we've got the brother staying here as well, have we?"

Of course he didn't know. I hadn't told him. "She's started talking."

I told him then about Eveline's brother and the bullet which Valerie found. I told him Valerie's tale about the man in the tree. My words rushed out, slipped over each other, giving voice to a suspicion that I was doing my utmost not to acknowledge.

My heart thumped in my chest. There were no extraneous sounds from the outside. No birdsong. Tom refolded the shirt and put it back in the cupboard.

"You've been here too long on your own Sis. I've asked too much of you. I'm sorry."

"I'm not making it up. The proof's upstairs, asleep. Eveline."

Tom started to crack his fingers, one by one, the sound ricocheting in the silence. It was something he'd been doing since childhood when he was at a loss as to what to do or say next.

"Don't."

"Eveline. You don't even know her name."

He gestured at the cupboard. "So are you trying to tell me that all these men, the men who left these clothes behind... are you telling me that they are all dead as well? Murdered by the Kumonos? Because that's what you're implying isn't it? Right bang here in the middle of France? And when it comes down to it — like when we actually look at the facts rather than supposition — all because of a bullet some Englishwoman found? For God's sakes!"

I wanted him to be right. I wanted to believe that he was right.

Tom enveloped me in another smothering hug. "You don't really know anything about the girl. All you have is her word."

"The passport could be her brother's."

He took a step back, disengaging from me. "You did get rid of it, didn't you?"

I was completely nonplussed. "But upstairs," I said, "you said couldn't remember me ever mentioning a passport..."

"Sis," He shook his head. "You're in such a muddle you're worrying me." That moment of truth was lost.

"Poor old you," he murmured, "having to deal with all this on your own."

"I haven't. There's Greg."

We sat at the kitchen table drinking coffee. Tom looked exhausted, the lines around his eyes and mouth etched. His hands, holding the hot mug, looked very sore.

"Your skin…" I began tentatively.

"Tell me about it. Stress. This business about lost brothers is the last thing I need."

"I'm sorry."

"Not your fault." He gave a weak smile.

I changed the subject. "Are you going to be here long?"

"Not sure."

"Do you know," I said jollily, trying to lighten the mood, "that this is the first time in I don't know how long you haven't been plagued by the phone?"

He smiles and pats his jacket pocket. "Switched off."

The phone upstairs began to ring. I stood up.

"Don't bother," Tom says, "it'll be for me."

"It could be Philip."

"Philip can leave a message like anyone else."

There was something in his tone which made me sit down again. Tom tilted back on his chair, hands in his pockets. We waited until the phone stopped ringing.

"What about Samantha and the children?"

"Just let the answering machine pick up. For a few days, that's all."

"Is everything okay?"

He smiled, a wide smile which didn't reach his eyes. "You know me."

"Does she know you're here?"

"Sam doesn't know about this place, remember? Unless you've let slip?"

I shook my head. "I've only spoken to her the once."

"She will only call if there's an emergency with the kids. Tell me," he changed the subject adroitly, "are there any other skeletons in the cupboard you have to show me?"

A cup of coffee and my brother was reenergised.

"Not real ones, you nit," Tom squeezed my hand affectionately.

*

I showed him the basement, where the washing machine was housed. "In there," I pointed beyond the ironing boards, "I've never explored. It gives me the creeps."

Tom had to crouch to get past the doorway. "Come on, I dare you."

"There's a torch on the washing machine."

"Scaredy cat," he mocked, blinding me with the light. I waited as he manoeuvred himself past the ironing boards and out of my sight.

"There's a door here," he called back, "bolted. Do you know where it goes?"

"I've only ever gone as far as the washing machine."

"So you didn't even know that there was a door? Have you got a wrench? Hang on…" He started hammering with something like a stone. There was the sharp clink of metal.

I heard juddering noises of an ancient door being forced open. I strained to hear what Tom was doing. "What luck!" His voice floated on an echo, like he was very far away. "It's all been left!"

There was a noise, a faint noise of glass smashing and I thought I could hear a gurgle. Then a deathly silence, save for a bird perched on the windowsill, cheeping.

191

I rushed past the washing machine, through the door Tom had found, and I stumbled, lurching over an unexpected step. A hand steadied me. The light from the torch in Tom's other hand danced across the walls. Then it was up on my face, dazzling me.

"Gotcha," Tom was shaking with pent-up laughter. "Are you okay?" He directed the beam downwards onto a broken bottle which had smashed against the side of a packing case, a dark stain on the earthen floor. The split wine smelt like Christmas cake.

"Is there a light?" He swung the torch around.

A single bulb illuminated racks and racks of bottles which stretched into the darkness, past the light's reach. They were curtained in cobweb. I sat down on the crate. The chill damp air made me shiver.

Tom pulled away the cobweb. He rubbed the dust off the labels, showing me dates which went back to the early years of the last century. I worried about the door closing behind us and being entombed forever.

"What a find," Tom crowed.

He handed over two grimy bottles of Mouton Rothschild. "Don't drop."

He selected a Château Lafitte off the rack. "I'll come down for some more later. But for now, I'm sorry Sis, I'm done in. I've got to go to bed."

He followed me, hauling himself up three flights of stairs. The house was utterly silent, totally unconnected to the outside world. Greg didn't appear. Eveline must have been still be asleep. In the corridor leading to the gym room, I saw a shadow detach itself from a wall and linger in broad sunlight for a second. I looked back to see if Tom had noticed, but he was stumbling along, like a drunk.

I offered him Greg's mattress as a bed. I didn't think he would make mine, up another flight of stairs. He swayed slightly because he was so tired but he was also punch-drunk with delight. Never in a million years, he repeated over and over again, could he have amassed such a collection of wine — the scarcity, the rarity, the value — not to mention the time and knowledge involved. "What a stroke of luck."

"I expect by rights it belongs to the embassy," I righted the fresh sheet I'd found for the mattress, and smoothed out the wrinkles. "I don't suppose the Kumonos bought it."

"No self-respecting Frenchman would have left that cellar." His face loomed into mine, upside down until I straightened up. He put his finger to his lips, backing away slightly, making a silly face. He flopped clumsily onto the mattress.

"Finders keepers," he winked. He pulled off a sock and shoe. "Never mind your panels. The wine alone," he pronounced, "makes the château worth it. You don't want the château, do you Sis, he added anxiously. "I know I said you could have it…"

He had fallen asleep. I pulled off his other shoe. One big toe with a little tuft of black hair on the joint protruded out of his silk sock. The skin between his toes was red and weeping. It made me feel sore just to look at it.

Something was up. I remember thinking that Tom was not a man to have holes in his socks.

Chapter 31

Tom was fast asleep on Greg's mattress by ten o'clock that morning. I needed fresh air to clear my head. I walked through the woods behind the château, listening to the rhythm of my feet, too tired at first to think of anything until I turned around to catch a glimpse of a buzzard in flight. Then I saw the view which Valerie had described, of a château with a tower and two lozenges of water: the ornamental pond and the smaller oblong of the swimming pool. Valerie must have been using binoculars to have seen Eveline.

Once Eveline's name popped into my head, I saw her everywhere — in my mind's eye, not in reality, not on the walk — stumbling up the scrubby path in the storm with Greg chasing after her. I managed to lose my bearings completely. I followed one woodland track and then another, looking up to see if I could tell into which tree the naked man had climbed and looking down on the ground for the little oyster silk pouch that Eveline had lost — was it only two nights before?

Eventually, I found the path back down to the stables.

Greg was repairing one of its walls. He looked at me truculently, a large furrow between his eyebrows.

"Do you want me gone?"

"And hello to you. Why should I want you gone?"

"With him about…"

"His name's Tom." I was sharp. Tom was due some respect. He was, after all, Greg's employer. "He hasn't told me how long he's staying," I added more softly.

"Well it's his gaff I suppose. The more the merrier."

"He's delighted with the house."

"Good." Greg looked grudgingly pleased.

After a while, he broke the silence. "You know the taxi driver? The one who brought him?"

I nodded.

"Sent him off without so much as a coffee." Greg mimed patting someone on the back, thrusting money into their hand. "There you are my man." Greg grinned, catching my expression. "No, he didn't say that. He didn't have to."

"He's not like that, Greg, honestly. And he'd have given a very generous tip."

My calves ached. A haze shimmered over the grass, it was so hot. I sat down awkwardly, in the ribbon of shade provided by the wall. I pressed my back into the cold of the stone. I thought about my garden back at home: a long narrow high-hedged strip of land with sycamore trees at the bottom, where the shade was always cool. I wondered how my husband was managing to fill empty evenings without me. Philip had always been such an industrious man. I expected that our lawn had been mown to within a millimetre of its life.

Greg gave up any pretence of work and joined me, his arm rubbing companionably against my shoulder.

"What's he like then, Tom?"

"How do you mean?"

"I dunno. Is he nice?"

I had to think. Nice wasn't an adjective I had ever associated with Tom.

"He's just Tom and he's a good brother. The best."

195

*

Tom had an uncanny ability to know when I really need him. When I was leaving for France, for instance. He picked up my call immediately.

"Where do I get the keys Tom?"

He knew exactly what I meant. He didn't say 'How come you've changed your mind?' or 'What time of the night do you call this?'

All he said was that as far as he knew, there was only one key to the château. "I'll find out and give you a ring in the morning."

Philip phoned me non-stop all the way down to Dover. He had come home from the park to find the house empty. I don't know what he had expected. It couldn't have been that I'd stay: not after being made to feel totally and utterly redundant, of no consequence whatsoever. Not after what I had done. I pulled over onto a lay-by and put the phone into silent mode. It didn't stop the blue light in my handbag pulsating in the darkness like a miniature siren.

Tom finally did call back just before I drove the car into the bowels of the ferry. When I'd finished the call, I hurled the phone with its blinking light into the sea.

*

Greg nudged me with his elbow. "Have you told him about Eveline?"

"Who?" For a second, I don't know whether he meant Tom or Philip.

"Tom."

"He doesn't believe the brother but he hasn't met her yet. I've told him about the passport."

"She could just make out that the passport was her brother's."

"But why would she?"

196

He shrugged. "Search me. She's a rum one."

The skin on Greg's fingers caught on my palm. My hands were almost as rough as his. He helped me to my feet and his eyes lingered on me. I could feel his eyes watching as I made my way up to the swimming pool terrace. I wondered how long it had been since Greg had a woman — a long time I remember thinking, if he was finding me suddenly attractive.

Eveline wasn't in the kitchen. I went up to the library and took the passport out of the desk. I thought that if I surprised her with the passport, I'd be able to gauge the truth in her reaction. I opened her bedroom door. Eveline was not in the room nor had she made her bed. I opened her curtains and caught sight of a shape down by the chapel which could have been her. I couldn't be sure. I put the passport back in the library, back in the desk, under lock and key.

I went up to my tower room. I was tired. Worn out by long nights and early mornings. I lay on my mattress, not meaning to fall asleep.

It took me a while to realise what had woken me; the acrid smell of smoke clogging my nostrils. A thick pall drifted past the open windows. For one panic-stricken second, I thought that the house was fire, then I realise that it couldn't be. The smoke was coming from outside.

A bonfire raged by the chapel, nowhere near the house — only there was a breeze which could lift a spark and set an old timber alight. Greg was at the scene, wielding a hose, dampening the flames, shouting at Eveline who was standing nearby, too close, doing nothing to help. I went down the stairs two at a time.

From the archway to the chapel, I followed bits and pieces of men's clothing, dropped on the ground. The stench of burnt plastic and leather was noxious. Greg and Eveline stood in silence by a smouldering heap. The fire had burnt a ragged shape into the grass, and blackened the chapel's one remaining wall. There were a few bits of singed cloth scattered about, blown back by the ferocity of the flames.

She crossed her arms and looked at me defiantly.

"You stupid girl." It just came out. Instantly I regretted it. "You could have burnt down the house."

She shrugged. I was so angry I struggled to speak. "You have no right."

Her eyes, for one unguarded moment, were full of disdain. "More right than you'll ever have."

Somehow she had managed to shame me again. I blushed.

"My brother's going to take a pretty dim view of this."

She shrugged again. Her expression blank.

"He arrived this morning."

"He's here?" Startled, she looked up at the château.

Greg gathered up the hose, winding it over his arm.

"She's right you know," he told Eveline. "It's like a tinderbox at the end of the summer."

"Sorry," she said, completely ungraciously. She turned on her heel and walked away.

"It's totally out of order," he said, staring after her.

"Maybe she just didn't want them dumped in some landfill somewhere. I can understand that."

I picked up the can of kerosene, thinking that I must put it away safely.

"Then you're as nuts as she is."

"That's it," I said, flushing for the second time in as many minutes. "I've had it."

I left the kerosene in the shade of chapel wall.

I caught up with Eveline by the stables.

She tried to shake me off. "I don't want to talk to you."

"Well you had better."

She looked down pointedly at my hand on her arm. I let her go.

"I felt like an idiot this morning," I told her, "with Tom. I know so little about you."

Her reply took me completely by surprise.

"So what do you want to know?"

"Everything."

"Everything," she repeated, sadly. "I wish I'd known my brother better."

She bent down to unlatch the gate to the woods. Before she disappeared up a track to the woods, she looked back.

"I've got to find my bag." She meant her diamonds.

Chapter 32

Tom slept through the fire. I spent the rest of that long afternoon painting the walls of one of the first floor rooms. I used an extension pole so that I could reach the ceiling. The repetitive act should have been mind-numbingly soothing, but I couldn't stop thinking about how, with one little slip, Eveline had betrayed her brother. I wondered how she remained sane. Was she sane? The bonfire was not a sane act. The pole swished back and forwards across the ceiling, painting out the blemishes, while my thoughts went around and around, never reaching a conclusion.

There was a knock on the door. Eveline looked unsure of her welcome.

I gestured her to enter.

With one fluid movement she sat, cross-legged on the bare floorboards.

"I am so sorry. I don't know what came over me." Her voice was barely above a whisper. "I have no money and nowhere to go."

I laid the roller back in its tray, determined that she would explain herself.

"What possessed you to burn the clothes?"

She looked up at me, her eyes huge, her lower lip quivering, her fingers plucking at the floor.

"They don't belong to you. I didn't want them just to be put in a black bin liner like they were rubbish…"

She buried her face in her hands and let out a long anguished wail. "You don't believe me about my brother!"

I was completely unnerved.

"I do!" I raised my voice above her crying. "In fact I'll show you…" I was about to go and get the passport but when I took a step towards the door my path was blocked by a tree with its branches being shaken.

It amazes me how I didn't question my own sanity because I could see the tree, even though I knew it wasn't real. It was little and compact, with dark green oak-like leaves and in its middle, a tall man, crouching down, thrashing the stubby branches.

"Hush," I said, cradling over Eveline, "I do believe you." The man was quite still, watching us, his eyes burning in his face. He moved then, he moved out of the tree and I shut my eyes for a second and when I opened them again, Tom was standing between us and the man from the tree.

"What the hell is going on? Is everything okay?" Red-faced and worried, he was shouting. He had changed out of his suit, wearing a shirt and shorts and loafers on his bare feet. Eveline raised her tear-stained face.

"This is my brother, Tom."

Eveline stopped shaking. She struggled to her feet. "Hello," she said, without looking at him. Unsteadily, and without a glance back, she left the room.

Despite his change of clothes, Tom still looked like a city slicker, still very tired, with dark indentations underneath his eyes. I got up off the floor and started to gather together the equipment. The man and the tree disappeared.

"I was outside," he said, "looking for you when I heard her scream." He shook his head. "God, it gave me a fright."

"I am going to have to show her the passport. It's the only way she'll know for certain if her brother was here."

"Are you keeping it safe?"

"Locked in a drawer in the library."

"Good," he said. "What was Greg thinking having a bonfire that near to the house?"

I'd been dreading telling him.

"Christ. She's completely unhinged. The sooner she leaves, the better."

"I've told her she can stay a while longer."

"What's got into you?" He looked at me speculatively. "What is it with this girl?"

"I think," I chose my words deliberately, "that it is in all our interests to find out what happened to the brother. I don't think that there will be any peace in this house until we do."

Tom picked up the hand brush which I'd left lying on the floor. He started to sweep desultorily, leaving two long arcs on the wooden boards before I stopped him for fear of dust on the wet paint.

He wiped specks of dirt and paint off his knees. "I've opened a bottle by the way, for this evening."

"Hell. I forgot to go to the supermarket. There's nothing to eat."

"There must be something."

"Tins. Or we could go to the restaurant? There is one, in the village."

"Tins are fine. I'm not particularly hungry anyway."

Nor was I.

As we go down the stairs to the kitchen, he asked about Greg's whereabouts.

"What time is it?"

He looked down at his chunk of a watch. "Ten past seven."

"He'll have gone home."

"Sis," he said gently. "Don't mention anything about the passport this evening, please. I couldn't bear another scene."

The wine from the cellar was glorious. Somehow, it made the food not matter too much: pasta and pesto, with a tin of bamboo shoots and two tins of artichoke hearts, all from château stocks. Eveline refused wine. In Tom's presence, there was a truculence about her, like a naughty child who had been caught doing something silly. She wouldn't catch Tom's eye. We ate in silence, chasing pasta shells around wide-rimmed plates. Tom and I gave each other occasional glances, when Eveline's head was bent. When Tom finished, he wiped his mouth with paper towel and looked steadily at Eveline until she had to raise her face and give him her attention.

"My sister tells me that you think your brother stayed here?"

She said nothing, mopping up the sauce with day-old bread.

"Eveline," I said. "Please."

Tom shot me a warning glance.

I shook my head. No, I was not going to mention the passport that evening.

Eveline didn't notice our unspoken communication. She looked steadfastly at Tom. "I know he did."

"Tell me," he said conversationally, almost changing the subject but not quite, "it's been puzzling my sister — just how did you arrive here in the first place?"

"My husband drove me." She told Tom what she had told me. "He's divorcing me."

"That seems a little brutal." Tom's tone was smooth.

"The marriage was arranged any way."

"Okay, let's start from the beginning." He wasn't rude, just firm. "With facts. What's your connection with the Kumono family?"

Eveline looked at her plate. It was empty except for the bamboo shoots.

"You have to talk," my brother said. "If you don't, my sister and I can't help you. You will have to find some other accommodation."

"Tom…"

He ignored me.

Eveline looked at him with her great, unfathomable eyes.

"Did you know the General?" she asked.

"Me?" Tom was taken aback. "Why ever would you think that?"

"You have his château." Eveline was very intent.

"No, not in as…" Tom chuckled unconvincingly. He looked to me for support.

"The truth," I mouthed, "tell her the truth."

Tom swirled the wine around his glass, playing a game with it, retrieving it before it slurped over the rim. "I met him a couple of times."

"All part of a marketing initiative," I smiled, giving him support.

"We pulled out years ago," Tom smiled back.

"What sort of company?" There was a very insistent quality to Eveline.

"Preliminary exploration. Nothing came of it. I tell you what Sis," he leant towards me. "Let's have one last glass outside. I'm so looking forward to a good catch-up with you."

"What were you looking for?" Eveline persisted.

Tom laughed. "Goodness, and I thought I was the one asking the questions!"

"It's my country," Eveline said stiffly but she got up and offered to clear the table and do the washing-up while Tom and I had a chat. "It will be nice for you and your brother." I felt horrendously guilty.

*

I glanced over at Tom who had been standing impatiently by the door, shifting from foot to foot, waiting for me. The luminosity of her beauty had suddenly registered with him. He couldn't take his eyes off her.

"Thank you." She allowed me to press her close.

"I am going to repay your kindness," she whispered, "by helping more around the house."

Tom and I sat by the swimming pool and watched as the sun turned an incandescent, putrid orange colour before sinking out of sight behind the mountains.

We were both lying on sun loungers. I remember that my legs were chilly and Tom insisting that it was warm still. It was growing dark. The cicadas were making a racket, as they did every evening.

"There is something extraordinary about her."

"Her beauty apart from anything else."

"It kind of ambushes you," he said distractedly. Then he sat upright.

"Sam's left me. For real this time. Oxfordshire is on the market. London's for sale. As she says, it's not as if the kids see much of me anyway."

I understood the psoriasis then. I stretched out my hand and he clasped it. His hand felt dry, flaky, almost reptilian.

"Why didn't you say something earlier?"

"I didn't want you to feel that you'd been wasting your time here."

"Don't be silly. I was grateful for the chance to get away."

He smiled but he couldn't hide the hurt. It was in the set of his shoulders as he turned his head away from me.

*

Years and years ago, I was at a function of Tom's. Philip wasn't there. He avoided Tom's parties if he could. He called him an asset stripper. He said that Tom was amoral. That he flew too close to the wind.

I was standing alone on the terrace, the party going on in the restaurant behind me. I was escaping the hub-bub for a minute, when my brother came up and put his arm around my waist.

"Beautiful, isn't it?" He always thought that he could surprise with his approach, but I always heard him coming. Stretched out in front of us was the night-time silhouette of London, from the Houses of Parliament to St Paul's with a barge chugging slowly up the Thames.

"It's fantastic." It was the first time I had spoken to him that evening. "Congratulations."

"I'm thinking of giving it all up. Spending more time with Sam and the kids."

My reaction was immediate. "You can't do that."

"Why ever not?"

"You're not the type for domestic bliss."

There was a pain in his eyes then, a sort of confusion. He knew I was referring to his many affairs.

"Honestly, you'd be bored. You'd miss the buzz."

He looked deflated like a little boy. "Do you think so?"

"Trust me," I laughed. "I know so."

Except that I didn't know and I wasn't about to admit, even to myself, that my brother's success was important to me. I liked him being rich. I loved being the sister of 'Tom Braid'.

What I didn't realise was that his business interests would expand to such an extent that his wife and children, never mind me, would rarely get to see him.

*

An owl hooted in the woods.

"And you," he asked, "how are you?"

"You haven't been seeing other women have you?"

"Give us a chance." Tom's laugh was genuine. "I haven't broken my promise to Mum yet."

"Mum knew about your affairs?"

"Why so shocked?" He was teasing me. "Of course I told her."

Tom and our mother had finally grown close during her final illness. They caught up with a lifetime of intimacy in a few short months — although he wasn't with her the cold November weekend six years before when she had died. Urgent business was the on-going story of his life.

"I thought I was the only one who knew."

"She weaselled it out of me."

Tom sensed my change of mood. "Come on, Sis," he said, picking up both empty glasses "of course she knew. She of all people." I was too tired to quiz him on exactly what he meant.

"You know," he said, as he gave me a kiss good night, "I don't believe that girl is married."

"Why ever not?"

He grinned tapping the side of his nose. "I see a lot of girls like her in hotel bars."

"You're wrong."

Up in my tower room, I couldn't sleep. I wedged a chair against the door handle in case the naked man tried to insinuate himself into the warmth of my bed.

Chapter 33

The following day, Tom's first full day at the château, he didn't appear until noon. I knew that he had already been out because of the way my car was parked — almost, but not quite in its usual spot — but when I checked to see where he was, he was sleeping like a baby on Greg's mattress in the gym room.

Eveline wasn't in her room. I presumed that she had gone up to the woods, in search of her diamonds. I was glad that she wasn't around.

"Is there anything for lunch?" Tom was like his old self again.

He turned up his nose at the cupboard full of tins and I found myself in my car with Tom at the wheel, hurtling down the hill to catch the last of the open air market in the village square.

We parked in a side street baking in the sun.

Tom made no move to get out of the car as I retrieved the baskets from the back.

"Aren't you coming?"

"I'll wait here for you."

"Why ever not?"

"Seriously Sis, I'm too tired."

"Come on. We'll be in and out in a jiffy. It's lunchtime, don't forget. Hardly anyone around."

He put on his sunglasses and levered himself out of the car, wincing when his fingers touched the hot roof.

The stalls hadn't quite packed up. We bought heaps of fruit and veg. It was just like old times, Tom and me, when our mother used to send us out together to do the shopping. I was experiencing the same heady sense of freedom.

We were at our last stop, at the ready-roasted chicken stall waiting for two chickens to appear from the back of the van, when a young Asian man with narrow-framed sunglasses approached Tom.

Tom was squatting, trying to find space in our baskets for the chickens.

The young man bent towards him. "Excuse me, but you're not Tom Braid are you?" His accent was broad Essex.

"Tom who?" Tom asked without so much as a glance up at the man. I stood by, silent and puzzled.

"Sorry," the stranger apologised, embarrassed. "It's just that we all work in the City..."

"What? You mean there is more than one of you?" Tom stood upright, his free hand shading his sunglasses, a string of onions dangling from the other.

The stranger pointed to three people watching us from one of the tables outside the Café de Paris. They waved. "They swore you were him, and I said you couldn't be not with all the rumours flying around London."

"I'm sorry to disappoint you." Tom transferred the oranges we had bought from one basket to the other.

"Actually," the stranger called as Tom and I hurried away, "Tell the bastard he deserves whatever he gets if you should see him."

"What did he mean by that?" The questions tumbled out as soon as we were out of earshot.

"I hope he isn't some arsehole of a journalist. That would be the last straw."

"What's going on?"

"It'll blow over. Has he gone?"

The man was still standing by the chicken van, hands in pockets, watching us.

"Why did he call you a bastard?"

"A minion from a rival company? Who knows?"

"But — "

"No buts," he said firmly. "I don't want to talk about it. I can't anyway."

"We can't leave the chickens."

"Could you go back and get them? Please. I can't go anywhere without being accosted these days."

I know what it is like to have unwanted attention from the press. When Tom made his first million with a lot of fanfare, I was button-holed by a spotty journalist who must have been as young as I was. I was aware — I took an active interest in Tom's businesses then — that there was speculation that the deal had been brokered with the help of some very shady people. This journalist though, had decided to approach his piece on Tom from another angle.

"So what does your father do? A philanthropist perhaps?"

He should have done his homework. The fact that he hadn't heard of our father's novels, meant that our father was dead in every way.

"No." It was sixteen years after the event, and I still found it impossible to speak of my father's death. "He's in fertiliser. Haven't you heard?"

And, until very recently — until two weeks ago to be precise — Philip and I have had journalists hanging around outside the house. They have gone now, thank God — leaving the street and our neighbours in peace.

*

We were to have the chicken that evening for supper, along with quiches, salamis, cheeses and salads. The table would be laden.

"It's a celebration," Tom said. He was stuffing the ends of five pink candles he had found in a box of fifty at the back of the sideboard into a tarnished almost black, candelabra. I was chopping up salad leaves. The kitchen was exasperating: we had five nut crackers, three ice cream scoops, two melon ballers but no colanders or potato peelers. Perhaps the French don't use potato peelers. Maybe the potato peeler is a purely British invention.

"For what?"

"For the château, finding the wine, for us — we're so rarely together these days."

"You're forgetting about Eveline."

"She's not our problem."

"She is, Tom. Like it or not, she's here."

"You seriously don't believe the brother nonsense…"

"I do."

Tom was trying to shove the last candle into its socket and it wouldn't go. "It's too far-fetched, Sis."

"Because," I said, "there was something about this house — something in the atmosphere — which I couldn't explain before she came."

"And now you can?"

I knew that I was going to sound unhinged, but I said it anyway.

"It's like the shadows in the house have been stirred up because she's here, searching for the truth about her brother."

He looked at me in mock astonishment.

"Shadows?"

I felt my face reddening. "I don't mean haunting. Not that."

Tom snorted. "You've been here too long on your own." Then he changed the subject. "What's going on between you and Philip?"

"We're having a trial separation."

Whatever answer Tom was expecting, it wasn't that one.

"You and me," he said eventually. "What a pair." He smiled. "At least we've got each other."

He came over and put an arm around my shoulder. I remember the stab of pain in my chest, every bit as real as Tom.

"I wonder how different it would have been if we'd had children."

There was nothing Tom could say. He had four children whom he saw rarely.

After a while, he moved away and placed the candelabra in the middle of the table. Pink and blackened silver made a pretty combination.

"It's not just a ploy to have somewhere to stay?" He was talking about Eveline again.

"You can't make that sort of grief up." I thought of Eveline scrabbling amongst the clothes. "Don't you remember with Dad?"

"Not really." Tom forced the last candle into place. "I was too young. What do you think?" He stood back to admire his handiwork.

I remembered our father lying dead under the apple tree with his blue eyes full of clouds, staring at the sky.

"Smell this." Tom had uncorked two bottles of red.

The odour was fusty and sour. If I hadn't known better, I would have said that the wine was undrinkable.

He showed me the label. "Château Latour. The year Dad died."

I remembered Tom up in the tree, before it happened, swinging from branch to branch. I remembered being annoyed with him, always grabbing as much of our father's attention as he could.

"Listen Sis," Tom said, "don't worry about Eveline. We'll sort something out."

That was the first time he called her 'Eveline'. Still though, it wasn't her name.

Chapter 34

So around eight o'clock in the evening, we sat down at the table: Tom, me, Greg and Eveline.

Tom had invited Greg to share our supper. He had sought Greg out during the afternoon, and paced the château and its grounds with him. He seemed impervious to the fact that the château used to belong to a dictator and that a young girl was searching for her dead brother there. Eveline's presence, I remember thinking, was merely an irritation. Nothing and no one was going to be allowed to taint my brother's vision of the place as a wonderful retreat for his family — not even his sudden lack of wife. For all his anonymous donations to charities over the years, my brother was a hard-hearted man.

Greg had been abroad too long. He'd gone back to the caravan and changed for the meal. Sitting next to Tom, he looked foreign. Greg also needed a haircut, and absolutely not another do-it-yourself job. He could have almost been attractive in the right light with the right haircut.

I, too, had changed for the meal. For the first time ever at the château, I was wearing freshly pressed clothes. My heart, though, had almost fallen out of my chest when I saw the neat pile of clothes on my bed. For a moment, I thought that they belonged to the man in the tree. They were my clothes, taken off the makeshift line I'd strung up near the swimming pool. Eveline had ironed them, when she returned after a futile search in the woods. She was being good to her word and helping around the house.

Tom insisted that I tasted the wine first. He stood beside me, one arm behind his back, a parody of a wine waiter. "And what does Madame think?"

"Madame," I said carefully, swirling the thin brown liquid around my mouth, "thinks it's wonderful."

"And Madame?" He turned to Eveline who automatically put her hand over her glass. There was a hint of eyeliner around her eyes and she'd painted her nails. The red varnish glinted.

"You can't do that," Tom said in mock outrage, "you may never again taste the vintage of '73. It wasn't a bad year for Bordeaux."

Whilst he served Greg, Eveline stretched her impossibly long neck and emptied the glass. I was surprised because the wine, despite what I said to Tom, tasted old and bitter. Tom looked momentarily horrified. Greg stifled a giggle. I glared at Greg. Tom poured Eveline another glass. She downed it in one.

"Eveline — " I was about to say: 'be careful. Don't get drunk.'

Tom interrupted me. "I can see you're a girl after my own heart." He poured her half a glass and wagged the bottle. "Let's leave a little something for the rest of us."

Eveline smiled and took a sip. Tom looked touched. Greg's face was a picture.

"Eveline," Tom offered her the plate of salami, "just picking up where we left off last night, how come your family were friends of General Kumono?"

"How come?" The question seemed genuinely to baffle her. In the silence which followed, her eyes wandered over the plates of food, wandered over all our faces, like she was searching out an answer in order to please Tom. I wondered if the wine had gone to her head.

"Tom means…" I said, in case she hadn't understood. But of course she had understood.

"My father was the General's architect." Her knife clattered onto her plate.

"Did you know him personally?" Tom's voice dripped with sympathy.

"Yes," she said defiantly. "But I was always frightened of him. He played stupid tricks, like the first time I met him."

"What sort of tricks?" Already, I was anxious for her, for what horror she might reveal.

"I was only small and I was sent out into the garden when he arrived. My brother was sent to play with me." She bit her lower lip, remembering. "He didn't want to, because he was twelve at the time and I was only four — but already, I think, our parents didn't trust the General. So my brother played shop with me, my favourite game. Do you know the game?"

"Yes," I said, "Tom and I used to play it when we were children. Didn't we Tom?"

Tom wasn't not paying any attention to me either. All his concentration was on Eveline.

"We got stuff from kitchen: tin cans, things like that. We made a display with the cans." Eveline drew a triangle in the air as an explanation, her eyes still on Tom.

"We did too. Don't you remember Tom?" I knew I was gabbling.

"Sis," Tom said gently. "Shut up." So I shut up. We waited. Tom nodded to Eveline.

"Anyway," Eveline continued. "General Kumono was leaving. He was nice to us. He gave us sweets. He had a pocketful of sweets. But at the gate…" Her voice wavered.

"Go on," Tom said softly. "You're with friends here."

216

"At the garden gate, we were waving goodbye beside our shop, with our parents there..." She faltered, and started again. "He took out a gun and whoosh! He shoots. Pow! Pow! Pow!" Eveline's palms and fingers aligned together like she had a gun, bullets scudding across the table. All the time, she was pointing at Tom with her two index fingers and their blood-red nails.

It was stricken, the silence, which followed. It was as if the General had joined us at the table; an overbearing caricature of a man who would have been laughable if he hadn't been so dangerous. Tom had met the man but Greg and I — we were familiar with the General from news footage. We had seen the images of the mass graves, the tidy lines of excavated bones. Eveline had brought his spectre to our table.

Tom played for time, lifting his glass up to the light and then swallowing the lot. Greg was quite still, his chin bent towards his chest, as if he were deep in thought. I pressed Eveline's hands back into her lap and held them there. I could have wept for her.

"What was the General shooting at?" Tom reached back and lifted a bottle of wine off the sideboard. He helped himself liberally. Greg roused himself, took the bottle from Tom, and poured himself another glass. Tom winked at me. He was trying to be light-hearted. The attempt fell flat.

"The cans," Eveline shrugged her shoulders. She was long past caring. "It was a joke. The bullets — silver bullets — they were only for the cans."

"Your poor parents."

She gazed at me solemnly. "My father put a hand over my mother's mouth."

"Are those the bullets?" I hazarded a guess.

"Yes. My father marked two and gave us one each, my brother and me — as a good luck charm, you know? It was his dream," she shook her head, unable to believe her father's naivety, "that we lived without fear. Of course we always lived in fear after that." She picked up her knife and fork, folded the slice of salami in two and popped it into her mouth, as if she hadn't been, two minutes before, taking aim at my brother. If those bullets hadn't been make-believe, my brother would have been dead, as dead as my father and her brother.

"Which is why," Eveline announced, "that I know that Zachary is dead. He would never have left behind the silver bullet."

Zachary. The same name as in the passport, hidden in the desk drawer in the library. Eveline's shadows swarmed around the table. It was they who were eating the glistening flesh of the chickens; they were scooping up the muddy-looking foie gras and savouring it, like Tom, on baguette; they who were chomping through tough endive, slicing through the flaccid moon of a ham quiche. Not us.

I pushed back my chair.

"Sis, wait," Tom said, half-rising. He knew what I was going to do.

He addressed Eveline. "Isn't Zachary a rather unusual name for your part of the world?"

Eveline wiped a droplet of oil from her lips. "My father heard the name when he was studying in Paris."

Tom's expression was completely neutral.

"My brother was here," she insisted. "I found his chain. The bullet proves it. I don't need more proof."

"I've got something to show you," I said, standing up.

"Sis!" Tom tried to call me back.

As I took to the stairs, Greg asked Tom how business was in London. Good old Greg. We had to maintain a semblance of normality.

Chapter 35

I upended the drawer. The papers scattered across the desk. No passport. I checked the two unlocked drawers underneath. I stopped my frenzied searching and thought back to the last time I had seen the passport.

There had been a stiff feeling to the cover — as if it was new but it wasn't; it was out of date. Most of the pages were blank and unused. Some were stuck together. I remembered the identity section, the photo of the young man, with Zachary as his first name and an unpronounceable name for his second.

I could remember dropping the key into the cloisonné pot, but I couldn't be sure if I had put the passport back because I couldn't recall actually, physically, locking the drawer. I was sure though, that Tom had taken the passport.

Back in the kitchen, I caught the tail-end of some joke of Tom's — something about all work and no play making Tom a poor boy. Greg looked puzzled. He hadn't understood the punch line. Eveline looked drained and in a world of her own. Tom stopped laughing when he saw me.

"Everything okay?"

"Can I have a word with you?" I kept my tone light.

He gave a mock groan. "Can't it wait till the washing up is done?"

Greg glanced up at me, then back to Tom and across to Eveline.

"We'll do it." He started to gather together the empty plates. "Are you alright?"

"I'm fine thanks," I said, locking eyes with Tom as he slowly rose from his chair. I thought he was directing the question to me. Later, I realised he was asking Eveline.

Tom and I walked through the archway and out to the front of the house, the only sound the scrunch of our shoes on the gravel. Tom strolled along, hands in his pockets, ostentatiously sniffing the night air, as if nothing was wrong. He was waiting for me to speak.

"Where have you put it?" We stopped in front of the ornamental pond which glittered with stars, like the sky.

"Put what?"

"Stop playing games," I said wearily.

Tom shrugged his shoulders. "An out-of-date passport isn't much use to anyone."

"What have you done with it?"

"Can't you see, Sis, that she would have claimed the passport as her brother's whether it was or not?"

"But it was his as it's turned out."

Tom put a finger to his lips. "You're shouting. It's called being cruel to be kind. She didn't know about it, did she?"

"Where is it?"

"Burnt," he said smoothly. "In the remains of the fire she started."

I closed my eyes and saw the man shaking the branches of the tree. I opened them and he was there between me and Tom. I shut my eyes again. I felt dizzy.

"Are you okay?" Tom's face was up close to mine, his eyes glistening with concern. "I can see how all this could do your head in."

"It was totally and utterly wrong of you."

221

"It was the right thing to do," he said firmly. "For you. You're the person I care about." I'd wanted him to take control and he had: he'd taken the decision and the relief I felt, the worry of what to do with the passport, sloughed off me — but I was still angry.

There was a soft 'plop' as something dark slid off a lily pad and scattered the stars.

"Hey, did you hear that?" Tom whispered.

"How did you know where I kept the key to the desk?"

"You've always kept keys in little pots. Remember the ballerina jewellery box which you had when you were small?"

The ballerina twirled to music. I'd kept the key hidden in a papier-mâché pot I'd made with a yoghurt tub at school.

Tom threw back his head and laughed. "And you never knew!" he crowed.

Always, he could make me remember how we once were: a naughty little boy and an earnest little girl.

He squeezed my hand as we make our way back into the house. "Seriously, it's best that the girl goes."

"With what?"

"I'll give her some money."

"It's not money she'll want. It's her diamonds."

He stopped so that I had to turn to face him again. His teeth gleamed white. "Okay," he said. "I'll go up to the woods with her tomorrow. Fat chance we'll find the diamonds but at least we'll have done our best. Either way, there will be absolutely no excuse for her to stay."

Back in the kitchen, back in the pools of light, Eveline was nowhere to be seen. Greg had opened another bottle of wine. A stack of shiny plates gleamed on the rack.

"I've been thinking," Greg said, "Claudine. Maybe she remembers if Eveline's brother was here."

"You're right. Valerie mentioned her." I couldn't hide my excitement.

"Who's Claudine?" Tom asked.

Greg told him.

Tom looked at me. "She sounds round the twist. There's no point."

"There is," I said as firmly as I could. "If we can get Valerie to come with us, she can translate."

"For Christ's sakes, nothing went on. It's a nonsense. This is hunting country. There are bloody bullets all over the woods."

"If something had happened to you, I'd…"

He cut me off. "Seeing the cleaner will be a waste of time!"

"We have no choice!" I shouted at his back, disappearing up the stairs.

"Do you two argue like this all the time?" Greg asked good-humouredly.

I told him the truth. "Only in this bloody place."

Chapter 36

There was a note propped against the plate of croissants telling me that Tom and Eveline had gone up to the woods — with a PS 'I've taken the car, hope you don't mind'. I did mind. I'd wanted to engineer a visit to Claudine. By taking the car, Tom had effectively marooned me at the château.

The day stretched out before me, with nothing to do except to do up a château. Greg was around. I could hear the squeak of the wheel barrow being pushed over the gravel.

I decided to finish painting the room on the first floor. All it needed was a final coat.

Greg slid into the room as I started on the last wall. He closed the door carefully behind him.

"Can you leave it open?"

The door open or closed, the room was still laden with heat.

Greg mopped his hair with one of my painting rags from the floor.

"You'll smell of white spirit," I warned.

"Who cares?" he said, grinning, watching me load the roller with paint and smooth it, self-consciously because he was looking, across the plaster.

"What was going on last night?" He asked, perching his bottom on the window ledge.

I told him that Tom had burnt the passport.

Greg whistled.

"But it did belong to her brother. She said her brother was Zachary and the passport belonged to someone called Zachary."

"So what now — will you still tell her that his passport was here?"

"What do you think?"

He considered his response carefully. "I think you'll have to — at some point."

I jabbed at the ceiling with the roller. "My bloody brother."

Greg laughed. "Careful!"

Then he said he had seen them sitting in the salon together after I had gone to bed. "Not talking, just sitting."

"He was probably trying to persuade her to let him help her find her diamonds."

"It didn't look like that to me." Greg grinned.

I put down the roller. "What do you mean by that?"

Greg's grin disappeared. "Nothing."

"Tom's a family man. He's got children." He wouldn't, I thought, not at the château. Not with her. He wouldn't revert back to his old ways so quickly. My brother was a better man than that.

"So have I," Greg said, "so what? She's an attractive young woman."

"I thought you…" and I was about to say something about Greg's previous denials that he found Eveline attractive, when I realised what he had said.

"You never told me."

"You never asked." He crossed his arms, belligerent with embarrassment.

"How many?"

"Just the one, back in England."

"How could you," I said as levelly as I could, "leave a child?"

"It happens."

What I thought must have been written all over my face.

Greg flushed beetroot. "I went do-lally, okay?" He made that awful twisting motion with his finger against his forehead.

In the silence which followed, he didn't take his eyes off my face. It was as if he was daring me to judge him.

I'd spent months with this man, and I know virtually nothing about him.

"I am sorry. Truly."

Greg's eyes were full of regret. "My best mate, he told me that the kid wasn't mine..."

I had an idea. "Let's get out of this place for a while. Go out. Have some lunch together."

Greg's face lit up. "Where do you want to go?"

I crossed over to him. I meant just to tease when I ruffled his hair. Where could I take a man who reeked of white spirit? Instead there was a shock — recognition that we could easily have sex right there on the bare floor. It registered with Greg as well. He smiled at me.

"Lunch. Where do you suggest?"

Chapter 37

Greg said that we couldn't go to the Café de Paris in case Valerie was there. I didn't question why he was worried about her whereabouts. "Okay then. Your place." He looked unsure. I told him not to worry, that I'd raid the château's fridge.

He took washing-up liquid from the sink and disappeared upstairs to wash his hair. I piled a basket with food.

There was sense of freedom as we walked along, a feeling of constriction removed — or maybe it was just the fact that the château was behind us and we were leaving it behind, like a fat toad on a lily pad, sitting on its hill.

Greg's caravan was under the shade of an enormous oak tree, in the far corner of a wide meadow, not far from the lake where the locals liked to swim. It was a rectangular tin box, too small for two and so stifling in summer that Greg slept outside, in a patched one-man tent.

I pulled a tartan rug out from the tent and laid out plates of quiche and salami. He brought out two glasses — they were chipped and slightly grey, like everything else in the caravan. It was obvious he had little spare cash. I was wrong about him. He didn't drink his money down at the café — he sent it back to England, for his child. Greg was a good man. He was very kind to me. He was kind to Eveline, despite his frustrations with her. He was one of those rare people who are simply, effortlessly, without an ounce of malice.

We lay on the rug, facing each other. Greg poured the pale yellow wine. Yet more insects hovered, attracted by its sweetness.

Greg fumbled in his back pocket and drew out his wallet. He flipped it open and handed it to me — showing me a photo of a little baby with enormous jug ears, just like Greg's.

I laughed. "She's yours, Greg."

He was pleased. "I'm beginning to believe it."

"And?" I asked, using one hand to move the glasses and the bottle back to the edge of the rug, where I deliberately left the food.

"Cheryl wants me back."

"So are you going to go?"

Greg considered perhaps the most important decision of his life, his fingers plucking up bits of tuft. I leant my face into his. I wanted to be closer to him, to comfort him.

The kiss took him by surprise. It took me by surprise. I'd never thought that I would — that I could — seduce a man, let alone so blatantly.

For a long time we just kissed. Greg won't let me do anything else. "There is plenty of time. Just relax." So I relaxed and the feeling of well-being — of being out in the sun, of being intimate with someone else — well, it was just blissful.

Eventually, he wriggled his arms out of his t-shirt and lets me slide it over his head. My t-shirt and bra came off in one smooth move.

I kicked off my shorts and pants.

Greg looked concerned. "Shit."

"Don't worry," I giggled, heady with nakedness. "I'm not going to get pregnant. I can't."

He unzipped his jeans. I pulled them down. He pushed first one leg and then the other, off with his feet.

His skin, where the sun hadn't touched it, was the colour of milk.

By then, we had moved off the rug. The smell of the earth was warm and pungent, and tassels of grass tickled. Greg treated me so lightly and so respectfully.

It was different with Philip. Our sex was for making babies. When we had given up hope, we gave up sex.

Greg smiled hazily and pulled me towards him — and still, I caught of a waft of white spirit, which made me giggle again.

Afterwards, we watched chinks of sky shift shapes in the canopy. I felt elated. Liberated. There was a passing thought about my father — then another about the man in the tree which I shut out of my head.

Greg stroked me on my cheek. "Can't have been easy splitting up from your husband."

"Who says I have split up from my husband?"

"Tom."

I was still too full of languor to take him seriously. "Well, that's another thing he's wrong about."

The atmosphere changed in an instant. Greg scooped himself off the ground in one, fluid motion, full of umbrage.

"I don't go with married women."

"That's good of you," I said, stung. "Glad you have some morals. What about Cheryl?"

"I'm not married to her."

Greg struggled to get his legs into his jeans. He disappeared into the caravan. I grew cold.

*

229

I put on my shorts and t-shirt, stuffing my bra into a pocket. I was so disappointed that what had promised to be so lovely had turned out so wrong.

I dumped the uneaten food into a plastic bag. I watered the grass with what was left of the wine. I found my shoes. There was a whistling from the caravan — of a kettle, boiling on a gas stove.

Greg re-emerged holding two mugs of tea.

"I am sorry. About the misunderstanding."

"When did Tom tell you that I'd split from Philip?"

"He didn't — not in so many words. I think he wanted me to look out for you. It was obvious you were upset when you came. I just assumed… it's all my fault." He looked miserable.

"When, Greg?"

"When he asked me to get the gas and electric reconnected and then he mentioned it again when he told me you'd be coming the next day…"

I started to laugh. Greg and I had had this conversation before. "But I didn't know I was coming!"

"It's probably not my place…"

"Go on."

"He's not always straight with you, is he?"

I had to admit that Tom wasn't. Not recently anyway. Not since I'd been at the château. It wasn't conceivable that Philip had told Tom about the affair. He disliked — distrusted — Tom.

"I haven't separated from Philip," I told Greg. "I just left him."

"Just like that?"

"It's too long a story." In fact, according to Philip it was a very short story of three months and five days.

Greg looked at me, waiting for me to continue.

230

I knew I owed him more. I took a deep breath. "He had an affair. But I think that, once the château's finished, I'm going to go back."

"He doesn't deserve you."

"I'm beginning to wonder if I deserve him." I surprised myself with that admission.

Greg gave me a peck on the cheek, all passion spent.

Chapter 38

Walking back up the hill, I wondered how well, truly, I knew my brother. Tom and I had never spent any length time together as adults — not until, that is, the château. I didn't know the intricacies of his life any more than he knew mine. I hadn't told Tom about Philip because I couldn't have borne the shame. I hadn't wanted Tom to know that his sister was capable of picking up a knife and lashing out... even then, as I thought about it, my face burned with the recollection. It still burns when I think of it.

Tom and Eveline weren't back. My car wasn't there. I was glad.

The château felt becalmed, like a great ship. The shadows stretched across the walls and floors as I switched on lights.

I went up to the dining hall where the telephone sat in solitary splendour on the white lacquered sideboard. Eveline had got rid of the clutter of old lampshades, books, balls of string and tangled ping-pong nets.

Philip picked up the phone on the first ring. "Is everything all right?"

"Does no one else ever call you?" I couldn't help the anger which still rose every time I heard his voice.

"Sorry," he said, "and no."

"Why shouldn't everything be alright?"

"I left a message for you yesterday. You didn't call back."

"No one told me. Did you speak to Tom?"

"So that's where he is. I did wonder."

I had better things to worry about. "Philip, did Tom know about you know what? You know…?" I couldn't give it a name. I couldn't give her a name. I still can't give her a name.

Philip sighed. I could see him taking off his glasses and giving the lens a quick clean while he thought how best to answer.

"Bugger," he said as I heard glass tinkle. "My whisky."

"Since when have you drunk whisky?"

"Since you left," he said bluntly. There was a silence before he started again. "Tom insisted that I tell you — blackmailed me, rather."

"Does he know about the abortion?"

"No, thank God." Philip sounded genuinely horrified at the idea.

"So how did Tom find out you and…?"

"Saw me coming out of a hotel lift."

"Is someone with you at the moment?" I could hear movement in the background.

"With me? No." Philip chuckled. "Only Pepper. She's wagging her tail so hard it's thumping against the cupboard. She can hear your voice."

He started again. "Tom said that if I didn't tell you about… He would. I couldn't have borne that."

"I love you," he said.

'And despite everything, I still love you.' I didn't say that.

Minutes trickled away, unspoken.

"I've got it!" Philip's voice blazed down the line. "He set me up to get you down to France to do up his bloody château. That's what happened. He banked on you leaving me, the bastard."

I couldn't stop the flare of anger scorching back in reply. "He was getting me away from you and for that, I'll be forever grateful."

*

Out in the corridor, a shadow passed by the dining hall's open door. The silence in the house was immense. Eveline's door clicked shut. I was sure it was Eveline's door, but Tom and Eveline hadn't returned. Then I wondered if the man was free of his tree. I wondered if I was mad, going mad, or just getting madder.

When I went to bed, I dreamt of the man in the tree. I was a child and the tree was full of parrots. He was beckoning me to climb up and join him. The man had Eveline's lingering smile. He had her long, long, fingers. I could hear a door slamming somewhere and a light laugh — Eveline's.

Tom's dark bulk loomed over me. "Sis."

There was an urgency — an excitement — in his voice, so I was immediately awake.

"Look." He bent down and unclenched his hand. Cupped in his palm were five little nuggets.

"We found them," he said, his eyes sparkling like the diamonds in the moonlight. "What luck!"

"How?" I asked. "Where?"

He pressed a finger to his lips. The upper part of his face was wreathed in shadow, the light catching his hefty watch and its illuminated dial. Half-past one in the morning. Where had they been?

"Tomorrow," he said. "Sleep tight."

Chapter 39

I smelt that slice of sun, the sharp tang of citrus fruit long before I reached the kitchen. I looked in on Eveline's room on my way down to the kitchen. It was empty, the bed a rumpus of sheets.

Tom was squeezing the oranges with an ancient, hand-operated citrus press which he must have found at the back of a cupboard. I'd never seen it before. He gave a brilliant smile on seeing me.

"Isn't it fantastic? Honestly, It was like looking for a needle in a haystack and then... Hey presto!" He was practically singing with happiness. "You know what this means?"

I looked for a glass. "Where is she?"

"Outside somewhere."

"I spoke to Philip last night."

Tom looked at me askance. "What's up?"

"You tell me."

He stopped squeezing the oranges. He was silent for a second, thinking. Then his face brightened.

"Yes. Sorry. Philip. He left a message for you."

Deftly, Tom halved an orange. "It completely slipped my mind. It was only for you to call him sometime. This business with the diamonds..."

"What's going on?"

"I feel like we've won the lottery and we have, Sis, in a way, the chances of finding them must have been a zillion to one." He smiled broadly. "Some luck, at last."

"Why all the intrigue?"

The smile disappeared. "I don't know what you're talking about."

"Not answering the phone. The guy at the market."

"I'm screening my calls, that's all." His tone was light.

"The chicken stall. What was all that about?"

"Just a bit of heat in London. Nothing for you to be worried about." He poured frothy juice into my glass. "Well?" He waited for my approval.

"It's delicious," I said reluctantly. "So what should I be worried about?"

He looked exasperated, almost angry. "Nothing. Eveline is going back to Paris. I thought you'd be delighted. What's got into you?"

"What's got into me?" For a moment, the pain is real, a sharp stab through the heart. "How come you told Greg about Philip's… before I even knew."

I'd have choked rather than have said the tawdry word.

Carefully, Tom poured himself a glass of orange juice.

"I didn't tell him. I just asked Greg to take care of you. Anyway, deep down you did know. You simply wouldn't acknowledge it." He took a sip.

"That's not true."

"Oh Sis," Tom put down his glass. He moved from away from the counter. "You need a hug."

"Don't you dare."

The space between us crackled with tension.

"How did you find out?"

Tom looked away. "The Fairfield. 6th March this year. 7 o'clock in the morning. Coming out of a lift together. I couldn't believe my eyes, honestly."

He looked at me then, with sorrow in his eyes. "I thought it would blow over. Philip, being an idiot, having a mid-

236

life crisis. So I left it but every time I called — remember? I was trying to persuade you to come down here? You sounded increasingly unhappy. I felt such a heel, knowing."

"So what changed your mind?"

"You. I had to get you out. You were coming apart at the seams. And that husband of yours wasn't doing anything."

"Did you know it was over by then?" I sounded so hectoring, so accusatory.

Shock registered on Tom's face. He hadn't known.

"No," he said slowly, "Philip didn't tell me… I'm sorry, but what matters," he raised his voice again, working himself into righteous anger, "was that he hadn't had the guts to tell you. Let alone tell you it was over. All these years, your husband has taken the moral high ground with me, always managing to make me feel some fly-by-night who can't be trusted. I thought, well, the boot's on the other foot now, mate, and you're making my sister very unhappy. The least you can do is put her out of her misery."

He banged the press down on the orange, practically flattening it.

"I was just glad that I had the château for you."

"You used our situation to get me down here. Why?"

He looked at me, bewildered by my hostility. Then he hunched over the counter, so his face was hidden.

"You're the only person I can trust." His voice was muffled.

"With what Tom?" I shouted. "What aren't you telling me?"

There was despair in his eyes.

My heart broke for him. I had never seen him so vulnerable, my swash-buckling, devil-may-care brother.

I leant into him. I curved my body over him. I sheltered him, like he used to do with me, all those years ago when I was frightened by nightmares in bed at night.

"I've made a mess of things," he said shakily.

"What's happening in London?"

"London," he sighed, straightening himself and me, up. He took a step away, pushed his shoulders back and jutted out his chin. "Good morning!" he beamed. "And how are we today?"

Eveline had just walked through the door, her arms full of flowers and foliage from the garden.

"It's wonderful about your diamonds." I gave her a smile, following Tom's lead.

"Isn't it just?" Tom crowed. "We spent most of the day tramping the woods and then they were there, weren't they?"

She nodded as she put down the flowers. She was proud and happy.

"Hanging off a branch," Tom said. "Snagged on a bush and you don't remember even being in that bit, do you?"

Eveline gave Tom a glance which looked suspiciously like adoration.

"What do you think Sis?" He was practically doing a jig in front of the citrus press, he was so full of his achievement.

"Well done."

"Thank you." He tried to juggle with three oranges but one bounced across the floor. Eveline picked it up and handed it back which he took, with a bow, as if he was on stage at the Royal Variety. He gave Eveline a glass of the juice.

"Is it okay Sis, to take the car again? I'm going to take Eveline to the train." He watched her anxiously as she drank.

All his talk and I still was completely taken by surprise. I looked at Eveline.

"You're not going are you?"

Eveline smiled. "It's time for me to go back to Paris."

"But what about your brother? What about Claudine?"

She looked at me as if I were quite mad.

"I don't want to see her. What would a cleaning woman," those words were said with such haughtiness, "know about my brother?"

"But…"

She put up a trembling hand. "No."

She scooped the flowers off the table and fled the room.

All Tom did was watch.

"Well, that's that then. I'll take her to the station."

"No it's not. What did you say to her?" I was furious that, once again, all my plans were being thwarted.

"She doesn't want to go. You should be pleased. Don't you want her to leave?"

"She can't bottle it now. Not after everything we've been through. I won't let her!"

Tom, too, was angry. "You're only thinking of yourself. Not her. Just because you've got a bee in your bonnet about that brother of hers, fact or fiction…"

I took a deep breath to compose myself. "I need to know what happened," I told him calmly. I couldn't tell him that I was frightened of being forever haunted by the man in the tree if I didn't discover what had happened to Eveline's brother.

"Be it on your own head!" Tom shouted after me as I took the stairs.

She was in the hall. The flowers were spread across the chest so that she could select which stem to put where in the empty vase.

"I thought I'd do this for you before I go." Her hands were still trembling.

I opened out my arms. Slowly, she turned into them. "I can't do it."

"You can. You are so near to finding out the truth."

"I don't know if I can bear to know."

There was man in front of us, a man in a tree, the branches of which were half-obscuring Eveline.

"You have to find out. Get him justice if necessary."

I could have squeezed the breath out of her, I was hugging her so tightly. "If you don't you'll spend the rest of your life wondering."

"You betrayed him once." It was a terrible thing to say.

She cried then, great wracking sobs and I held her, like she was a sapling blowing in the wind.

"Okay," she said. "Okay."

We went back down to the kitchen to tell Tom.

Tom turned on me, hissing with anger as soon as Eveline left the kitchen to retrieve her brother's photograph from her suitcase.

"What the hell do you think you're up to? You're just fuelling the girl's fantasies."

I stood my ground. "I don't understand you. One moment you're forcing Philip to tell me the truth and the next moment, you're trying to stop Eveline from finding out the truth about her brother."

He thumped his glass down with such force it cracked. "Don't say I didn't warn you. You're playing with fire." His laugh was mirthless. "It's not as if she hasn't already started a bonfire."

Before I could think of a retort, Greg entered the kitchen. Apart from a perfunctory "good morning" he said nothing. He looked as if he had been up all night worrying. He didn't offer Tom a reason for being late and Tom was too preoccupied to ask for one. Instead, he poured Greg a glass of orange juice and insisted that Greg accompany us to Claudine's.

"I don't know what use I'll be." Greg was reluctant.

Tom snorted. "Just having another man around may be useful."

Tom's mood was so thunderous that neither Greg nor I dared challenge him.

Tom drove. Greg, sitting beside Eveline, bounced up and down in the back, green at the gills.

Valerie was surprised to see us.

"You must be Tom Braid."

Tom's mood had changed. He was back to his old, familiar self.

"Yes," he grinned. "The brother."

Before Valerie could say anything more, Tom strode past her, into the sitting room, marvelling at the glorious panorama of her garden.

"Have you fully recovered from your fainting fit?" Valerie asked Eveline. She gave Greg a cursory nod of acknowledgement. He looked uncomfortable.

Valerie's sitting room was very pretty, very English in style, the sofa and two chairs covered in chintz and a coffee table laden with books.

Tom was all charm. "Do you mean to say you do this all by yourself?" He shook his head disbelievingly. Tom wouldn't have known a lavender plant from a sunflower. "How long have you been here?" He was flattering

241

Valerie. Greg had already told him that Valerie has lived in the area longer than any of the other British.

Behind Tom's back, Greg rolled his eyes at me and I smiled.

Valerie succumbed. "Would you like to see the garden?"

"Love to." Tom opened one of the French doors. "After you."

Eveline, Greg and I were left standing in Valerie's sitting room unsure if the invitation extended to us. I could see my father's last novel on top of a narrow pile of books and when I looked more closely the four beneath were his as well. It was my father's entire oeuvre and the slightness of his life's work dismayed me.

"Are you lot coming out?" Valerie called.

It felt even more awkward in the open air. Too tense to engage with anyone, Eveline wandered off, down a path.

Greg and I were totally superfluous to the conversation as Tom and Valerie focussed solely on each other. She grew visibly more attractive by the minute, cheeks flushed, eyes sparkling.

"Sis, here," Tom told Valerie, "wants to find out more about the château's very recent history. She has this wild idea," he grinned over to me, "about going to see the former cleaner. I don't think it's a good idea."

Valerie bristled, ever so slightly. It was her suggestion after all, to go to see Claudine. "I think it's an excellent idea."

Tom's face showed his disappointment.

"I'll come with you if you like," Valerie offered, as if to soften the blow.

"I know where she lives," Greg said mischievously.

"Her accent's very thick," Valerie said icily. "I don't think your French will be adequate."

Tom led Valerie down to the shadiest corner of the garden, out of earshot. Greg gave a derisive snort. He and I made a pretence of being interested in a plant with small daisy-like flowers. He rubbed the leaves roughly, releasing the pungent smell of aniseed.

Tom was standing at the end of a path with Valerie, telling her about Eveline's brother. Valerie listened closely, occasionally glancing over to where Eveline was standing.

"I've had her, you know," Greg gave a curt nod in Valerie's direction. "I can't stand the woman. Breakfast, lunch and dinner. She wore me out."

"I thought you didn't go with married woman?" I teased.

"She's divorced." Greg's reply was very serious.

Tom saw us, watching.

"What's the big secret?" he called.

"You tell us," I joked, delighted that Tom had finally accepted that we were going to go to Claudine's.

Chapter 40

Valerie sat in front.

As we rattled along, Tom ignored the rest of us, squashed behind. I was in the middle. The other two looked as if they were about to fall sleep. Greg's eyelids flickered. Eveline's eyes were closed, her head bumping against the window.

"All this fuss because of that bullet you found," Tom grumbled to Valerie.

"True," Valerie replied hesitantly. "But the chances of the bullet I found matching your guest's must be pretty remote."

There were a couple of hills between Valerie's house and the village. The château was built on the lower of the two. We climbed up the higher hill, the one furthest away from the village — but very accessible, across wooded terrain, for the château.

"This cleaning woman..." Tom murmured.

"Claudine?" Valerie was pert.

"How long did she work for them?"

"How many years did they own the château? Ten? She'd have been there nine, at least."

"So was she daily?"

Valerie gave her light, tinkling laugh. "Let's ask her, shall we?"

"Sis." Tom wrenched up the handbrake. Both Greg and Eveline opened their eyes with the car's sudden stop.

"I'm not so sure that this is a good idea, digging into the past."

"That is a mistake so many people make," Valerie began earnestly. Unbeknownst to him, Tom had lit on one of her pet themes.

Greg cleared his throat. "The sooner we find out what happened — if anything happened — the better really for all concerned." He glanced over at Eveline. I could feel her body stiffen but she looked ahead, her profile unmoving.

Tom released the handbrake and we moved again. His hair shone greasily, polished with the sweat that was dripping down the nape of his neck.

Dappled trunks of trees glided past as the car strained against the steep slope.

We abandoned the car half way up the woods and walked the last kilometre to Claudine's. Flies swarmed around us, buzzing at our faces. Tom found a stick and whacked back bits of dry undergrowth.

"You're not worried about snakes, are you Sis?"

"Are you?" Valerie turned round, curious for any snippet of information.

I lied.

The track was rough, uphill, and littered with flaky animal droppings which made my shoes slip.

"Are you sure this is the right way?" I called out to Valerie who was being coy out in front with Tom. I was walking with Eveline coaxing her along. She looked more anxious with every step. Greg brought up the rear.

"I come here in the autumn," Valerie called back without stopping, "to search for truffles. The terrain's not so difficult then."

245

"Truffles?" Tom was full of interest. Already, I could see him shipping boxes and boxes of truffles from Château de Tom to smart London restaurants. I shut my ears to Valerie's voice droning on and on.

My body felt, after the sex with Greg, as if it had been run over by a double-decker bus. It had been the first time in such a long time.

The path continued relentlessly upwards. Finally, we caught up with Tom and Valerie in the thickest part of the woods.

"Here," Valerie proffered a small, brown bottle. "Put a dab or two on your temples."

"What is it?"

"Something to calm you and Eveline down. You both look so tense. Don't argue."

Tom watched with amusement as I did as she said, before handing the bottle to Eveline.

I could have almost enjoyed that part of the walk, out of the sun, if it hadn't been for Greg, bursting into occasional snatches of nursery rhymes like 'Twinkle little star'.

"Don't you think '*Frère Jacques*' more appropriate?" I asked him. "Since we're in France?"

Eveline gave a slight smile.

"Not for much longer," he said starting to whistle 'Oh what a beautiful morning' with the two notes at his disposal.

"Shut up Greg."

"I have a daughter," he told Eveline.

She didn't respond.

I asked what was her name.

"Like what's Eveline's?" He joked.

For a moment, she looked as if she was going to run back down the hill. I glared at Greg.

246

"Jess," he said, grinning.

He was happy. How I wished for Eveline to have happiness, to find a way of living without self-recrimination about her brother.

I honestly thought that we were doing the right thing in going to Claudine's. I still think it was right. There was no other option.

Chapter 41

It would have been impossible to find Claudine's house without Valerie's help. It blended, I can imagine an English estate agent's description, 'beautifully with its surroundings'. It was a pitiful hovel, made up of a concoction of wood and odds and sods salvaged from building sites, in a clearing in the woods.

"It used to be a woodman's hut," Valerie said, her voice low. She, like the rest of us, was conscious of the sudden stillness and wary of disturbing it. Eveline hung back by the trees with Tom and Greg. I beckoned her and with slow, reluctant steps she joined Valerie and me. I caught her hand in mine. I gave her an encouraging smile. "Almost over."

Valerie banged on what passed for a door, the sheet of corrugated iron.

"Claudine!" Crows wheeled, cawing raucously above the trees hemming the clearing. "Are you there?"

Valerie tried again. "Claudine!"

We heard shuffling noises. The sheet of iron was scraped back — enough for a shrivelled face to appear in the gap, eyes blinking furiously. Instantly, I recognised the old woman who accosted me in the kitchen. Valerie spoke rapidly, explaining who we were. The eyes lingered on me. I blushed. I could tell she remembered being chased down an avenue three months before. Eveline was unflinching under the scrutiny.

Valerie indicated the edge of the clearing. Tom and Greg stood sheepishly as they too, were examined. The old lady seemed to recognise Greg. Her eyes lingered over Tom until he got impatient with the scrutiny.

He broke the silence. "This is ridiculous. I've had enough."

He started back through the trees, hands in his pockets.

"You can't chicken out now Tom! I'll never forgive you!"

He stopped, the set of his shoulders resolute. He tilted his head to look up at the trees. After what seemed like an age, he turned and retraced his steps. "I warn you, nothing good will come of this."

"Tell Claudine," I said hurriedly to Valerie, "that we'd like to know a little more about the Kumonos."

As soon as I uttered the name, the old lady tried to shut the makeshift door. I blocked it with my foot.

Valerie shot me a look of pure exasperation. "Thanks. I was getting to the sons." I realised then that she had been very careful not to mention the name.

I hurried over to Tom. "You've got money."

"Christ's sakes. No."

"Yes. The sooner she talks, the sooner we can get out of here."

He held my gaze as he pulled his wallet out of his back pocket.

Claudine watched the money in my hand. Her voice was vociferous, rasping with effort. Eveline evidently understood the old lady. Her body was taut, poised for flight. I put my arm around her waist.

The rheumy eyes looked up at Eveline. The old head nodded slowly.

"Do you understand what she's saying?" Greg asked no one in particular.

"She says," Valerie said breathlessly, "that the Kumonos killed her dog before they left. They slit its throat and left it to die in the sun as a warning for her not to talk."

"But the Kumonos are dead," I said. "Doesn't she know?"

Valerie translated. The wizened face relaxed. Tom, Greg, Eveline and I waited. Claudine responded.

"She says," Valerie relayed, "that she knows nothing, but what she knows she'll tell you if she has the money first."

All of us, even Claudine, looked at Tom. His expression didn't need any translation. Muttering, Claudine began to heave the door closed again.

"What's she saying?" I asked Valerie.

"She's calling Tom a bastard, amongst other things."

"Okay," I blocked the door again. "Tell her she wins."

"I'll wait for you out here," Tom said. "I've given over my money to that old witch. I'm not taking any more insults."

Tom stayed outside. Greg, Valerie, Eveline and I — we took up all the available space in the cramped interior, jostling for position around Claudine who sat at the only table on the only chair in the centre of the shack.

An oblong of sunlight fell through the open doorway. The rest of the hovel was in shadow — and it smelt of the rank odour of a life lived without recourse to fresh running water. Claudine ignored us, hunched over the banknotes fanned out across the table. They looked lovely: pink, crisp and clean under her misshapen fingers. I found Eveline's hand, slippery with perspiration, and held it.

"Could you tell her for us please," I asked Valerie, "that we're looking for the brother of a friend of ours who disappeared while staying at the château."

Valerie's voice was cajoling. Other than a sharp glance at Eveline, it was as if Claudine wasn't hearing her, that we didn't exist, that we weren't crowded around the table, waiting.

I had no choice. "Tell her that he was a guest of the Kumonos."

Claudine stiffened and her frightened eyes looked up again at Eveline, searching her face. The silence seemed to last forever.

Then, for a moment, we were cast into semi-darkness. Tom blocked the doorway before taking the ten or so steps to Claudine's table. He pushed between Greg and Valerie. He started bundling the notes together.

"I've had enough of this game."

Slowly, unsteadily, Claudine levered herself to her feet. Her face swam close to Tom's, the wrinkled mouth pouring out harsh invective. Eveline's whole body stiffened. I held her hand steady.

"What's she saying?" I had to shout to be heard by Valerie.

"She's cursing him."

There was no point in asking this bitter old woman anything. Tom was right. It was useless.

"Leave it Tom!" My voice rang out. "We'll go."

Claudine clutched him by the forearm. He could easily have pushed her away but it was as if he was mesmerised, a snake under the spell of the snake-charmer. He stood stock-still, his face redder and redder. Claudine ranted on, while Valerie watched her, open-mouthed and wide-eyed.

Eveline shoved her brother's photograph into Claudine's hand. Claudine barely gave it a glance and then something in the young man's face attracted her attention. Abruptly she stopped shouting. She sank back into her seat, peering at the photo a couple of inches from her nose. After a couple of minutes she started to talk again, her voice much softer, the tone laden with regret.

"She says," Valerie again, "that there were other young men who were guests of the Kumonos. They lounged around, getting in her way."

"And?" My throat was as dry as a bone.

"And what?" Valerie riposted.

Eveline shuddered and leant into me. I supported her. Claudine gave us both a sharp glance.

"This is insane," Valerie muttered.

Addressing me, a torrent of French spewed out of Claudine's mouth.

"She doesn't know anything," Valerie reported.

"Right that's it. Let's get out of here." Tom said.

"Come off it, she must." My voice pleaded. Holding on to Eveline, I was becoming very hot and sweaty.

"People came and went all the time. It was very difficult to clean the château, a security man stood over her as she did her work. The young men were nice enough, but careless, and as for the Kumono brothers — " Valerie imitated Claudine's hand gestures, "she doesn't like to speak about them. They were monsters."

Eveline was trying to pull away from me. I held her tight. I had to go on. For her sake, I had to finish what I had started.

"Tell her," I asked, "that we found a cupboard full of all sorts of old clothes, all beautifully ironed."

Another volley of French from Claudine. "She says," Valerie said, "that the Kumonos told her to tidy the château, after they'd gone. So she ironed the clothes and put them in the large cupboard in the room off the archway. She was too frightened to disobey them after her dog."

"The ironing boards," I said. "So many. Why?"

Valerie's eyes widened. "The Kumonos had a thing about ironing boards. Often as not she had to use a fresh ironing board as the sons had a habit of dismantling them."

"Hells bells," Greg whispered.

"So bloody what!"

"Shut up Tom. Just shut up."

I took a deep breath. "What happened to the young man in the photograph? What did they do to him? Why was he never seen again?"

"Christ, Sis!" Tom looked horrified.

"We all know what they were capable of!"

Valerie was also angry. She was angry with me, practically spitting with rage. How dare I, she shouted, nothing like that ever went on at the château. The village would have known. It would never have been allowed, what I was implying...

Eveline struggled to release herself from my grip. I held fast.

"You're the one who told me about the naked man in the tree."

"He was a druggie," Valerie said flatly.

"So they told you. You said yourself something about a hunt being on."

Eveline gave a strangled cry. She wrenched herself out of my grasp and ran out the door.

Greg swore, turned on his heel and chased after her.

Valerie's eyes were wild. "For God's sakes," she whimpered. "This is sick."

Greg's shouts for Eveline grew fainter and fainter. In the silence, all we could hear was Valerie's breath heaving. I felt ill. I couldn't believe how unthinking I'd been in front of Eveline.

"That was despicable." Tom's voice was bitter. "I warned you. You've given her nightmares for the rest of her life."

Claudine paid us no attention. Her concentration was absolute, the photograph a couple of inches away from her nose. The bespectacled young man smiled up at Claudine, trustingly, trusting in his future. A light breeze floated through the shack, bringing some relief. We waited. Eventually she looked up.

"They used the ironing boards as makeshift crucifixes and the irons like branding irons…" Valerie put her hands to her ears, tears in her eyes. "This is unbearable."

Tom started to crack his fingers, one by one. The sounds were little puffs of gunshot in the stillness. Claudine looked at him sharply. Tom stopped, but she kept on looking, examining his features — almost as if she were seeing him for the first time.

"I'll wait outside," he said but Claudine gripped his arm again, like before.

She looked back down at the photo. She looked up at Tom.

"I assure you it's not me," he said, trying to make a joke.

Claudine started to speak.

"He tried to leave," Valerie's voice faltered. "So they punished him by taking away his clothes. Then they let him escape again," Valerie clapped her hand to her mouth, "so that they could hunt him for sport."

Valerie had to lean in, until her ear was level with the old woman's mouth. "They were terrible men. They used anything lying around."

Valerie straightened up so suddenly that she almost hit Tom on the chin.

"I can't go on."

Neither could I. I couldn't listen anymore. I wanted to find Eveline, to tell her how sorry I was.

Tom angrily thumped on the table, sending most of the money spiralling to the floor. "I have never heard so much crap. What does the old crone take us for? Mugs?"

Gabbling incoherently, Claudine grabbed at Tom, battering his chest with her feeble hands. Shocked, he backed away from her, his hands up. She was telling him in no uncertain terms to get out of her house. Then she turned to Valerie and fired off a barrage of French. She sank back into her chair, laid her old head on the table and wept.

"Is it true?" Valerie addressed Tom, who was blocking out the light again, in the doorway.

"I don't know what you're on about."

"That you were at the château when that man disappeared?"

"I've never heard anything so ridiculous."

"She says you were a guest."

"She's a mad old woman." He had backed completely out of the hovel and was standing in the sunlight.

"It's the way you crack your fingers. It drove her wild all weekend. You saw her scrubbing out the bloodstains. You know what happened to the young man. They strung him up."

For a split second, I saw a little boy who had been found out.

"She is totally and utterly mistaken, I assure you." He strode back into the shack and over to the table.

I'll never forget that moment. I felt cold, wretched and totally alone. I watched the old woman shrink away from Tom as he bent down and picked up the notes from the floor.

He placed the money on the table.

"Tell her I'm sorry." He addressed Valerie but looked at me. He knew he had no place to hide but nevertheless he tried. "I haven't set eyes on the château, except in photographs, until a couple of days ago. I've never been here before — ever," he enunciated each word with great care.

"Sis here," he said, smiling at me, "will vouch for me."

Claudine grabbed the bunch of notes and shoved them into his hand. She spat at him. Then one by one, she started to curse us and it felt extraordinary that the world as we knew it hadn't ended. Sunlight continued to fall through the open door. The cawing of crows continued unabated in the trees.

Chapter 42

We slipped and stumbled down the track. Tom was out in front with Valerie, a hand pressed solicitously against the small of her back.

The idea that he would spend a weekend holed up in an uncomfortable château, in very provincial France with the sons of a dictator, was ridiculous. Ridiculous, the word rolled through my mind, making me feel surer of myself, that somehow the old lady was mistaken.

Red-faced and panting, dripping with sweat, Tom and Valerie eventually waited for me where the path levelled out. I avoided Tom's gaze.

"I am so thirsty." Valerie's voice quavered.

"You're not the only one," I said shortly, focussing on the shimmer of heat in front of us.

She continued on a rising note of hysteria. "How that woman could make such things up!"

Valerie huddled into Tom's chest. Tom's eyes bored into me over Valerie's bent head.

"You were right," I said, looking at Tom finally. "It was a bad idea."

Relief shone from his eyes. "That's okay," he said, accepting what he took to be an apology.

"She's made completely unfounded allegations before. A few years back, she said three boys raped her," Valerie muttered into his chest.

"Poor lady," Tom murmured. "Anything for attention."

Finding Eveline was foremost in my mind. "We've got to get back to the car."

Valerie lifted her face towards Tom. "The sons did have guests though. I used to see parties of them in the woods occasionally, hunting." She gave a long shudder. "Perhaps she mistook you for someone else?"

Tom eased her away from him.

"Well, that would be difficult," Tom said jollily. "As I wasn't here." He started down the track again.

I thought Valerie's expression looked calculating as she watched his retreating back before following him.

Halfway to the car, Tom let Valerie go on ahead and waited for me.

"Sis…" he said.

I batted his hand away. "This isn't the place or time."

Valerie called back. "We should have met the others by now."

"I expect," Tom answered Valerie soothingly, "that Greg has found Eveline and they're making their way back to the château."

Valerie nodded agreement. "We can pick them up en route."

I insisted on driving my car.

Reluctantly, Tom handed over the keys. He sat with Valerie in the back. I drove recklessly, childishly, bouncing over the potholes. I didn't care if my brother's head bashed against the car roof. The harder, the better.

Greg's tall spare figure moved into view, trudging along the road back into the village. I sped up and drew alongside.

"Where's Eveline?"

"Isn't she with you?" He ducked his head into the interior to check.

"Where could she have got to?" Valerie wailed.

"She hared off track and I lost her." He slipped in beside me.

"What do you think you're doing?" Valerie asked as I embarked on a three-point turn to go back to the woods. "I've got an aromatherapy client in half-an-hour."

I ignored her.

"It's all very well for you. I need the money. I can't afford to let my customers down."

"Let's get her home, Sis," Tom's voice was calm.

Greg grunted his agreement.

We drove on in silence, my thoughts focused on a distraught girl running through the woods, out of her mind with anguish. The man in the tree lodged himself in the back of my brain. "Sorry," I said softly. "Sorry. Sorry."

"Let's pay a little more attention to the driving," Tom shouted.

"Hells bells!" Greg swore as I swerved out of the way of an oncoming lorry.

"I'll tell the police," Valerie announced as we drew up to her house. "I'm the only one who speaks French."

Tom helped her out. "They won't thank you for wasting their time. All we have to go on is an old witch's ravings."

"There's the silver bullet."

"A bullet," he shrugged contemptuously and steered her towards her front door. "Let's just check our facts before involving the police."

They disappeared into the house together.

"I hope he's not going to be long," I said. "Every minute not searching for her is a minute wasted. God knows where she is."

"And the cow doesn't even invite us in for a drink of water. I could kill for a beer."

259

"It's unforgiveable what I said back there."

"Listen," Greg said. "Don't blame yourself. You've done your best. You've fought her corner when others wouldn't."

"Justice," I said, thinking back.

"What's this about the police?"

He listened in stunned silence. I told him everything except Claudine's assertion that Tom had been at the château. It would have been too painful to watch Greg process his disbelief.

"That fucking door," he said eventually. "We should never have opened it."

"It was all there in front of us even before." I blinked back tears. "The clues were there all along."

I remembered a detail which made me want to retch. "Those boxes and boxes of tongue scrapers, what were they for?"

He looked green.

"And," I continued remorselessly, "you took the hook out of the ceiling."

"Don't," he held up his hand.

"You knew about the Kumonos. Didn't you think?"

"I did my job. I wasn't paid to think. And aren't you forgetting something?"

I didn't know what he meant.

"Your brother. What does he know that he's not telling you? He got the place at a knock-down price. I mean why? Something stinks with the whole set-up."

"You're working for him."

"I've got to eat."

A cold finger ran down my spine. Years before Tom had offered Philip a job which Philip refused, saying that he wasn't prepared to end up in jail. I hadn't asked Philip why. I was just furious that he'd snubbed Tom.

"Actually," Greg said, "I've got nothing against your brother. He's a nice man but I'm going to go home, you know, back to Cheryl. You don't need me now, not with Tom around."

He gave my knee a sympathetic rub.

"What about Eveline?"

"She needs more help than I'll ever be able to give."

Tom reappeared grinning broadly. He tossed me a bottle of water, another to Greg. "With compliments from Valerie."

"Sorted," he said to me, sotto voce, as he slipped into the seat that Greg had vacated. Greg was now sitting in the back. Tom buckled himself in. "Valerie has agreed not to say anything to the police. What about you, Greg?" He looked over his shoulder. "Do you think the police should be involved?"

"I don't go near the police."

"Good man. I thought so. First things first, we've got to find Eveline." His glance at me was oblique and pointed as if the situation was wholly my fault. If I hadn't allowed Eveline to stay with me, if I hadn't allowed myself to become as obsessed as she about her brother, if I hadn't been so desperate to rid myself of the man in the tree — if I had done just what Tom had asked and revamped the interior, the slightly uncomfortable atmosphere would have been painted over and relegated to the shadows. We could have lived with it. I had lived with it, before Eveline came.

My brother's touch was reptilian. I couldn't bear him next to me. I had to go home soon as well, back to

London, and I would ask Eveline to come with me. It was the least I could do.

Chapter 43

We arranged to reconvene within the hour.

Tom took the track which led to Claudine's. Greg went downhill to the left and I picked my way slowly uphill to the right, glad of the canopy shielding me from the sun. For the first time ever, out in the open, I forgot about the possibility of a snake.

Our shouts for Eveline echoed each other. They were met with a stillness, underpinned by birdsong and the crackle of leaves being crushed by my feet. I couldn't stop myself from thinking about Tom when he had turned up, without warning, at the château. I'd needed explanations and I couldn't ask the questions. Everything he had said I'd accepted at face value. I'd been too frightened of the truth.

After a half-hour or so of futile searching, I came across Tom sitting on the trunk of a fallen tree, a couple of hundred metres from Claudine's shack.

He lifted his head up at my approach. "There's no use, she's not here — or if she is, she doesn't want to be found."

"I never thought you'd lie to me." My voice choked. "You knew all along where the stables were, where the wine was kept. You'd seen the gym before."

I couldn't have gone more than five paces before Tom grabbed me from behind. Roughly, he spun me round. His expression was so calm and so remote that it frightened me.

"I couldn't tell you. I could go to prison if it was ever found out that I had dealings with them."

"So you were here."

"Not when that boy was supposed to be. I swear it. I never set eyes on him. Do you think I could have stayed..." He scratched the crook in his elbow so frantically that he drew blood.

He was a little boy again, who got into terrible scrapes through his own fault.

I wanted to believe him with all my heart. "No," I said. "No. Of course not."

"They were ghastly," he pleaded. "Spoilt brats. I was the butt for their practical jokes. Infantile. I mean, a dog's turd in the bed? But murder, here in France?"

I giggled with relief. At last, I knew he was telling the truth. "I found it, the turd sitting on a pile of crockery, shoved under a cupboard. I thought it was real."

He laughed out loud and the tension between us evaporated. "You are a one, sometimes, Sis!"

"So the old lady did know you?" I was still anxious for the whole truth.

He shrugged his shoulders. "Maybe. Though I can't recall ever seeing her."

And, as if in response, a low keening lifted on the air. It freaked us both — a sound so desolate, it felt like a call for the dead to rise from the grave. I was rooted to the ground, the hairs rising on the back of my neck. Tom grabbed me by the elbow. Swiftly he propelled me away from the forlorn little hovel with its old woman whose life was mired in her past.

I stopped us halfway down the path. "We can't tell Eveline. It's too dreadful."

He agreed. "It would break her heart. No point in mentioning the lies about me, either."

Greg was waiting by the car. He looked upset and disgruntled. "No joy," he said. "I'd laugh if she is at the house."

Chapter 44

Back at the château, Tom parked in the shade. The house looked as tranquil as ever, the soft brick lit by the spun gold of a Provençal sun. The rows of windows were precisely aligned. The roof was in place. A late rose provided a cloud of pink by the archway. The weathervane had swung round. It pointed north, towards England.

The men searched the grounds while I checked the house. If she was nowhere to be found, they would comb the woods behind. As Greg said, she could have sprained an ankle.

I remember how, after the harsh sun, the cool of the archway fell around me like a cloak.

I checked the locked room, the furniture repository. Nothing. The kitchen too was still, the shadows motionless, pinned to the walls.

I took the kitchen stairs. In the hall, light from the huge window spilt across the floor. I went down the short dark corridor to Eveline's room. I knocked on the door, hoping for a soft voice to bid me 'enter'. I opened it, half-anticipating a slight silent figure curled up on the bed. I was met with the ordered silence of an empty, tidy room. She hadn't been back.

Tom and Greg were sheltering in the shade of the Cyprus tree. "No joy?"

I shook my head.

Tom waved his mobile at me.

"Ring me if she appears."

"I'll come with you."

"Could you make some food? If we find her, she'll be starving. I know I am."

Almost an entire day had passed since breakfast. I was glad to have something practical to do to occupy myself — to stop the thoughts whirling around my brain about Eveline and her brother, my brother, the sad little boy who had lost his father, and the Kumonos.

The phone rang and I ran into the dining hall, buoyed by the hope that Greg and Tom has already found Eveline. What luck!

"Tom? Have you found her?"

"Hello? Hello?" There was someone. There was the rustle of someone's breath, like someone breathing through leaves of a tree. I waited, listening, the receiver pressed hard to my ear.

"Tom Braid?" A broad West Country accent barked.

"Who's calling?"

A chuckle gusted down the line. "Colin Wareing. I've called enough times."

"Can I take a message?"

Another chuckle. "I've left him one."

There were thirty-five incoming messages: five from Tom on the night of the storm, sounding more and more desperate, urging me to return his calls; two from Philip although one message wasn't a message at all — it was the conversation we had when Philip told me that the General didn't have a daughter; ten were from Tom's secretary, sounding increasingly fraught; and all the others were from a journalist on an English broadsheet who has the same voice as the man who has just called the château twice. He wanted Tom's 'side of the story' as a matter of urgency. I deleted them all.

267

The phone started up again and I waited for the outgoing message to click into action and when I heard the voice — presumably a Kumono son's — I couldn't believe that I had ever found it attractive. I deleted it mid-flow. Whoever rang the château now, would receive a beep, but no outgoing message.

The phone continued to ring for an hour or more, starting up again as soon as it rang out — I went back down to the kitchen, going back up and down the stairs constantly, checking for messages.

Tom came back alone, completely despondent. Greg, he said, had decided to return to the caravan.

The day in the woods had ravaged Tom's skin. I rubbed cream into his hands and bound them tight with the crêpe bandage from the first aid box, leaving only the tips of his fingers and his thumbs free. He waved his white paws and I laughed and then stopped — shocked that I had laughed.

I uncorked the wine. "We should go to the police."

"With what? Even if we knew her name, she's an adult."

I'd prepared pasta and made a tomato sauce with a tin of tomatoes. Tom sniffed at it and told me to add some capers. He fished a tin of black olives out of the back of a cupboard.

"Are there any anchovies do you know? Pasta puttanesca."

The phone rang and Tom started for the stairs two at a time.

I called him back. "She doesn't have the number here. It will be a man called Wareing, Colin Wareing."

All the energy drained out of him in an instant. He clutched the banisters, whey-faced.

"Who is he?" His reaction alarmed me.

He looked at me dazed. Then he fumbled for in the pocket of his shorts and withdrew his mobile.

"Fuck me." He laughed.

"What's the joke?"

"I had it on silent and no vibration. Look."

He came back down the stairs to show me. The phone upstairs rang off.

The screen on Tom's mobile was chock-a-block with missed calls. He pressed the button to switch it off and tossed it into an empty paint can on the dresser. "Stuff it. The bastard's found me. God knows how." He said his P.A. wouldn't betray him. "No one else knows about this place."

Philip does, I thought, as I dished up the pasta and poured out the wine.

All Tom said was that the journalist had been nosing around for years for dirt on him. If the banks hadn't stopped lending on account of the financial crash, he would have been alright. He talked so fast that I found it difficult to follow him.

He grew visibly more frustrated with my lack of comprehension. He looked at me as if I was an idiot.

"It's all gone! Up in smoke. Caput." He waved his bandaged hands.

The employees would lose their jobs but he hadn't one jot of sympathy for the shareholders. "What's that warning Sis? Your financial investment can go down as well as up?"

I felt a surge of anger. I had persuaded Philip to invest in Braid Industries out of loyalty to me.

Tom tried to tackle his pasta but the fork and spoon slipped from his hands. I cut up it for him.

"I suppose me having to come down here was the start of the rot. You know I even had to take the plane to see those goons?"

"What was so urgent?"

"A deal that saved the company for the next five years. It was a business meeting Sis. The writing, in hindsight, was already on the wall."

"So why take on the château?"

"I was given it for free. The new government owes us money. It would have gone into the administrator's black hole. So I took it. Greed, madness, call it what you will. I knew by then that I'd need a bolthole.

He hadn't taken the taxi all the way through France for me after all. "No more talking, Tom. I've had enough."

Tom gave me a long hug before he turned to go down the corridor to his room. "We'll find Eveline tomorrow."

And upstairs in my turret room I saw a hump in my bed. The man in the tree was sleeping on his side, turned towards the wall. I was consumed with rage. Stealthily, I picked up the pillow discarded on the floor. I leant over, pillow raised, and then a hand reached up and gripped my arm. I lost my balance and toppled onto the mattress. Screaming for Tom, I thumped and pummelled while I was struck and scratched in retaliation.

Tom manhandled me, hoisting me bodily off the mattress. "What the hell do you think you are doing?"

Eveline sat bolt upright in my bed, gasping for breath, her eyes dark shadows.

"Oh my God!" I cried, "I thought you were the man in the tree!"

She said nothing, her chest heaving.

Tom knelt beside her. He cradled her in his arms. "Everything is going to be alright," he said soothingly, repeating it over and over again. Eventually she settled back on the mattress. He drew the sheet over her shoulders and I followed him down the spiral staircase.

Chapter 45

Tom made cocoa, clumsily. Eventually he became so exasperated with his hands that he ripped off the bandages. He whisked the milk round and round with a spoon. He handed me the mug and then he settled into the chair opposite me, still without a word.

I told Tom how, ever since Valerie mentioned him, the man in the tree had stalked me and hidden himself in my brain.

"It never occurred to me that Eveline would take refuge in my bed."

"But you checked the house?"

"I did, but not my room." Tears trickled down my face.

"You've been cooped up here too long."

I took Eveline's bed because she had mine. Tom lay beside me and, just like old times, held me. I remember burrowing in to him, breathing in the security of his scent. Then in my sleep, the man in the tree came and wrapped his arms around me, telling me that everything would be alright, that soon I could go home, and not to worry too much about Tom. He leant forward to kiss me. I could feel his breath on my lips which was warm and comforting and somehow so very familiar until suddenly I felt that I was drowning in his darkness. I screamed to catch myself awake.

Tom stroked my forehead, his hand as light as a feather, pushing away tendrils of damp hair. My hair was wringing. My pillow wet.

"Darling Sis. I thought you'd grown out of nightmares."

All those years ago, after our father died, only Tom could stop the nightmares. He'd have to climb in my bed and hold me.

Tom lay beside me, his arm crooked around my shoulders. He murmured things, keeping the darkness at bay. I clung onto Tom like he was a life raft but he left, when dawn broke.

When I woke again, Eveline was kneeling on the floor a little way from the bed, sorting through the clothes in her suitcase. She was still in the t-shirt and shorts from the day before. They were filthy. I was horrified to see a long scratch down the side of her cheek.

I sat up. "Did I do that to you last night?"

She touched her face. "This? No. What did you mean about the man in the tree?"

"I am so sorry…"

She stopped me from continuing. "The man in the tree," she repeated, her tone harsher.

I told her only what Valerie told me about the man in the tree. I didn't tell her what Claudine had said.

It was awful enough. Eveline's face grew paler, the shadows under her eyes deeper.

"It's obsessed me," I said, "which is why, last night, when I saw you in my bed…"

"I don't want your pathetic excuses. I want to know what that woman said about my brother."

I was completely panicked. I didn't know what to do for best.

"If you don't tell me, I'll ask her myself."

I told Eveline. I told her because I had no right to be the keeper of the truth. That truth. My voice was clear, strong and detached. If I hadn't told, she would have had to endure more agony searching for half-truths about her brother. I told her so that she could set herself free. I didn't tell her what Claudine had said about Tom.

Her face aged before my eyes. The t-shirt she was holding dropped unnoticed onto the floor.

When I finished, there was a feeling of shock in the room but everything was unchanged — the sun seeped through the drawn curtains, my clothes were still at the end of the bed, the water in the glass on the bedside table, untouched. Everything was unchanged except for Eveline. She looked shrunk. She glanced down at the floor and saw the t-shirt by her feet.

Automatically she bent but instead of retrieving it, she remained crouched on the floor. She wrapped her arms around her head, as if she was shielding herself from physical assault.

I got up off the bed and crouched beside her. I put a tentative hand on her rigid shoulder. She shook my hand off.

"I guessed yesterday," she whispered.

I didn't know how long I stayed with her but it was long enough for my legs to start to cramp and I had to bite my lip to stop crying out. I shifted so that I could sit.

Eventually Eveline looked at me, her pupils large and dark. "I'd hunt them down if they weren't already dead."

She stood up then, abruptly. "I want to be alone."

The pain in my legs was intense. I scrambled to my feet. I glanced back before I closed the door. She'd moved onto the bed, staring into space. The t-shirt was still on the floor.

"I can't bear to think of how much he suffered."

"Listen," I told her with as much vehemence as I could muster. "He's no longer suffering. You have to hold onto that. He's at peace."

Tom came flying into the kitchen while I waited for the kettle to boil. "She's gone from your room." There was panic in his voice.

His stance changed suddenly then, his eyes fastening on a point beyond my shoulder. He reworked his face to give a wide, welcoming smile. "And look who's here!"

I swung round.

Pale and composed but with strain etched in every facet of her face, Eveline ignored my brother's welcome. She took a few more steps into the kitchen.

"Did you get my brother's photograph back from that woman?" The question was directed to me.

We'd forgotten about it. She could tell as much from our expressions. "I'm going to go back."

I didn't think that I could feel any more guilt for what had happened at Claudine's, but I did.

"I'll go," I told her. "It's the least I can do."

Visibly, she relaxed. "It's the only one I have of him."

"Hang on, Sis. Let me. I don't trust that old lady." Tom.

It was my turn to feel relieved. I didn't want to go back up to the woods.

"I'll come with you."

"Hold the fort here."

Tom stood up, stuffing the mobile into his back pocket. He gave Eveline a friendly pat on the arm as he left the kitchen. "Don't worry. I'll get it for you."

I dialled home.

"I've been trying to get hold of you. You're okay?" Philip could hardly contain his anxiety.

"Tom's told me about the business."

275

"How is he?"

"Under a lot of strain."

"They'll be after him you know. He won't be able to stay in France."

"You shouldn't have given that journalist his number."

"No," he sounded troubled. "It was a spiteful thing to do." He didn't know what else to say and I didn't want to make it any easier for him, so for a while we said nothing.

"I'm going to come home soon," I told him, eventually. "When things have calmed down, I'll start checking on flights."

Philip was completely taken by surprise. "What about the car?"

"You do want me to come back?"

"Of course I do. You've no idea…"

"Tom will drive the car over, when he comes."

I heard my car disappearing down the avenue and, as the sound faded, so my fear grew. I hoped that Tom would not lose his temper with Claudine. I reassured myself, thinking that I had never seen Tom raise a hand to anyone — but then I remembered I had.

Chapter 46

Our mother had been dead a year by then, the day of Uncle Mani's funeral. We were in the cemetery, Tom and I, the only ones left. It was a cold February afternoon, with the wind whipping up flecks of snow and the sun sinking behind the blocks of flats on the housing estate nearby.

At first, we couldn't believe what the men were saying. "Our Mam told us that our Dad was shacked up with an English whore," the smaller of the two hissed. There was a sharpness in the silence which followed the insult, before Tom brought the man to the ground, crashing the stranger's head into the concrete path with a sickening crunch.

The man spat a tooth out at Tom's feet. "You're an animal."

"Leave it, Seán," the other brother said. "These people are nothing to us."

*

"Why did you come?" I shouted after them, two tattered figures stumbling through the falling snow.

"To make sure the devil was dead, that's why," one of them shouted back.

"Bastards," Tom said, "fucking bastards."

"They're not the bastards. Did you hear what they said?"

"Don't give me that," Tom's eyes were wild with rage. "No man is ever going to call my mother a whore and get away with it."

We talked long into the night, that night.

"Perhaps we should have asked more questions."

"We were only children."

"I thought they told each other everything."

"She didn't tell him how Dad died."

"How do you know?"

Tom shrugged. "He asked me."

"And?"

"I told him to look at the newspapers of that time. It was for her to tell him." His eyes shifted away from mine. "Besides, I was too young when it happened."

*

In all the weeks I had been at the château, I'd never been down to the lake. I decided to go for a swim. I asked Eveline if she would like to come with me but she said she would wait for Tom to return. She lay on her bed, looking utterly exhausted.

I walked through the gates except there were no gates — the lack of gates would now be Tom's worry, not mine. I went down the hill. I crossed over the bridge. It couldn't have been more than a fifteen minute walk.

Already, family groups had taken all the shade of the trees by the water. There was no shade left for me, so I picked a spot on the gravelly sand of the man-made beach and, using my towel, peeled off my clothes and got into my swimsuit.

A little girl, who couldn't be more than three years old, joined me on the shoreline and solemnly contemplated the water lapping through my toes. I threw a pebble into the lake for her, and we both watched as the water closed over it. She toddled back to the mother who had hoisted herself up onto her elbows to watch us. The woman flopped back onto her back as her child approached. Someone had started to play music, not loud enough for words, but loud enough for a beat.

I sliced my way through the thick water. It was cold and welcome. I could feel the sweat sloughing off my back. I swam out towards the middle where it was deep enough for me not to churn up the muddy bottom.

I looked back towards the shoreline and see the château, perched on top of its hill. The Kumonos' music swirled through the village and yet, according to Valerie, people were too intimidated to complain. I wondered if I would have been as unquestioning — of course I would. I thought about seeing someone in London about the man in the tree. I probed my brain very carefully, but the man in the tree had gone. I felt elated; the obsession had gone. What had happened the night before with Eveline had set me free.

Someone was waving to me from the beach. Greg. His eyes ran over my body in my saggy black swimsuit. I didn't mind. The sex that afternoon had liberated both of us in a funny sort of way.

Thin and spare, he passed me my towel.

"Great to see Eveline is back. What happened to her photo?"

I wrapped the towel around me, suddenly chilled with the sun beating down on my head and shoulders. "What about the photo?"

Greg contemplated the mountains in the distance and when he did answer me, he was abrupt. "I went up to tell you and Tom that I'm leaving. Eveline was having a right old ding-dong at Tom."

"But Claudine did have it!"

He looked at me with disbelief. "Hells bells. How could you leave it behind?"

I put on my shorts and t-shirt over the wet swimsuit. I'd be dry by the time I got back to the château.

"So I'll see you around. I'm catching the ferry tomorrow."

I threw my arms around him, giving his bony frame a tight, damp hug. "Good for you. Is Tom okay with you going?"

"He didn't say. He seemed to have more important things on his mind."

"I'll miss you."

He pulled away from me, pleased. "Gotta go."

He sloped off though the trees, in the direction of the field where he kept his caravan.

But before he'd gone too far, he turned back.

"You don't have any readies on you do you, by any chance?"

"Hasn't Tom paid you?" Greg's wages were due earlier in the week.

"He didn't have any spare cash on him."

"Well that's odd, he had loads yesterday."

"He paid off Claudine, remember?"

"Yes," I was about to tell Greg that she had returned it — and besides I'd only given her half the notes in Tom's wallet but I stopped in time. Greg had gone after Eveline by then and I'd have had to explain why Claudine had refused Tom's money.

I rolled up my towel, gritty with sand, anxious about what was happening back at the château.

Chapter 47

Halfway up the avenue, I heard the sound of a car engine behind me. Valerie drew alongside.

"Tom left his sunglasses yesterday."

"Thanks. I'll take them for him."

She leant over, one hand on the steering wheel.

"Hop in. You're tired."

She was right. I was too tired to argue.

"I feel responsible," she said, shifting the gear into first. "If only I hadn't agreed to come with you…"

"We already knew about the Kumonos."

"Yes," she said, "but there's knowing and knowing isn't there?" She gave a little shudder.

The house, bathed in sunshine, looked serene, idyllic even. There wasn't a sound in the air and the lack of any sort of noise was so eerie, it made me feel even more apprehensive. Valerie parked her car under the cypress beside mine. I couldn't think of a good enough excuse not to invite her in for a cup of tea. I don't know, even now, what I expected to find inside the château. As it was, I needn't have worried.

The kitchen was wreathed in gloom after the sun outside. As soon as he saw us, Tom jumped to his feet. Eveline remained sitting at the table, her face streaked with tears.

"What are you doing here?" All his focus was on Valerie.

She gave her tinkling little laugh, scooping his glasses out of one of her pockets. "I thought you might miss these."

He accepted them, I thought, rather ungraciously. "What happened at Claudine's, Tom?"

He glanced over at Eveline. "Burnt. The old witch burnt the photograph."

"What for?"

"How should I know?" He was trying not to shout. "She's mad."

Eveline laid her face in her arms and started to sob.

"I don't know what to do," he said, gesturing at Eveline.

"I have an idea," Valerie said brightly, beckoning for Tom and me to follow her out to the archway.

"The girl needs closure. She thinks her brother is dead." Valerie's eyes darted from Tom to me and back again. "If we take her to where I found the bullet at least that's somewhere physical, rooted in reality, something not in her head. It might help. What do you think?"

"I'm not sure…" I said.

"It might cancel out the awful image of a hunt," Valerie said tartly.

"Okay," Tom made the decision. "Let's go for it."

Back in the kitchen, Tom declared in a tone which brooked no opposition that we were all going for a drive.

Eveline acquiesced meekly. All her energy had gone. She watched listlessly as Tom threw two spades into the boot of Valerie's car.

I was horrified. "You're not!"

"Of course we bloody well are," he retorted. "We'll do the job properly. There'll be nothing there."

Eveline didn't react. She had completely shut herself off from us.

Valerie's car was even smaller than mine. Eveline and I were crammed, legs at acute angles in the back. Eveline kept her eyes closed, her head knocking against the window. As she drove, Valerie made light, inconsequential conversation with Tom. I could tell from the set of his neck that he was taut with tension.

We took a different route up into the hills than that we took to reach Claudine.

Eveline opened her eyes. "Why are we going into the woods?"

"Tom," I interrupted Valerie, "Eveline wants to know where we are going."

Tom pushed his face past the headrest. "We are going to the spot for you to see where Valerie found the other bullet."

Eveline stiffened.

He turned to face the front again.

Suddenly, patches of sunlight were travelling past on the woodland floor. I grabbed Eveline, not certain if the door was open by intent. Neither of us said a word. Tom was alerted by the sudden rush of air and the flap of the door hanging on its hinges. He jammed his shoulder in the space between the two front seats, and held onto Eveline's thigh.

"What's going on?" Valerie cried. "If I stop, I'll never…" The car swerved dangerously towards a line of trees.

"Just keep your eyes on the road," Tom yelled.

Eveline lunged away from me. She crushed my legs, trying to swing her legs out into the open space but the foot well was too cramped. She strained her upper body instead, her head and shoulders right out of the car, pulling me over with her.

"I can't stop the car!" Valerie shrieked.

"Just keep it going!" Tom shouted.

With great difficulty, I leant across Eveline and using the side pocket, manage to swing the door closed. I heaved myself back into sitting position. Amazingly, the car was still travelling forward. Eveline slumped her head against the window, energy spent.

"Well done, Sis!" There was relief, admiration even in Tom's expression, as he relinquished his hold on Eveline.

"What the hell is going on?" Valerie.

"Eveline just wanted to exit the car," I said.

"What was that all about?" Tom asked Eveline.

Eveline tried to shift away from me. Fat chance. The car was too small. There were beads of perspiration on her upper lip. "I don't want to come. You can't force me to."

Tom gave Eveline a huge reassuring smile. "You'll be okay, we'll look after you. You know that."

We continued our journey in silence, the car bumping over ruts, wary that Eveline might at any moment throw herself out the door. We were so ineffably British. Finally, the car came to a halt.

Valerie heaved the spades out of the boot. "It's a pity Greg's not around."

"He's not coming back," I told her. "He's returning to England."

It was a small pleasure to see surprise register on her face.

Tom took one spade and made me take the other. Valerie marched out in front. We walked for ten minutes or so, me lagging behind as usual. Eveline allowed Tom to hold her hand, allowing him to draw her alongside. She needed comfort, I thought.

Valerie led us to a trickle of water following a course past rocks and logs.

"In the spring this is a stream. I found the bullet lodged over there." She pointed to a spot a few inches from the edge of the bank.

"You're sure?" Tom asked.

"Of course I'm sure," she said, watching me.

"Let's get to it then." Tom glanced round for Eveline who had moved fifteen, twenty feet away, her back pressed up against a tree like she was waiting to be shot. Her eyes were fixed on Tom, as if her life depended on him.

Valerie gathered her skirt around her and hunched on the ground, waiting for us to begin.

"Come on, Sis."

I took one last look at Eveline and start to dig. The earth was hard. Tom and I stood on the blades of our spades, trying to force them in but the deeper we managed to dig, the denser the earth became. Tom grunted with the effort of turning over the soil.

A frog hopped out of nowhere and darted into the undergrowth. For a moment I was petrified. Tom noticed. "No snakes would hang around here, Sis, not with the noise we're making." Valerie wandered off to look for a plant which was good for arthritis. She was going to treat Claudine's arthritis for free.

"Nothing," Tom announced when we had dug a hole about two feet deep. He looked around. "What about over there?" He pointed to a small mound of heaped up earth further down the stream.

We started again, our spades clunking against tree roots, conscious of Eveline's eyes on us. I felt really self-conscious and my arms ached.

285

When Valerie returned with her arms full of plants, she was outraged. "What are you doing? This isn't the spot."

Tom showed her the first of our two-foot holes. Doubt flickered across her face. "Further upstream," she said. She dumped the plants on the ground. "Give me the spade."

Eveline's eyes were still locked on Tom.

"Here." Valerie set to with a manic energy. Tom looked at me over the curve of her back, a suspicion of a smile on his sweaty face. Obediently he bent over the spade again and started shovelling earth.

I left Tom and Valerie to it, and joined Eveline by her tree trunk. There was a strange silence in the wood, like the half-light filtering through the canopy above us. We could hear the whisper of water running across the almost dry bed, the occasional birdsong, and the clink of a blade hitting stone.

Tom eventually called a halt. "It's futile. What did I tell you?" I rejoined him and looked down into the hole.

"I did find the bullet here." Valerie was annoyed.

"You finding another silver bullet was just coincidence," Tom assured her.

"Yes," I said sarcastically, "there are silver bullets sprinkled all over the woods in France."

"My brother died at the château," Eveline's voice carried clearly. "I don't know why you have brought me here."

Fury surged across my brother's face — only to be obliterated by something smooth and obsequious.

I realised then that he was intent only on trying to persuade Eveline that her brother had never been at the château. That she was completely mistaken. It was Tom, not Claudine, who had disposed of Zachary's photograph, just as he had destroyed the young man's passport. Tom was telling lies and it sickened me.

He wrenched his spade from the earth. His anger smouldered all the way back to the car.

Chapter 48

Valerie sped away as soon as Tom had retrieved the two spades from the boot. I left him and Eveline standing on the gravel and went up to my turret room. I had a headache. I was terrified that the man I knew as my brother was someone I didn't recognise at all.

I sat in the lower room and contemplated the grisaille panels of Cupid and Psyche. I could see exactly why Valerie thought that they were not beautiful. The truth was that they weren't. Their value was in their rarity. It was a sleight of mind to endow them with more. I was indulging in my own vanity by calling them beautiful.

Eventually I heard slow steps approach the door. I'd jammed the chair underneath the handle to prevent it from being opened.

"Sis," Tom said. "I've made some supper. Are you coming down?"

I didn't reply.

The handle rattled as it was pressed down. "Let me in."

"You're a liar."

There was a long drawn out expulsion of breath. "Okay. You win. That fucking old woman wins."

"I know you Tom! You burnt the photograph, not Claudine!"

"For God's sakes keep your voice down and let me in!"

I unhooked the chair from the door. I didn't look at Tom. I went back to my place on the stairs.

"I didn't, Sis."

"He was here."

"There isn't an iota of proof."

"Not now."

"There never was. It's bloody hearsay from someone you can't exactly call balanced, can you? Can't you see it from my perspective? I want the kids to come here… don't you understand?"

"What about Eveline?"

"I'll do my best for her. Are you going to come down?"

I shook my head but he didn't leave, as I had expected. He lingered in the doorway.

"Sis, you've got to understand. I wouldn't have done business with them. Had I known what the régime was up to — what we know now."

"But why did you have to come here, to the château?"

"I had to rescue a deal which was going badly wrong and with people like that — like the Kumonos — it all boils down to the relationship they have with you. Price in the end is of little consequence."

"Couldn't you have sent someone else?"

"No one else would do, not for that lot. I had no choice. The steel market was in freefall at the time."

"It was worth it," he said, as if he could tell what I was thinking. "A factory didn't have to close down, saving a couple of hundred jobs. All it was to supply spare parts. Little bits and bobs. I have hundreds of people to keep in employment — and that's hundreds of families, which is a bit of pressure, if you let it get to you. If I could turn the clock back, I would never have supplied them. If I had known what's been uncovered during the last few years, of course…" His voice petered off.

Of course I believed him. "Poor Tom. You were in a bind."

He came over, knelt and squeezed my hand, grateful for the sympathy. "But Sis, though, I tell you nothing happened at the château. I would have seen, heard something… Nothing happened here, I tell you." He was so fervent, he was like a child; if he said something hadn't happened, long enough and hard enough, it couldn't have happened. That the child really didn't eat all the sweeties in the sweetie jar.

"But there was a young man," I reminded him, "found in the woods, frightened out of his wits who was brought back to the château and from what Claudine says…"

The frustration exploded out of him. "For Christ's sakes!"

"Actually," he started again, after a long silence, "very few people know that we had links with the régime and I'd like to keep it that way. The smokescreen they insisted upon — well, it's worked out to our advantage."

Tom waited for me to say something.

"The embargo." I'd forgotten about the embargo until then.

"It can't come out, please, that I was here. I'd be ruined — exactly what Wareing wants." There was panic in his voice. "Eveline's brother wasn't murdered here. I'm certain of it. Those men wouldn't have shat on their own doorstep."

There was too much at stake for him.

"You won't tell anyone?" he asked.

"That you were here doing a deal when there was an international embargo?"

He looked shamed.

"Put like that, yes."

"I'm your sister."

"You won't tell anyone? Not Philip? Not Eveline?"

290

"No one. Promise."

He was wrung out, exhausted suddenly. "Thank you."

He clambered to his feet. "I've told you everything now. No more secrets. I bloody well wish I'd never heard of the Kumono Mining Company. Are you coming down for supper?"

I shook my head.

"Suit yourself then," he said flatly, stung by my rejection.

I woke in the middle of the night to the gentle rumbling of snoring, one floor down. My father snored. I liked the sound of it as a child, waking up and knowing my parents were near. I went down the stairs carefully, the sheet trailing behind me, stepping over the shadows which lay motionless on the treads.

I stood over Tom in the gym room, lying flat out on the mattress. The exercise bike was nearby, eerie in the moonlight. It could have been Tom's tethered horse from the Gingerbread House of our childhood. Snores shunted in and out of his slack mouth and every so often, he snuffled one back through his nose. Either way, the noises spilled into the room and out to the rest of the house. I looked for the little boy who shared my childhood. I looked and looked from the tip of the receding hairline to the edge of sheet half covering the hairless chest, and I couldn't see him. I couldn't see him at all. It was as if he had been cannibalised by the stranger in the bed.

Tom's eyelids flickered open. His face was glazed with sleep. "Sis," he mumbled. He pulled away the sheet, about to get up. "Something wrong?"

Always, I thought sadly, he had some misplaced notion of protecting me.

'You're a duplicitous bastard.' I didn't say that. Instead, I said "Nothing. You were snoring."

He flopped back onto the bed and closed his eyes. I pulled the sheet up around his shoulders. I didn't know for whom I felt more sorry: him or me.

Tom grunted and rolled over to face the wall. I tiptoed out of the room, back to my turret through a silence heavy with shadow.

Chapter 49

I didn't emerge from the turret until after midday. I dozed, off and on, listening to the activity outside. Tom and Eveline were gardening, from the sounds of the wheelbarrow rattling across the gravel, the occasional grunt from Tom, and Eveline's light voice, questioning.

When I eventually looked out of the window, I couldn't believe my eyes. Heart pounding, I ran down the stairs, wrenched open the front door and ran down those steps.

I hadn't been hallucinating: there were six long, oblong heaps of earth dotted around the vicinity of chapel's ruined wall.

Tom and Eveline, with their backs to me, were sitting on a knoll of lawn nearby. They were wedged close to each other. He had his arm around her. Her head rested on his shoulder. Tom heard my feet crunching on the gravel. He turned his head. "Nothing."

He smiled up at me, tired and triumphant. Eveline looked miserable. She got up onto her feet and dashed past me, disappearing through the front door which I'd left open in my haste.

"Poor little girl," Tom said. "She's seen reason at last."

"You've ruined the lawn."

"It will mend. Like she will now. Valerie was right. She did need closure."

"You're Machiavellian."

He laughed. "No. I just survive."

A series of clanks rumbled out of the château. Eveline was having a bath.

"I wish you'd warned me about the plumbing," he said, giving a mock groan.

"This is just bonkers Tom. Why here, by the chapel?"

"She insisted. Said that she felt his presence. I tell you she needs professional help."

"Have you heard anything more from the Wareing man?"

"No," he said sharply. "The phone's disconnected remember?" He shielded his eyes with his hand. "Isn't the view glorious?"

Tom proposed a dip in the pool.

"I can't be bothered to go up to the tower again to get my costume."

"You've got your bra and pants."

"Pants," I considered myself in my baggy grey pants which have been chewed by the château washing machine too many times.

"I'm your brother, Sis, not Greg." He gave a knowing grin.

So we moved through the pulsating heat to the swimming pool terrace. Tom took off his t-shirt and shorts. His soft body, streaked with earth from his digging and clad only in a pair of boxers, glowed white in the sun. Tom slipped into the water. I stood hesitantly by the side. He dipped his head and shoulders beneath. "It's great!" he shouted, striking out.

I peeled off my clothes.

"What do you mean about Greg?" Dirt from my feet eddied through the water like chocolate sauce.

"Don't tell me you didn't notice him mooning over you."

"I didn't actually," I say, which was true up to a point. "Not until you came, anyway."

Water sloshed over the sides of the pool as Tom ploughed backwards and forwards. I didn't try to keep pace. I enjoyed the rhythm of my arms and legs, breaking through the shimmering reflection of sky. Eventually, Tom turned onto his back. "This is the life."

"If you have a life. Unlike Eveline's brother."

"Please, don't go on and on."

"I wonder where Eveline is?"

"You're very possessive of her aren't you?" He kicked some water at me, teasingly.

"I like her. I can't imagine what she has been through."

"It's more than that. You're half in love with her."

"Don't be stupid."

"Anyway, she is going tomorrow. Nothing more to keep her here. Job done."

I was about to argue with him. I didn't like the note of satisfaction in his voice. He turned on his back again with a hefty splash to gaze at the sky.

"There you are!" It was a call full of cheer and undisputedly directed at us. For a second I thought they were little old men, hunched over by the heaviness of their rucksacks, as they came alongside the pool — then I recognised the high forehead as Harry removed his trilby.

Chapter 50

"Who the hell are you?" Tom charged through the water like a bull.

Harry and Serena were in the same clothes that they were wearing before: same shabby green shorts and shirt for Harry, and Serena in the swirly skirt with tiny mirrors embroidered on the hem.

Harry took a step back, nearly toppling with the weight of his rucksack. "We thought the place was deserted at first but then we recognised the car round the front…"

"And then we heard your voices!" Serena smiled, unhitching the straps of her rucksack from her shoulders. "I hope you don't mind."

"It's okay," I called over to Tom as he was about to heave himself out of the pool. "I know them. They're students."

Tom splashed back into the water and glared.

The prospect of getting out of the pool was not appealing. I really didn't want Serena's sympathetic gaze lingering on my improvised bikini. I made the introductions from the water, Tom alongside me.

"This is my brother, Tom Braid."

Tom, I knew, was waiting for the exclamation of recognition. It never came.

"How come you know Sis?" Tom sounded quite jolly, welcoming even.

"Your sister gave us a lift," Serena explained breathlessly, "and when she mentioned that she was staying in this village, it… well…" She looked to Harry.

Tom was out of the water, looking around for the towels which we hadn't thought to bring.

"It piqued our curiosity," Harry finished what Serena was going to say, "and since we've seen all the major sights provincial France has to offer, we thought we'd come, take a look."

"Nothing better to do?" Tom rubbed himself brusquely with his t-shirt.

Harry gave Tom a look full of admiration for his frankness. "I suppose you could say that, yes." He changed the subject adroitly. "This is the Kumono château, isn't it?"

Tom took me aback with a simple "Yes."

Harry shook his head in disbelief. "Wow."

It was easy to see that Tom had decided to deal with the Kumonos' connection to the château, as a matter of fact. Nothing more and nothing less. Reluctantly, I clambered out of the pool.

"How fascinating." Serena turned to me as I once again put dry clothes onto wet skin. "You never told us you were actually living here?"

I pretended not to have heard her. I left Tom to give our unexpected visitors a tour of the château. He took them round to the front so that they could see the chapel. He'd make up some story to explain the dug-up earth. It wouldn't be the truth. I knew that for certain. I went back in the house.

Eveline wasn't in her room nor was she in the bathroom. The tub was still full of water. I pulled the plug, plunging my hand through the oily surface of the tepid water. I

297

picked the damp towel off the floor, with the monogram 'CH' beautifully embroidered in a corner. I hung it on one of the pipes running across the wall. All the while, Tom's voice floated in through the open window with the resonance of a tour guide's.

The doors on the first floor swung open onto silent rooms. Most showed signs of Greg's recent industry: a swipe of fresh plaster, a dismantled radiator, a new floorboard with the old one propped up against the wall. I pictured Greg's little daughter, her arms outstretched, her face beaming, her short legs running towards the father who had bent his long gangly frame to catch her up in his arms — but she couldn't, I thought. Greg's daughter wouldn't know who he was.

There was a shout of laughter from outside. I looked out the window. Harry was larking around on the edge of the pool — fully dressed and wildly showing off, I would have said, for Eveline's benefit. No wonder I couldn't find her. She was in the pool with Serena, finally in her bikini. She looked lovely: wet hair slicked back from a face lit up by a smile. Harry was pretending to teeter. Serena reached up, trying to grab his ankle. Her voice carried clearly.

"Come on Eveline, let's get him!"

Tom had introduced her by the only name he knew. Harry toppled in. The girls jumped on top of him.

Tom was on the pink lounger, far enough from the pool not to be splashed. He was back in his swim trunks. He had a glass of wine in his hand and was smiling with amusement, watching the antics in the pool. The bottle was on the ground beside him.

I leant out. "Everything okay?"

All four faces looked up. Eveline waved. Tom waved as well.

I went up the stairs to the second floor. Tom, despite his protestations about a bad back, had turned the gym room into a makeshift bedroom. The exercise bike was draped with clothes. A towel was slung over another machine. His bedside table was a suitcase, a travel alarm clock within easy reach. No wonder Tom rose early in the morning, the alarm was set for six o'clock. The clock told me that it was five o'clock in the afternoon, which was right, given the slant of sun across the floor.

I switched on the treadmill, set it at an impossibly high speed and listened to it whir; a clackety-clack sound. I left it running. There was a lot of choice, a lot of machines.

I decided on the shoulder press. I brushed the layer of dust covering the plastic seat, put my elbows on the outside of the pads and tried to push them together, as demonstrated by the helpful diagram. Nothing moved. The weight, I discovered, was set at twenty kilos. I moved the weight to one.

So there I was, my arms moving backwards and forwards, squeezing the minutes away and thinking about how both Tom and Eveline had an extraordinary ability to switch personas much in the same way as a chameleon reacts to its surroundings, when it occurred to me that Tom's mattress was not flush with the floor. I remember smiling because, as a little boy, he had stuffed all his treasures under his mattress in the vain hope that I wouldn't find them. It didn't occur to me not to investigate. Respect for my sibling's privacy simply wasn't part of the childhood memory which propelled me, with infantile delight, to slide my hand underneath the mattress. I dislodged bundles of newspapers.

Tom, it would seem, the five days he had been at the château, had bought every single copy of every English

299

newspaper carried by the newsagent down in the village. Puzzled, I looked through them. Why? My little brother was literally front page news in a back issue of the Daily Mail. There he was in black and white, times five, because there were five copies: my brother Tom and Samantha, looking impossibly glamorous, smiling out at me. My mind seized up. I had to spell out the words of the caption — times five: 'Braid Bust'.

I examined and re-examined the photo which must have been at least ten years old. Tom seemed so young.

I saw page seven as per instruction. I read black words such as 'fraud', 'tax evasion', and 'pension deficit'. In fact, I didn't have to read them; they leapt out at me, up off the page.

Page three of a broadsheet had a headline with the word 'Braid'. Colin Wareing's explanation was convoluted: Tom had been using money that he didn't have to buy companies. If the banks hadn't started to call in loans, no one would have been any the wiser.

Another newspaper talked of breaking bank covenants and investor panic.

The most recent edition discussed of Tom's disappearance — not even his 'estranged wife' knew where he was. There was concern for his mental and physical welfare.

No wonder he had rushed down to France. No wonder he had wanted to keep the château secret.

The alarm shattered my concentration. My hand slammed down on the clock, breaking it, silencing it forever at six o'clock.

I stuffed the newspapers back under the mattress and sat for a while, listening to the silence. Only birdsong filtered in from outside. The treadmill had ground to a halt.

According to Colin Warcing, my brother was a thief. The pity of it was that I wasn't surprised. I'd suspected as much for a long time but, true to form, had never acknowledged my suspicions. I couldn't hide from the truth any longer. It was a relief. It was a relief too, to realise that knowing what I did, I still loved my brother. I thought then that my love for my brother had passed the ultimate test. How wrong I was.

I heard Tom's voice, Harry's voice and Serena's voice, their shoes crunching over the gravel. A car door slammed: once, twice, three times. My car, not Harry's and Serena's, fired up. The noise faded as the car went down the avenue. I wondered where Tom was taking the youngsters. It worried me, I remember, that he was too drunk to drive.

I got to my feet. The lights on the console blinked furiously like there was an emergency. There was, in a way, an emergency going on in a château which used to belong one of the world's most dissolute dictators, and which now belonged to a man, who, from what I had read, would have to spend some time in prison.

He hadn't wanted me to know. With no internet access, TV or radio, I could only have found out through a newspaper. He'd have guessed that the resident English would be too circumspect — and too afraid to be seen to be prying — to tell me. It was a small crumb of comfort.

The swimming pool was deserted, a child's faded plastic ball floating on its flat surface. The sight of it, bobbing about like a bald man's head, made me shiver. There was an empty wine bottle beside the lounger and four dirty glasses. I passed through the archway, past the furniture store and out onto the gravel in the front.

Eveline started when she heard her name. She turned round and watched me approach. She had been sitting gazing at the view across the valley, by the ruined walls of the chapel.

"I thought everyone had gone." I sat down beside her. The sun was low enough in the sky to make the graveyard on the opposite hill glint, like a myriad of little fireflies in the light. The tranquillity of the scene belied the frantic activity of only hours before; the heaps of earth in front of us.

"They've run out of oil for their car, so Tom has taken them to a garage."

"You didn't go?"

"I wanted to be alone."

I told her that I was going to go back to England sometime soon. "Come with me."

Eveline turned away from me, back towards the panorama.

"Harry has offered me a lift to Paris tomorrow."

"So they're staying the night?" I was surprised that Tom had invited them.

"And from there, I am going home. I am going to tell the authorities what happened." Whether they believe me or not... there is so little proof."

"But what if they put you in prison? Aren't you running a terrible risk?"

She shrugged her shoulders. "I have nothing to lose."

I longed to run a finger down the nape of her neck, feel the bones beneath the skin. To have her. To comfort her. I wanted to tell her that there had been a passport which would have been sufficient proof. I didn't. I didn't want to add to her distress. I didn't want her to think of Tom as a heartless monster. I thought that maybe Tom was correct, that it would be better for her not to know for certain that her brother had been at the château. Whatever the reason, in that small moment of longing, I failed her.

"My brother was here, despite what Tom says. I know he was here. Finally," she turned her head and smiled at me, "I have peace."

"What about your husband?"

"My husband," she said, as if it were a joke, that she had a husband. Then she asked when I would return to London.

"Soon." I would have liked to explain about me and Philip, about me and Tom, about what Tom is presumed to have done — but it was too inconsequential compared with what she had had to face.

"I needed to know about my brother. Nothing else mattered."

"Be careful," was what I wanted to say to her. I didn't.

Chapter 51

Tom helped his two guests heave two mattresses up into a room on the first floor.

"This is lovely," Serena said admiringly, although there was nothing in the room except dead flies and dust behind the door.

"Sheets, Sis. Where are they?" Tom seemed to be doing everything in his power not to be alone with me.

He asked the students to give him a hand with supper.

"There's no food," I warned.

"What about the stuff we bought the other day?"

"Stale. Gone off."

He sighed heavily, as if it were my fault that the fridge was on its last legs.

"You can't stay holed up here forever," I said deliberately.

Instantly he guessed. It was there, in his eyes. I'd as good as told him that I knew. He smiled, making a challenge out of what I had said. "So be it. The restaurant then."

Harry and Serena were enthusiastic. Who would have turned down a free meal at their age? Any age?

Later, Tom, Harry, Serena and I were in the salon, waiting for Eveline to appear. The young people sat bunched together on the sofa in front of the fireplace. I was sitting adjacent to them. Tom had given us each a glass of champagne, Dom Pérignon 1985. Harry and Serena hardly touched theirs. Harry twirled the end of

Serena's fat plait like a paintbrush, she absentmindedly stroking one of his bony knees. Tom paced the room, knocking back the champagne like lemonade. Serena watched him without really looking, a half-smile on her face. He seemed less tipsy than he was in the afternoon.

"I'd rather stay in," Tom announced. "Take our chances with whatever food is left in the kitchen."

"Is there any truth in what Colin Wareing is saying?" I asked lightly, as if making small talk.

He forced a laugh. "I should have known I couldn't have secrets from you. Tell me," he asked Harry and Serena, "do either of you have bossy older sisters?"

"Please Tom," I said before either of them could answer.

"I could see the mattress had been moved. You wouldn't make a good spy, Sis."

The youngsters' eyes focussed on me with renewed interest.

"To be honest," Tom gave in and answered my question. "I haven't read what he has written. I expect it's rubbish. But as with everything I expect there is a nugget of truth in there about Braid Industries."

He put down his glass. The mask — the successful, debonair Tom with the Midas touch — slipped for a second. My brother was frightened. Tom was Braid Industries. It carried our name.

I couldn't go over and comfort him, because we were having this awkward conversation in front of two strangers who were aware without comprehending, that something important was being communicated.

Harry jumped up, almost knocking Serena's glass out of her hand with excitement.

"You're the Tom Braid? I should have guessed!"

"A celebrity!" Serena giggled. Harry laughed as well. The two of them look at Tom with something akin to admiration.

With that comment, the atmosphere changed. It was visible in the set of Tom's shoulders, in the way he snapped the foil off another bottle of champagne, in the way the cork popped with the resonance of a bullet.

"Is that why you're here, you two?"

"We didn't know you were here, honest." Harry sat back down on the sofa. "We just came here because we met your sister... we didn't know her name."

"It just seemed," Serena said softly, "a fun thing to do."

I believed them. They were just joyous that they had met someone who had the capacity to make headlines. They didn't care how.

Tom too, he believed them. They might have been very clever but they were also stupid.

The evening had begun to draw in. The shifts and glitches in the ancient glass in the salon's window panes gave the gardens a surreal air in the twilight. Inside, shadows had begun to form: a pool of dark around the standard lamp, a clump of shade on the floor which was Serena and Harry, my shape, more etiolated than Tom's, across the worn Oriental rug laid in front of the fireplace. Serena's attention seemed to be drawn by something in the corner of the room, so I looked, dreading the return of the man in the tree, but there was nothing there. She shook her head, almost imperceptibly.

"Soon it'll be time to have a fire," Tom gestured at the enormous empty grate, a proprictorial hand on the baronial mantle.

"There's a woodpile down by the stables," I drained my glass and proffered it to Tom.

"Where is that girl?" He demanded with mock exasperation.

"I'm here." None of us had heard her enter the room. Eveline faced us, her back pressed up against the door. There was a sharp intake of breath from us all. A pang of regret went straight through my heart. I felt as proud and as apprehensive as any mother when confronted with a daughter's startling beauty.

"You look stunning," Serena said admiringly. "Doesn't she Harry?"

"Let's go," Tom said and he frogmarched us down the hill.

Chapter 52

The buzz of conversation stopped as soon as our group entered the restaurant. Tom threw back his shoulders so that he stood absolutely erect. He needn't have worried. All eyes were on Eveline. She was dazzling, radiantly overdressed in her silk dress with her green shoes and their pink rose detail.

We were shown to the last remaining table in the far corner, by the kitchen door. Tom, in the old days, would have made a fuss. I made sure that he and I were seated with our backs to the rest of the room.

Eveline ordered for us all in perfect French: soup to start with; steak for her, Harry and Serena. I had duck in memory of Greg. Tom requested chicken.

Harry and Serena did most of the talking, regaling Eveline with tales of university life.

"And what about you Eveline?" Harry asked. "What brings you here?"

Eveline gave me an oblique glance. "My brother."

"I didn't think there was anyone else staying at the château?" Serena was puzzled.

"He's dead." Eveline smiled at them both.

Embarrassed by the mention of death, Harry swiftly changed the subject, relating some exploit of his and Serena's in a cathedral town in Northern France.

"What are you going to do?" I asked Tom as the crème brulée was cleared away.

Tom looked at me vaguely. He had hardly spoken, taking no real interest in the meal, not even in the choice of wine.

"I'll have to go back to London at some point... sort things out."

"And Samantha?"

"For the last few years, she's only been in the marriage for the money." He looked drained. "I can't say I blame her. Are you sure about going back to Philip?"

"What about the children?"

"They'll see as much of me as they ever do."

I became aware that the others had stopped talking, but they weren't listening to my conversation with Tom, their eyes were focussed on a point somewhere above Tom's head. They looked puzzled. Tom's expression was impassive. Perhaps — most probably — he had spent the entire meal waiting for something to happen.

Slowly, Tom turned to face the man who had been standing silently behind his chair.

He was about my age this man, smartly dressed with greying hair and angry, burning eyes. I didn't recognise him as one of the local British.

"I don't know how you have the cheek to show your face in here," the man said to Tom. "Here or anywhere."

With difficulty, Tom pushed back his chair and stood up.

"I don't recall having met..."

The man ignored Tom's proffered hand.

"My mother invested everything she had in Braid Industries," he hissed. "And by the looks of things, she's going to lose the lot, you bastard."

"What are you going to do about it?" The man's voice cut across the restaurant hub-bub. In the hush, everyone looked at our table; at the man angrily leaning in on Tom.

"Everything I can, mate," Tom put up both hands in a gesture of surrender. "I'm so sorry."

The man jabbed Tom in the chest. Startled, Tom took a step back and knocked against the table. A glass smashed to the floor, but no one cared — the stranger had grabbed Tom by the shoulders and started to shake him. It was as if he was trying to jerk Tom's head off his neck with Tom offering no resistance.

And, for what seemed an age, I watched. Harry, Serena and Eveline, they watched. The people in the restaurant. The waiter. We all just watched.

"Stop it," I pleaded, finally putting out a hand, putting my fingers around the demented man's thick, hairy wrist. "Please, stop it. There's no point. I assure you that my brother will do everything in his power…"

The man stopped. His scornful eyes raked our table — over me, Tom, Serena, Eveline, and Harry, who had half got out of his seat, hesitant about what to do.

"Your brother is nothing more than a common thief."

He turned on his heel, took a couple of steps away from us, turned his raging face back towards us.

"First thing tomorrow 'mate'," his voice was laden with derision, "I'm telling the police where you are."

He swaggered self-consciously out of the restaurant, aware that everyone was looking.

Tom rubbed his neck. He looked — not to make too much of a pun — shaken. Then what had happened before, happened again: he pulled himself together; reworking his face and his stance, quite visibly, for all to see.

Eveline, sitting on the other side of Tom, tugged at his shirt. He sank back into his seat. She closed her hand over his, sympathetically. He gave her a weak smile.

"Well," he said, when the noise level was back to normal, "let's get the bill, shall we? My treat." He waved and a waiter promptly appeared.

"Here," Tom selected a card from his wallet. "Use this to cover our bill and — " he beckoned the waiter to bend closer, "after we have left, give everyone a glass of champagne with my compliments — and apologies for the inconvenience caused."

"The house champagne?" The waiter murmured.

"No," Tom said. "The best you've got. Give yourself a tip as well."

As soon as we stepped outside, we were lit up by flashes from a camera. Tom put his arm to shield his eyes. When my vision readjusted, I could see the solitary figure of man, smoking in the shadow of one of the plane trees on the square. It was too dark to see his face.

Tom shrugged his shoulders. "All part of the territory," he murmured to no one in particular.

*

We walked back up to the château, Harry and Serena loitering behind, whispering fiercely; Tom, Eveline and I out in front.

"Thanks, Sis," Tom broke the silence between us.

"You're my brother."

"I'll pay every penny back. I'm not a thief."

I could hear the distress in his voice. "But was it really necessary to give everyone champagne?"

"I might have maxed out on that card. I hope not. My name really would be mud."

He took my hand. He took Eveline's hand. He walked us home.

Amazingly as soon as we got back, Tom regained his bonhomie. He slapped Harry on the back. He joked with

312

Eveline about her shoes. He called Serena 'Rapunzel'. He slit the foil on another bottle of champagne. It was his idea to have a midnight swim and the others were glad to be propelled along by his enthusiasm. They wanted to forget the incident in the restaurant. I felt heavy with tiredness. I wanted to go to bed. Eveline darted off to find candles. Harry was despatched to locate the lanterns that Tom had seen, but couldn't remember where. Serena looked frantically for her costume.

"I had it earlier," she kept on repeating, bewilderment in her voice.

"Then it can't have gone far," Tom said. "Or use your underwear. Sis, are you going to join us for a dip?"

There was a devilish glint to his eyes. I wondered if he had hidden Serena's swimsuit for a joke. He was on a maniacal high.

I went to bed and fell asleep with the sound of laughter drifting up from outside.

And to my horror, I dreamt of the naked man in the tree. My heart wept because I thought he had gone forever. I couldn't get away from him because of his branches. I could feel his weight pressing on me, like he was falling from a great height, like he was pressing the life out of me and eventually I found my voice through the leaves of the trees and I screamed and screamed to chase him away.

Harry and Serena stood by my mattress. She was draped in a sheet. He was clutching a towel. Their faces were suspended in the darkness, lit by the candle Serena was holding.

"Are you okay?" she asked.

"For a second, we thought someone was being murdered." Harry said gruffly.

"I'm fine. Sorry. Just a nightmare."

313

"This house is full of nightmares, isn't it?" Serena's voice was soft with wonder.

"Serena," Harry began to admonish.

"Other people's nightmares," she corrected herself.

"It's okay," I told them both.

When they had gone, it was difficult to get back to sleep. Drenched in sweat, I was cold.

Chapter 53

There was a hush in the house in the morning, the deep hush of other people sleeping. Harry and Serena had left the door to their room open. They lay entwined, her hair fanned over the pillow, cascading across the floor. I closed the door gently. There was no sign of Tom, nor of Eveline.

I walked down to the boulangerie, past the familiar houses with their balconies and pots full of pink geraniums. Although the sun was shining, it was noticeably more chill and heavy clouds were banking up behind the hills. I tried a little French and Madame smilingly corrected me. She gave me another pot of jam.

"You know," I wanted to confide in her, "my husband had an affair."

"Ah, an affair." The Madame of my imagination would have given a very Gallic shrug of her shoulders. "So what?"

My heart sang. I would stay at the château, only for as long as Tom needed my presence, and not a moment longer. I would be a good sister and then, back in London, I would be a good wife. I was so looking forward to getting home.

I passed a round little man with a lank grey hair walking down the hill as I was going up. He acknowledged me with a slight, almost apologetic smile as if I should have known him. I didn't recognise him but I knew, in a heartbeat, who he was. I hurried on, desperate to tell Tom. When I reached the château gates, I couldn't help but look back. The man hadn't continued on his way. He was standing stock still, smoking a cigarette, watching.

I opened the door to the gym without thinking of knocking. There was the smell first: the smell of two people who had been in close contact. Then there was the tangle of sheets on the floor. The exercise machines encircled the mattress like sentries.

I must have stifled a cry because Tom slowly propped himself on his elbows. I can't remember. Even now, I can't remember. He regarded me gravely without uttering a word. Eveline, curled beside him, shifted in her sleep.

I shut the door.

"You missed a lovely time," Serena said happily, wiping down the kitchen table. "We ended up skinny dipping."

"Even Eveline?" The image of Eveline lying naked with my brother was blistered on my brain.

"She couldn't be persuaded — unfortunately." Harry was sitting at the table, hands clamped around a mug of coffee, watching Serena bustle. Serena gave him a playful swipe with the dishcloth. "Harry's got a hangover."

"Are Tom and Eveline up yet?" Harry asked.

Serena saw how I stiffened at the mention of their names.

"Harry…" Serena said, giving me a brilliant smile.

She gestured at the two fat rucksacks propped against a wall. "We're just waiting for Eveline."

When Eveline eventually did come down with her suitcase, she was wearing the same black jacket and jeans as when I'd first set eyes on her, lying on the ground by the gates, except there were no gates. She looked happier than I had ever seen her. No, she said smiling, she didn't want breakfast, and they should be on their way.

I was so angry. "I need to speak with you."

I could tell she was startled by my tone.

"Let's get the baggage in the car," Serena said, giving Harry a prod.

Harry picked up Eveline's suitcase. "Crikey, what have you got in here? Bricks?"

Eveline appeared not to have heard him. Harry gave her a searching look to which she also seemed oblivious. He shrugged and lugged the suitcase out through the archway door.

Serena disappeared upstairs to the bathroom. The sun disappeared from the windows, leaving the kitchen in a twilight. I switched on the overhead light.

Standing in the centre of the room, Eveline looked around, as if she was trying to imprint the kitchen on her memory. I looked with her: at the table beneath the windows, the dresser cluttered with paint pots, the chipped cabinet by the door, the battered old range, the even more antiquated fridge — and felt even more alive with rage. I had given her sanctuary. Cared for her. In return she had betrayed me with my brother.

"You know," I said, "you've proved Tom right. He always wondered if you were a prostitute."

Her eyes darkened. "How dare you."

"I don't know what you thought you'd gain by sleeping with my brother."

"Whatever he's done, he's a better person than you." She spat the last word out with utter contempt and started to walk towards the door.

I wanted to hurt her. I wanted to hurt Tom.

I grabbed her wrist. She gazed at my pale fingers with a moue of distaste.

"He burnt Zachary's passport."

317

It was as if she had been hit by a bolt of lightning. She had to steady herself. She gripped my arm.

"No."

"Yes."

Her eyes searched mine.

"Zachary's passport was here all the time?"

"I would have shown you but you were so fucking rude."

"It's not true." She was pleading with me.

"Tom thinks so little of you that he thought you'd just lie and say it was your brother's anyway and do you know what? I think he's right. You'd use anyone and anything…"

"Burnt. Why?" She sank into the nearest chair. She put her hands over her ears to shut me out.

"Leave me alone," she whispered.

I left the kitchen, still enraged but calm.

Harry and Serena were chatting by their car.

"She'll be along in a second," I said, after saying my goodbyes. I went back into the château, through the front door. I watched from a salon window as Eveline emerged, without a backward glance at the house. She exchanged a few words with Harry and Serena. Whatever she said, it seemed to cause a flurry of consternation but eventually, they settled themselves in the car. Serena reversed, and started to drive down the avenue. Harry caught sight of me and gave me a thumbs-up from the back. Serena thrust her arm out for a valedictory wave. Not Eveline, who was staring straight ahead.

A drop of rain landed on the window pane. Then another and another. The sky was the colour of concrete, pressing in on the château. I went to find my brother.

Chapter 54

Tom wasn't in the gym. I opened all the windows and let the grey air with a few flecks of rain roll in. Outside, it was very still with a two-dimensional quality: the trees stiff like cardboard cut-outs on a painted landscape.

Tom was no longer bothering to hide the newspapers — the pile was on the floor, not too far from the mattress. The bottom sheet was half off the mattress, displaying stained ticking which made my stomach turn even though I knew that the stains had been there long before Greg had slept on it. I sat on the mattress and flicked through the papers, so taut that I couldn't concentrate enough to read.

The noise of the plumbing trying to belch out hot water eventually subsided and in the silence, I listened for Tom's footsteps to come down the corridor. I listened as they came nearer and nearer before coming to an abrupt halt. I caught the look of apprehension which flitted across Tom's face but I knew he wasn't surprised to find me waiting. I held up the alarm clock for him to see.

"I broke this yesterday."

"Sis…" He started.

"How could you? She's a child."

He walked across to the exercise bike.

"She's twenty-two. She can look after herself." He turned his back to pull on a pair of underpants. "I heard you having another nightmare last night. Everything okay?"

"We owed her a duty of care," I kept my voice level.

"That's bollocks. She's better able to look after herself than you are. How do you think she has survived so far?"

He reached for the pair of shorts dangling on the bike's handlebars, and pulled them on. "You forget she's the pampered darling of a discredited régime."

"You're unbelievable."

"Look, if it makes you feel any better, nothing happened, I promise."

"Tell me another."

"A girl looking for her long-lost brother."

A drop of rain smacked against a window pane, followed by another and then another. They cascaded down the glass, in front of an unrelentingly grey sky.

I watched Tom thread a belt through the loops on his waistband. He studiously ignored me, until eventually he said:

"Look, I'd never hurt her — anymore than I would you."

"Why did you have to climb into bed with her?"

"Hang on a minute," he said. "It was the other way round. She came to me."

For one long bewildering moment, it was as if he had stabbed me through the heart. I'd thought he had cajoled her.

"You're a two-bit opportunist, apart from anything else."

"Do me a favour."

"It's the truth, Tom."

"You're jealous. You should have seen the way you looked at her sometimes."

"You don't care whose life you fuck up."

"If you say so." His dismissiveness hurt. How dared he?

"You fucked up mine big time."

He laughed. "I don't think you need help on that front."

"Not many people kill their Dad."

Tom's laughter died in his throat. He looked at me, aghast.

*

No longer was it Eveline between us. It was the long shadow of what had happened thirty-six years ago on a gloriously sunny afternoon in Devon. The picnic — my special picnic as promised by my father — was laid out in the shade of an enormous oak tree. Tired of waiting for our mother who had gone down to the stream to retrieve the cooling bottles of pop, I had wandered into the sun. It was so hot, I remember, that the sun painted stripes on my back through the thin cotton of my dress. There wasn't a breath of wind. My father was stretched out on the rug, lazily swatting flies away from the food. He was a very handsome man, our father: chiselled jaw, dark lock of hair flopping onto his forehead. Tom was above him, leaves rustling, climbing to the top of the tree.

Our father called up to Tom, remonstrating. "You'll break a leg you silly monkey!" Tom swung higher and higher.

Sighing, our father stood up, feet carefully positioned between the plates of food. He cupped his hands around his mouth. "Come down! Now!"

Tom flung himself from branch to branch. "Look Dad! Look at me!"

I heard cracking. I saw a flash of blue and green t-shirt plummeting. I saw my father with his arms outstretched. One shout. I saw my brother knock my father off his feet. In the silence which followed the sun would never be in the same place in the sky again.

Tom stood up shakily, up off our father's head. He started to cry. I screamed.

Our father lay spread-eagled across our picnic. His eyes were wide and staring. There were leaves everywhere. An arm had squashed all the scotch eggs. A foot had ruined the chocolate sponge cake he and I had made that morning.

Our mother rushed past me. She knelt beside her man. "Darling. Darling." She leant her face into his. She ripped open his shirt collar. She pressed two fingers against his neck. She pulled Tom towards her. "What happened? Tell me what happened." She looked to me but I couldn't speak.

She flung her arms around Tom. She rocked him backwards and forwards, tears cascading down her cheeks. "My poor baby. Poor, poor baby." She scrambled to her feet. She looked up into the huge canopy above us.

And in that room, that improvisation of a gym in the château, our mother's terrible cry of loss reverberated down the years.

*

Forwards and backwards Tom paced, between the bike and the treadmill, the tracks of his feet in the dust. He didn't hit me, of course he didn't. I couldn't tell what he was thinking, because he kept his face averted.

I wanted him to burrow under the covers with me again. I wanted to hold him, hug him. I wanted to say how sorry I was. The sunlight had completely gone from the room. I wanted the easy intimacy we used to have — so long ago. Such a long time ago.

A drop of rain smacked against a window pane, followed by another and then another. They trickled down the glass, in front of an unrelentingly grey sky.

Tom stood in front of me. I looked at his feet, the bare vulnerable toes with the tufts of hair.

"Dad had a heart attack when I fell out of the tree. He had a weak heart. Don't you remember Mum telling us?"

I shook my head, unable to speak.

Tom crouched down. He took my hands. His one brown eye and his one green eye — they weren't angry any longer. They were full of pity.

"When she came back from the hospital, she sat us down, each on a knee and told us that it wasn't our fault, that we shouldn't blame ourselves... you can't remember?"

"It was my picnic." I could see the little girl, I could feel her fear — and then she was blanked, whitewashed, scrubbed out by my brain.

"She never spoke of how he died again, as far as I know. She blamed herself. If it hadn't been for her, they would never have gone down to Devon."

*

I remembered being woken up by my father. I remembered being tenderly cajoled into putting sleepy arms into sleeves, sleepy legs into trousers, sleepy feet into shoes. I remembered sitting in the back of the car, Tom asleep beside me, looking at the backs of my parents' heads. I remembered speeding out of the city in the grey dawn light.

*

"She had had an affair," Tom said. "Dad had found out and insisted that they leave London."

"It wasn't a proper holiday."

"Somehow," Tom said, "Even as little children, I think you and I knew that."

How much our father must have loved our mother. Sometimes, I'd take the cup of tea up to her in the morning, when he was busy making our breakfast.

323

Carefully, I'd ascend the stairs, trying to stop the tea slopping against the china rim. I'd offer it, wobbling in its saucer, to my mother who looked delicious propped up in bed. She would reward me with a kiss and ask me to 'tell Daddy that Mummy loves him very much'.

Tom rubbed my hands between his. "You are cold, aren't you?"

He sat on the mattress beside me. Together we watched the rain cascade down the windows. It was like a curtain on the world, shutting it out.

"Poor Sis," he said, "you've lived with such a burden."

*

I can still see the bulk of my father sitting at the gate-legged table in Devon, hunched over his typewriter. I can see the slender shape of my mother with her arms draped over his shoulders, dropping kisses onto the top of his head. I can't hear the clackety-clack of the machine, the constant refrain of my childhood, so suddenly truncated.

*

"That's why," Tom's voice was muffled because he'd buried his face in his hands. "Mum found me so difficult. I reminded her of her guilt, me being the one who caused his death. If she hadn't had an affair, if we hadn't gone down to Devon, Dad might have stayed alive."

"She said that to you?"

"No, of course not." Tom wept, tears trickling through his fingers. I wanted to weep too, for him. I didn't. I was too angry with the pretty, fey, young woman who was our mother.

"I tried so hard," Tom whispered, longing in his face. "To make it up somehow."

"She found you difficult," I told him, "because you were a little boy who had lost his father. Nothing and no one could ever make that up to you."

"So she didn't hate me?"

"No," I told him. "She loved you. She loved us. She just wasn't much of a mother, being crippled by guilt and grief."

The truth, finally. Our father would have died young, regardless.

Other than the piles of paper and the typewriter, our father's writing table was clear, Spartan in its simplicity but in order to get to the table, you had to wade through sheaves of white paper, crumpled into balls which no one was allowed to clear in case my father had written a nugget of pure gold on the rejected page. By the time of his death, the balls of white paper were like a lake, held back from spilling into the hall by the dining room door.

*

There was an exasperated shout from below. "Anyone at home?"

Tom dashed to the window. "What the hell does she want?"

Chapter 55

Valerie's cheeks were flushed. She could barely contain her excitement. She addressed Tom. "There are a lot of questions being asked in the village about you."

Tom didn't bother to conceal his distaste. "That doesn't surprise me."

Valerie cocked her head. She looked like a hen: sharp-nosed and sharp-eyed. "I heard about the restaurant. By all accounts it was a set-up. That man and the journalist travelled down together."

"I can't believe you've come all the way up here to tell us some village gossip?"

I didn't understand his open hostility.

Valerie gave one of her tinkling laughs, turning her back on Tom. She opened her hand for me to see a silver bullet, gleaming in the dim, sodden light. "I'm giving this to Eveline. It's hers by right."

She was very surprised when I told her that Eveline had gone and was on her way to Paris.

"But I thought I saw…" Valerie shook her head. "Maybe I'm seeing things. Never mind. Take it anyway. You're more likely to see her again than me."

Tom marched her to the front door. This time though, there was no solicitous hand guiding her and definitely no kisses on the cheek.

"She blackmailed me," he said, as he pushed the door closed. "You know the time I went in with her and left you and Greg in the car? Then. She cleaned me out of the rest of my cash. She'd dug up some tripe on the internet. Threatened to contact Sam. I can't have my wife and kids involved."

I told Tom about meeting Colin Wareing on the hill.

"This can't go on," was all he said.

Once I'd mentioned the journalist's name, the feeling of being under siege — of helplessly waiting for him — wasn't helped by the weather. Visibility from the windows was almost nil. A mist of rain rose from the ground and pressed against the windowpanes.

Tom occupied himself by making a roaring fire in the huge fireplace in the hall. He stood in front of it, watching Greg's logs hiss, spit and throw tawny flames into the cavernous chimney. He told me that he was going to tell Colin Wareing the truth. "I can't keep on running forever and there are mitigating circumstances."

I put my arms around his waist and tried to squeeze all my love and sympathy for him into that hug. He smelt of wood smoke. It was a smell which brought back my father.

He leant his head on my shoulder. "At least, they won't be able to touch the château."

"Come down to the kitchen," I said. "We need to eat." Neither of us had had breakfast.

In the kitchen I made a lunch of salad leaves with a tin of tuna. I sliced the baguette which I had bought only that morning, but which seemed a lifetime ago. Tom went down to the cellar and reappeared with a bottle of white wine. He wrenched out the cork. I laid the table with two knives, two forks and two plates — my favourites, white with a burgundy border patterned by lacy gold.

"One more thing," Tom said. "I didn't sleep with Eveline, I promise."

"I am so sorry. I was just so angry…"

"What if Claudine was correct? That her brother did die a horrific death here?"

I looked at him, stunned. "So you did believe her? Despite everything you've…"

He interrupted me. "It doesn't matter what you and I think, it's what Eveline believes — and I couldn't have her believing that. It would have been too much for the girl. For anyone."

"In a way, I was trying to bury him for her here. To stop her futile searching. Whatever happened to that young man can't have been good, don't you see?"

All along he had been trying to protect Eveline and I'd betrayed him just as she was leaving. I had done him — and her — a grave injustice.

"That's why you got rid of the passport."

"Yes," he said.

I remember hoping, reasoning that there was no possibility of him ever finding out that the sister he trusted had proved so unworthy in a fit of spite. I have no way of knowing what I might have said because just then, the door to the archway, which had been shut tight on account of the weather, crashed open, hitting the wall.

Startled, Tom and I jumped up from our chairs. Eveline, scarcely recognisable, hung from the door, chest heaving, her eyes locked on Tom. What was shocking was her face. That beautiful face was ugly, truly ugly, with hate. She panted, gulping in air, her eyes never leaving Tom.

I didn't dare go to her. I didn't dare speak. I couldn't. I remember the silence punctuated by her heavy, rasping breathing.

It was as if I wasn't there. That I didn't exist. Only Tom existed for Eveline.

Tom didn't move, didn't utter a word. A deep flush flooded over his cheeks. He knew.

Eveline used the sleeve of her sodden, blood-splattered jacket to wipe away the rivulets of water running down her face. A puddle was quickly forming around her shoes.

"Let me get you a towel," I said gently, taking a step towards the kitchen stairs.

"Sit down." Her voice was like a lash.

"I want you," she said, speaking to me, but with her unwavering gaze still fastened on Tom, "as a witness."

I sat down at what used to be Eveline's place at the table.

Tom didn't move at all. It was as if he was caught in a spell which rendered him immobile.

Eveline walked over to Tom. My brother's face took on a wary, hunted look. His eyes looked anywhere but at her as she came so close that her little breasts left a smear of mud on his shirt.

"Your sister," she said. "told me this morning that you had burnt Zachary's passport."

Slowly, Tom's eyes turned in my direction. His sense of shock — of betrayal — was unbearable. I stood up.

"He was only thinking of you," I said to Eveline, "you've got to understand…" She didn't allow me to finish, shoving me back into the chair with such force that the chair toppled backwards with me following it to the floor. I remember lying there stunned, looking up into the innards of the table.

Tom moved then. I saw his hand reach out. I saw her feet in the wet trainers take a couple of steps across the flagstones. A sound reverberated around the kitchen like a gunshot. She had slapped him on the face.

Shakily, I hauled myself onto my feet. Tom was bent, holding onto the table for support. He was as white as a ghost, the full force of her blow reddening one cheek. She stood beside him, her hands clenching and unclenching. I thought she was going to punch him. He collapsed into a chair. He hid his face in his hands while she looked down on him, scorn written all over her face.

It wasn't just my legs trembling. I was juddering with shock. I righted the chair. I, too, sat down. Eveline stood behind Tom, one hand pressing down on his shoulder. She yanked his hair to force him to sit upright. His eyes started with fright.

Her chest heaved with the effort of having had to grapple with him.

She used me, sitting at the other end of the table to her and Tom, as her audience. Her tone was almost conversational.

"Remember yesterday," she said, bending close to his ear, "when you told me that Claudine had burnt Zachary's photo? It puzzled me. It didn't make any sense. Why would she burn it? But I accepted what you said. You were a nice man."

Eveline looked at me. "And then your sister told me what you'd done — and I thought, why would you do that? I didn't believe her."

Tom gave me a look of utter despair.

"I'm sorry Tom," I said, crying. "I don't know what came over me."

"What?" Eveline jeered. "Did you tell her not to tell me?" Viciously, she jabbed a finger in his ear. He screamed with pain.

"To continue," she said. "I thought then that you simply hadn't gone to Claudine's. You'd palmed me off with a lie. I thought that maybe Zachary's photo was still there. Harry and Serena gave me a lift up to the woods."

She gave his hair a sharp tug. "I hope you're listening."

I was horrified, mesmerised by the cruelty.

"Speak when spoken to."

"Yes," he said.

"So where are Harry and Serena?" I asked, hoping against hope, that maybe they were outside in the car, waiting for Eveline.

"On their way to Paris."

"What about your suitcase?"

"Who gives a shit about my suitcase?" She let the clump of hair and scalp float to the floor.

Chapter 56

We could hear water gushing out of the drainpipe beside the window. With her standing behind him, Tom couldn't see how all the hatred had left Eveline's face. I allowed myself a little hope then. It was completely blank, a beautiful blank just as it had been when I first met her. Her hand, though, was still clamped on Tom's shoulder. Neither Tom or I dared move.

After a couple of minutes, Eveline's attention returned to Tom.

"But you weren't lying about the old woman were you? She had burnt it. Destroyed the only photograph of my brother. She didn't want to be involved." Eveline's voice rose, her face twisted with fury. "Because she was in this house, like you were, when they murdered him for sport."

She jabbed Tom in the neck. "Armistice day. Six years ago. You didn't stop them. You didn't report them. You did nothing. Just hid in your room."

The realisation of what she had said enveloped me, like an icy tide.

He looked at me, shamed, but still I struggled to cling onto his lies.

"Tell her it's not true!" I screamed. "Tell her Tom."

He said nothing.

Our mother had died on that day. Tom had been on an unavoidable business trip.

Eveline gave me a glance full of contempt.

"Your brother deals in falsehoods. Haven't you noticed? Little lies that trip off the tongue."

Claudine had been telling the truth. The way he clicked his fingers — he'd been doing it as Eveline's brother died.

My heart broke for the young man — and for the fatherless boy who had grown into a middle-aged man corrupt to the core. I tried to save him. I swear I did. He was still my brother.

"He wasn't here. On my life. You've got Tom all wrong. Telling little lies as you put it is very different to being complicit in murder."

Tom shifted in his seat. With my support — we were a team again — he would refute Eveline.

"I'm listening." She let go of his shoulder. She pulled a chair away from the table. She positioned it so that she was sitting about a metre away from both of us and a metre away from the table. It would seem that that was the closest proximity to us that she could bear.

Tom no longer looked frightened. He rearranged himself in his seat, smoothing down his hair and wincing. The imprint of Eveline's fingers was beginning to fade from his cheek.

Oblivious to the wet, bloody clothes stuck to her body, Eveline folded her arms and crossed her legs. I wondered if she were cold, I remember.

"I don't know how you can believe the rantings of a mad old woman," he said earnestly. "I wasn't here."

"Do you honestly think," Tom continued, leaning forwards, like he was trying to reach out to Eveline, to be sympathetic. "That I would witness something like that and not go to the police?" He stops to think. "I mean, why didn't Claudine go to the police?"

"She had good reason not to."

Tom pointed his finger triumphantly. "Exactly. And you take her word over mine."

He smiled over to me, confident for himself. The length of the kitchen table from one end to the other, suddenly seemed enormous. Another world.

All the time, Eveline watched him, her gaze never wavering.

"What was it that made my brother's life worthless to you?"

Tom looked at me. Looked at her. Hope drained out of him. "You have to understand my position. I did what was best for my employees in that particular company. I ensured their futures. If I hadn't the company would have gone down the pan. You have no idea what it is like to be responsible for so many lives, so many mortgages, children…" It's like he had been rehearsing this speech for a court of law.

"So you did business with murderers."

"We didn't actually know then…"

"You knew enough."

"Yes." His voice was barely above a whisper.

"So what about my brother? Why didn't you report his murder?"

Tom looked at me despairingly. I shook my head.

"The embargo," he said. "I was never supposed to be here."

"So?" Eveline asked.

He took a deep breath. "So," he repeated.

Eveline and I both waited as he searched for the right words. "So," he said again, "I couldn't risk prison. I had to think of my wife and children."

He saw the look of utter contempt on Eveline's face.

"For God's sakes," he cried. "How do you think the world operates? It's all compromise."

"What's that about compromise?" A male voice asked from the top of the kitchen stairs.

Chapter 57

Colin Wareing hesitated halfway down the flight of stairs. He was looking down on a scene which he couldn't have expected: three dishevelled people, one of whom was soaking wet, sitting at various distances from a kitchen table on which a meal had been laid for two.

"I hope you don't mind," he said pleasantly, continuing his descent. "I knocked four or five times before trying the front door." He tilted his head, waiting for an answer. It was obvious that the journalist thought that his unexpected entrance had struck us dumb.

Wareing laughed, stepping off the bottommost tread. "I'm not gate crashing a party am I? I would have come earlier, but I thought I'd dig up some background info so went up to see a lady... I believe her name was Claudine?"

At the mention of Claudine, Tom stood up with such force that his chair toppled to the floor. My brother lunged at the journalist, trying to force him out into the archway. I found myself between them, trying to stop Tom's flailing arms. Only when he inadvertently landed a blow on me did he come to his senses. "Christ, Sis, I'm so sorry." Colin Wareing patted himself down. When he looked up, his expression was sneering.

Tom glanced in Eveline's direction. She is still sitting in the same chair, her eyes blankly fixed on some point on the ceiling, completely removed from the commotion. Eventually Tom straightened himself up. He ignored

Wareing. "Just make sure he leaves the grounds. I'll handle the situation here."

Out in the archway, Wareing seemed amused by his treatment. "What situation? Who's that girl? She was with you last night, wasn't she?"

"Please leave."

He followed me out to the front of the house.

"What's going on?"

The rain had stopped. There was a slice of blue sky amongst all the cloud.

"You are trespassing."

At a brisk pace, it took ten minutes to walk down the avenue. Wareing had perfected the art of being a complete irritant. He dawdled. He stopped to look at the chapel. He lit first one, then another cigarette. He seemed to think that if he spent long enough with me, I would let something slip. I maintained a stubborn silence. He would never know how grateful I was for his arrival.

Wareing might as well have been talking to himself. He said that Tom would almost certainly go to prison. "With a good lawyer, he's looking at three years."

But when he said that it puzzled him that there were no gates to the property, "given that the château, used to belong to the Kumonos," I reacted.

"So what?" I said lightly, pleased to have the opportunity to put the odious little man in his place. "Gates don't keep bad news out. The likes of you will always find a way in."

He smiled. He had had a reaction. "My gut tells me that there's more to the Kumonos and your brother than meets the eye…" He stopped for a moment, thinking. The tone of his voice completely changed. "I would have come earlier but I had to deal with the police. You see when I went up

337

to interview the cleaning woman I had the shock of my life."

A jolt of fear stopped me in my tracks. "Why?"

"She'd been stabbed. I found her dead."

I started to run, fear propelling me back along the avenue we'd just come.

There was nobody in the kitchen except shadows, floating in a lifeless silence.

"Tom!" I screamed. "Eveline!"

I took the stairs, two at a time, and hurried through the dining hall. I went into the salon. I looked in the library. No one in Eveline's room. I screamed for Tom. I heard Colin Wareing shouting up at me and I shouted for him to check the basement and outside in the stables.

I flung open every door on the first floor. I ran up the stairs to the second, barely touching the banisters but when I looked down at my hand because it was sticky, I saw it was smeared wet and red. I tried to scream but my throat was choked.

I saw then the splashes on the dark stairs, the smudge of a palm print going up the wall. I fell, stumbling up the last few stairs. I could feel the weight of the château closing over me.

I stood on the threshold of the lower of the two tower rooms. Tom was lying on the floor. He tried to say something but his head fell back. His hands were over his stomach. His chest was covered in blood. His eyes stared at the ceiling.

He came up to the highest point in the house, in a doomed effort to escape.

I knelt in a puddle of his blood. I leant my face into his, like I watched my mother do to my father. There was no breath. I ripped his shirt open, to the chest. I pressed two

338

fingers against his neck. I took his hand. "Don't leave me Tom."

I was already bereft.

I heard footsteps then, soft and light, coming down the spiral staircase from my room. They came towards me and stopped, behind my back. I felt the cool steel of a blade pressed against my neck. I was too terrified to breathe, let alone turn my head. I knew too that if I did, I would beg her to spare my life.

"You are as bad as he is."

I felt the tip of the knife lightly score my skin. I felt the trickle of blood between my shoulder blades. I felt a movement of air, as if she had raised her arm and I stiffened, waiting.

"Isabel!" Colin Wareing shouted from far below. "Where are you?"

She left the room then, stopping for a moment — by the door, I think. "I'll be back."

I don't know what he can have said to her — what she can have forced out of him at knifepoint. She wanted the truth. He never told me the entire truth. I could hear my car churning up the gravel. I heard it roaring down the avenue.

I cradled Tom, my man in the tree, the little boy in the tree who killed my father, my beloved brother, and the château's shadows kept me company. They grieved with me and then the silence through which they gently moved was ripped apart by heavy feet thundering up the stairs.

They crashed into the room. Another stricken silence. Then Colin Wareing's voice was soft in my ear. To my surprise, he had tears in his eyes.

"He wasn't a bad man." He could never have realised how much that comment meant to me — still means, as the inquiry into Tom's business affairs continues.

I hope that Tom never knew about the shackled slaves used by the Kumono Mining Company.

My car was recovered at Marseilles, wiped clean of fingerprints.

Chapter 58

So I sit here, at my desk, looking out at Christmas trees twinkling in the windows of tall narrow houses, just like mine. I watch and wait for Eveline. My brother could never have survived. He was stabbed fifteen times, twice through the heart.

I don't know what will happen when she comes. She'll notice, of course, my stomach, the burgeoning of new life. Perhaps we'll have tea. Perhaps Philip will come in after a long day at the office and I'll introduce him to the woman who killed my brother. Perhaps she'll try to kill me — but I do hope not, because of the baby. I wonder if he'll have jug ears, like his father.

I am no longer frightened of the unknown. I know who I am. Besides, I have taken precautions with another life at stake.

I remember Tom. I can see my young brother, with the looks of my father, one eye green and one eye brown. I can feel his hand around my waist and my head resting on his shoulder as we dance, the beat of the music binding us together, lost in the ecstasy of being in rhythm with someone whose heartbeat you know better than your own. Outside it is night and the windows are all open and I'll remember thinking, all those years ago, how no one and nothing mattered more than the two of us, and then I'll see Eveline, more beautiful than ever, standing by my study door.

"What about me?" she will shout though no words will come out of her mouth. "How can you live your lives and shut me out? How can you exploit me and my countrymen for your gain? How can you seek to be rich on the backs of others? All this because your father died? People die. My brother died." I will realise that she is covered in blood.

And I'll betray Tom again. "But my brother died too, isn't that enough?"

Whatever happens, I'll beg her forgiveness with all my heart.

Printed by Amazon Italia Logistica S.r.l.
Torrazza Piemonte (TO), Italy